MW00880121

Dorm Life

An Undead Ultra Novel

Dorm Life

Undead Ultra Book 2

By Camille Picott

Copyright 2019 Camille Picott
All rights reserved.

www.camillepicott.com
camillepicott@gmail.com

ISBN: 9781093981483

Contents

Prologue
Outbreak

JENNA

"Friday pop quiz," I announce to my boyfriend. "What should we do tonight? We've spent all our money on the van, so the movies are out. The CDC goons have a blockade on the north end of town, which means the beach is out. And there's martial law curfew in effect, which means spray painting the back wall of Safeway is out."

Carter sprawls on a sofa in the dorm common room with a tablet, reading reviews of the latest craft beer releases. He sits up as I speak, pushing his shaggy hair out of his eyes.

"Babe, has anyone ever told you you're a buzzkill?"

"My sisters." I plop down in his lap. "And my mom."

"They're idiots." He kisses my neck, his bushy beard tickling my skin.

"Let's see, the last time I talked with Rachel and Lisa, they brought up the time I left Stephanie Ryzer's party early and embarrassed the family. My mom—"

"Forget them." Carter silences me with a quick kiss on the lips. "I heard Beta Sigma Epsilon is throwing a blockade party."

"You mean, there's a CDC blockade and the frat boys needed an excuse to throw a party."

"Pretty much. Wanna go?"

"I never thought I'd hear you propose an outing to a frat party, but okay." There aren't many fraternities at Humboldt State University; the general populace frowns on anything resembling traditional establishment.

"I may have overheard my lab partner saying one of his frat brothers spent last weekend driving to a bunch of different microbreweries getting kegs," Carter says sheepishly.

"Ah. Now the proposal makes more sense. Count me in, babe."

An hour and a half later, the two of us are snuggled up on a grungy sofa watching a Ping-Pong drinking contest. We each have a red plastic pint glass in hand. Beta Sigma Epsilon does not disappoint in its beer choices.

"You look gorgeous, babe." Carter smiles at me over the rim of his plastic cup.

A normal girl would appreciate her boyfriend's compliment. Not me. I can't find a way to break the old habit of blowing off compliments, even if Carter is unlike any boy I've ever dated. To be precise, he's a thousand times better than any boyfriend I've ever had, but even that isn't enough to remake me.

I ignore the comment and say, "Let me have another sip of that." I take the pilsner out of Carter's hand, downing a long draught. I close my eyes and savor the golden liquid, blocking out the disappointed crease between Carter's eyes and wondering if I overdid it with the low-cut top. I wouldn't have even bought it if I didn't like the flowery pattern of the fabric so much.

"Oh my God," I say, lowering the cup. "Babe, we have to try and make something like this." I give him a quick kiss, hoping he'll see how into him I am.

"I was thinking the same thing." Carter's frown disappears. He snugs his arm around me. "Let's call it the Elite."

"Elite, as in, elite runner?"

He nods with a grin. "Exactly. You're picking up on ultrarunning jargon fast."

I pull out a small sketchpad, my pencil running in delicate lines across the blank page.

Carter leans in, one arm around my shoulder as he watches me draw. I've never let anyone watch me draw before. My mom and sisters give me crap for wanting to study art, so I made it a point of keeping it private most of the time. With Carter, instead of feeling self-conscious, I enjoy sharing the process with him.

I draw a medal with the word "elite" on a graduated diagonal across it. Around the medal, I draw beams that shoot out from all sides. Except they aren't beams of light; they're roads, complete with dotted yellow lines down the middle, but disguised to look like sunbeams.

"That's awesome, babe."

I smile in thanks, both pleased and embarrassed. "You're just saying that because you're drinking good beer."

"I'm saying it because my girlfriend is a kick-ass artist and I can't wait to have her labels on our beer."

I snuggle deeper into the crook of his arm, the sketchbook balanced on my knee where we can both see it.

"I might play around with the letters of 'elite.' I'm not sure I like the corners." I take a sip from my beer. "You have to try this. It's that lime IPA from Eureka."

"I didn't see that one." Carter takes the cup and drinks. "Damn, that's good. I don't love our IPA recipe. We need to tweak it."

"We did tweak it," I say with a laugh. "We just haven't had a chance to try it yet."

"I'm telling you, we should see about getting some lees from one of the wineries by my house back home. It will give us a richer flavor, plus it will be totally unique."

"We're targeting ultrarunners," I say. "Do you think they want beer made with wine lees?" Lees are the leftover sediment usually filtered out of wine before it's bottled.

Carter shrugs. "If it tastes good, why not?"

"Okay, then we should try it. Do you have any winery contacts who can hook us up?"

"Yeah. My friend Todd works in a tasting room. His brother's girlfriend works in the winemaking lab. I'm sure one of them can help us get lees."

"Nice. Find out when they can get us lees and we'll take a road trip to pick it up." I look at him out of the corner of my eye. "Maybe I can meet your mom if we're down that way?"

Carter hesitates before smiling at me through his beard. "Sure. She'd love that."

"You don't want me to meet your mom," I say flatly. His recalcitrance hurts. I don't think his mom even knows about us.

He shakes his head. "It's not that, babe. You're awesome. I know my mom will love you once she gets to know you. It's just . . . I think on some level she'll feel like she's losing me. Like she lost Dad."

"Having a girlfriend isn't the same thing as your dad passing away." I can't believe he'd compare us to his father's death.

"I know that." He looks away, a clear signal he wants to change the subject. "I'll send a text to Todd and see if he can hook us up. I—"

A howl rends the air. I turn in time to see a small girl in a minidress covered with Cheshire Cats body slam a much larger frat boy onto the Ping-Pong table. The people gathered around give a collective shout of surprise and fall back. Beer cups fall to the ground, splashing golden liquid across shoes. The girl in the Cheshire Cat dress leaps onto the pool table and pins the frat boy. Red lipstick is smeared all over her face, her mouth twisted in a snarl of determination. Her eyes are an eerie eggshell white. They roll discordantly in her face.

"What the hell?" I mutter, tightening my grip on my beer cup as I take a sip. I will not be one of the losers who spills her drink. This beer is way too good to spill.

"I'd say she's pissed," Carter murmurs. "What do you think—?"

We both stop short as a cry of agony goes up from the boy sprawled on the Ping-Pong table. The crowd scatters, many of them tripping over one another in their haste to get away.

That's when I see it.

The girl in the Cheshire Cat dress crouches on the Ping-Pong table like a predator, her face buried in the boy's neck. She rears back, letting out a growl of pleasure. Gripped between her teeth are chunks of flesh and sinew. Blood—not lipstick—paints a red rictus around her mouth. Gouts of blood spurt out of the boy as he flounders and convulses.

"Shit!" I leap to my feet. My beer falls to the ground, my concern for it going out the window in light of the current circumstances. Carter reaches for me and shoves me behind him.

Several frat boys close in on the scene, each of them grabbing a different limb of the girl and trying to drag her off the boy. She doesn't resist. Not at all. Instead, as soon as they grab her, she turns on them.

She lunges straight at the boy who holds her wrist, sinking her teeth into his shoulder. From where I stand, I hear the sound of tearing fabric and flesh being gouged.

I watched my fair share of horror movies in high school and junior high. I've seen countless scenes like this. Although, it's one thing to see it in a movie and another thing to see it at a frat party. Even though I know what I'm seeing, I can't form the word in my mind.

Carter grabs my hand. I squawk in surprise as he swings us into the melee of fleeing students.

It's pure panic in all directions. Students yell and scream in fear and confusion. I cling to Carter as he drags us toward safety.

We're almost to the door when another girl charges into the crowd. Blood smears the front of her tie-dyed tank top. There's no question this time if the red around her mouth is lipstick.

The crowd surges. I'm thrown forward—right into the path of the raging girl. I scream as I'm ripped from Carter's grasp and thrown to the ground.

I'm going to die. The thought flashes through my mind as the crazed girl lunges for me. Her eyes are smooth, eggshell white. They roll in different directions in her sockets.

Carter seizes a wad of the attacking girl's tank top. He yanks back ruthlessly. I scramble to my feet. Fleeing students split in a stream around us, desperate to get outside.

Tie-dyed girl swings her attention to Carter. She bares bloody teeth. Carter releases her and kicks out hard. She flies backward, knocking over a few other students in her wake.

We don't stop to see where she lands. We don't try to help the kids she knocks over.

Carter grabs my hand, and we run.

1
One Week Later

JENNA

"How long do you think she'll sleep?" Reed asks, running his hands through his afro and puffing it up.

"I don't know," Carter replies. "She's never run two hundred miles before. Usually, after a hundred-miler, she spends a day or two in bed."

I stand with my roommates in the common area of the dorm suite. All of us cluster around the short loveseat where Carter's mom sleeps. Every one of us is fixated on her, staring at her like she's an exotic zoo animal.

"Dude, that means she might sleep another two days," Reed says.

"I wish she'd gone to sleep somewhere else," Eric grumbles. "It's kind of hard to play *Call of Duty* with her on the couch."

"Dude, don't be an asshole." Lila flips her long black hair over one shoulder. "She just ran two hundred miles to find Carter. She deserves a little sleep."

"I wonder if she'll let me write her story." Johnny, never without a pen, chews on the plastic end.

"We were just about the get the Scorpion Key!" Eric barely manages to tamp his shout down to a whisper-yell. His shirt has come untucked around his burgeoning potbelly.

Camille Picott

"Your dumb solar panels won't last long enough for you to get the Scorpion Key," Lila snaps.

"Did you guys see her feet?" Johnny asks. "I could write an entire novel about her feet."

"Dude, why are you even looking at her feet?" Reed frowns in disgust.

"They look like they've been run over by a lawn mower. There's a story there."

I tune out the whispered conversation, taking in the near-catastrophe that is my boyfriend's mom.

Two pillows are shoved under her calves, effectively elevating her legs. Her shoulder-length brown hair is washed but uncombed; she'd been too tired to comb it after she staggered out of her bucket shower last night. Gray roots show close to her scalp. Her exposed arms are covered with cuts, scratches, bruises, and poison oak.

There's also a bullet wound. The stitches look like they were administered by a blind person, the threading uneven and crooked.

Carter has been fretting about the wound since he found out about it. He hovers near her arm, staring down at the dirty, puckered red skin and scabs encrusting the black thread. He wants to dump disinfectant all over it, but we don't have any.

Her feet, the current topic of conversation, are bare. There are more blisters than I can count. Some have been lanced and sealed with Super Glue. Others are big lumps of clear fluid, others dark disks of blood. A few of her toenails are missing. The soles of her feet are cracked and scabbed. At some point during her two-hundred-mile trek, she rolled an ankle. It's swollen to twice its normal size.

All in all, my boyfriend's mom looks like hell.

I've heard so much about this woman, but I don't know what to make of her. It was obvious to me early in our relationship that Carter and his mom are close, even if she sounds a bit weird. I can't fathom getting along or

8

even liking a parental figure, but I want her to like me.

"She's lost weight since I saw her last," Carter says in a low voice while Eric and Lila argue about the merits of the solar panels stolen off the university campus streetlights to power the Xbox.

"She just traveled two hundred miles on foot in three and a half days," I remind him. That's a crash diet for sure. If the world hadn't turned upside down, Carter's mom could slap a fancy name on it and market it as the new weight loss fad. Hell, my mom and older sister would be the first to sign up. Half of Southern California follows diet crazes the way beagles follow the scent of dead animals.

I try not to think about my family in Los Angeles. It's been a few days since cell phone service went out. I imagine them safe in our family cabin at Big Bear Lake. The last I spoke to them, that's where they'd been headed.

"I have to raid some of the other dorm rooms and find first aid supplies."

I must not be hearing well with all the whispered arguing around me. I turn to Carter with a frown. "What?"

"I have to raid some of the other dorm rooms and find first aid supplies for her. My mom needs calamine lotion. And some disinfectant for her blisters and cuts and the bullet wound. An Ace bandage for her ankle would be good, too."

Okay, maybe I did hear him correctly. "We don't know which of the rooms are empty," I say, returning the argument I've heard every time I pitch the idea of raiding other rooms for supplies. None of my companions, not even Carter, has felt a compelling need to secure the rest of our building or organize supplies.

"We'll have to use the attack and stack method to draw them out," Carter replies. "Like we did in this room."

"Sure, okay." I guess if Carter's mom is what it takes to get him and everyone else mobilized, I can't complain.

"Cannabis oil can help with the poison oak," Lila pipes up from the far side of the couch. Her dark eyes brighten at the challenge of creating yet another marijuana recipe for healing. "I'll see if I can make a salve."

Eric snorts. "You think pot cures *everything.*"

"Mom, my dick won't go down," Reed says in a high-pitched voice. "Can I have some marijuana lube?"

Lila plants her hands on her hips, almond eyes narrowing at Reed and Eric. "Laugh now, assholes. When I'm living in a mansion, you losers will still be drooling over *Call of Duty* and working deadbeat jobs at the local mini-mart."

"When you're arrested for breaking federal law pedaling marijuana salves, we'll send you a care package in prison," Eric replies.

"Cannabis is legalized in more and more states every year. It's only a matter of time before the federal government legalizes it. And who are you to criticize me for wanting to make and sell cannabis products? You used to trade pot brownies and pot butter for term papers."

I suppress a groan, not in the mood to listen to yet another argument between Lila and Eric. They hadn't liked each other before the zombie outbreak; now that the two of them are stuck in the same dorm suite, the arguing is endless.

Eric spreads a palm over his heart. "I make products for recreational pleasure. I don't ride around on a high horse because I know how to grind a few buds with a mortar and pestle with some coconut oil."

"There is *way* more to my recipes than buds and coconut oil!"

"You two need to get high and fuck already," Johnny says.

That shuts up everyone. Lila, red-faced, storms off

and slams her bedroom door. Eric stalks into the kitchen and bangs around in the cupboards, rifling for something. He makes enough racket to wake the dead, but Carter's mom doesn't stir.

"Way to go, bro." Reed exchanges a fist bump with Johnny. "I thought they'd never shut up."

"It's called shock value," Johnny replies. "A valuable writing technique when employed effectively."

Reed heads toward the door. "We going on a raid, or what?" he says to Carter. I'm surprised he even heard Carter's plan above all the arguing.

"I'm going," I say. No way do I want Carter venturing into other rooms without someone to watch his back. I don't trust our stoner roommates.

"Room raid?" Eric stops his banging in the kitchen. "I'm going, too. I'm all out of brownie mix."

Reed snorts with amusement. "Planning to make some of your famous brownies just to needle Lila?"

Eric grins. "Maybe." He jams his feet into worn sneakers.

"Woah." Carter holds up his hands. "This is a raid to help my mom. That's it."

"Dude, we can help your mom *and* get brownie mix," Eric says. "Besides, if we need to take down any of those things, you know I'm good with my spear." He hefts a sturdy chair leg from the pile in the entryway. The handmade weapons, created on the fly when we were trapped in a dorm room, have become our go-to zombie-killing weapons.

"I'll stay here," Johnny says, scratching at his enormous sideburns. "Someone has to look after our new roomie." He indicates Carter's slumbering mother, who has yet to stir in all this commotion.

"Why are you coming?" I ask Reed.

"I'm bored," he replies, once again fluffing his afro with his hands.

"Look, this isn't a joke," Carter says. "You all know

what we could encounter in the other rooms."

"All the more reason for you to have backup." I smile sweetly at him, shoving a chair leg spear through my belt. "We're going to help you, babe. Get over it."

2
Clearance

JENNA

"You're risking your life to help your mom." As soon as I say the words, I realize how lame they sound. Families are supposed to help one another. That's what normal people do.

Carter glances up as we file into the hallway. There is exactly one other confirmed empty dorm room on this floor. The only reason we know it's empty is because we'd been hiding in it until it caught fire and we'd been forced to clear it. Unfortunately, a search of that room yielded a handful of Band-Aids. We have to raid more rooms to find the things Kate needs.

"She almost died to keep our family together," Carter replies. "The least I can do is get her some calamine lotion and other stuff to help her heal."

"My mom once ran two red lights to get me acne cream before prom," I reply.

Carter chuckles, leaning down to plant a kiss on my lips. I wrap my arms around his waist and return the kiss. I don't think this boy has any idea how crazy I am about him.

"Don't worry, babe," Carter says. "I'll kill zombies to get you acne cream if you need it."

I whack him on the shoulder, grinning despite myself.

Carter always knows how to make me laugh. "If our cell phones still worked, my mom would tell you to get me makeup and skin toner while you're there."

"I'll add it to my list."

"We should check out Kevin Cassidy's room," Eric says. "That guy wanted to be a medic. I bet he has first aid stuff."

"Good idea," Carter says, heading three doors down.

I follow him with the others, tightening my grip on my spear. We should have done this days ago instead of huddling inside the safety of our room. There are valuable supplies in the other dorm rooms, supplies we are eventually going to need.

We cluster in front of the plain brown door, staring at it in silence. After a moment, Carter raises his spear and raps it against the wood.

At first, nothing happens. Carter raps several more times.

Something thumps against the door. We jump back, all of us instinctively raising our spears.

A few seconds later, another loud thump vibrates the door. Through the wood comes the sound of moaning.

"There's at least two of them," Carter murmurs. "Eric, you brace the door. Try only to let one of them come out at a time."

Eric nods. He grips the door handle, positioning his feet on the floor.

Reed, Carter, and I form a half semicircle near the opening. This method of clearance has been dubbed Attack and Stack. We learned it from Kate. It means stacking our opponents in a narrow opening so they can't all rush us at once.

As I raise my chair leg, holding it like a spear, I feel like a different person. I'm not the daughter of a plastic surgeon who grew up in high-speed Southern California amid people who spent their days worrying about fashion and hairstyles. I'm not the girl who dreams about graduating from college and starting a business with her boyfriend.

That girl doesn't kill people. That girl is a person who likes to draw, paint, and antagonize her materialistic mother.

This girl who wields a wooden spear is someone from a different world. This other person is necessary. She has to come out from time to time to survive.

At Carter's nod, Eric turns the door handle.

A zombie throws itself into the opening. Eric shoves his weight against the door to keep the thing from barreling into us. The creature's shoulder gets lodged in the doorway, its arm swiping out at us.

I dart forward and jam my spear through the narrow opening. I get a brief glimpse of a face, one white eye exposed as the zombie snarls and tries to reach us. I recognize Kevin, the medic-in-training.

My stomach clenches, but I force myself to act. I sink my spear into his blind eye, grimacing at the squishy feeling as the wood punctures his brain.

I yank my spear free. Kevin slumps down. A second zombie clambers over him, pushing against the opening. The door swings open another few inches.

"Hold it!" Carter leaps forward. He attacks the girl in the opening. I recognize her as Kevin's girlfriend. I think her name was Jennifer. Carter's spear smashes her nose and pierces her face. She thumps to the floor, dead.

"Now *that* is a perfect Attack and Stack," Eric says, wiping sweat off his nose. "Your mom would be proud, Carter—"

"Look out!" Carter shouts.

A third zombie smashes into the door. It flies open, throwing Eric off his feet. A boy named Stewy, half of his arm chewed off, launches himself straight at Reed.

Carter and I surge forward as Reed is thrown to the ground. He has just enough time to raise his spear, but it bursts through Stewy's midsection. The zombie lands on top of Reed, snarling and snapping.

With a shout, I shove my spear downward. It glances off the side of Stewy's head, only managing to scrape off a portion of his scalp.

Damn it! I haul my arm back, preparing for a second strike. Reed is screaming, pushing desperately against Stewy's sternum in an effort to keep from getting bitten.

Carter's spear punches through Stewy's skull. Blackish-red blood spatters everywhere. Stewy gives one last snap of his teeth before collapsing.

"Fucking shit!" Reed shoves Stewy away and leaps to his feet. "Motherfucker." He swipes at his face and clothing, presumably to clear away the blood. All he manages to do is smear it. "That guy and I used to get high together."

"You all right?" I ask.

"No, man," Reed replies. "I need to get high. You guys are on your own for this shit." He turns away and heads for the stairwell, the heavy metal door banging shut behind him as he heads downstairs to the lounge. Reed has a favorite couch down there where he likes to nap after getting stoned.

"You guys okay?" Carter looks me and Eric up and down.

"I'm okay," I reply, peering into the dark interior of the dorm. "Do you think it's empty?"

"Nothing else is charging out at us," Eric observes.

"If there is something else inside, it's probably behind a closed door or it would be here with Stewy and the others," Carter says. "I think it's safe for us to go in."

I draw in a breath to steady my nerves, reminding myself we're eventually going to have to clear every room in this building if we hope to pull together enough supplies to survive for a while. It's been a growing point of frustration with me that no one has been interested in taking a serious look at the dwindling supplies in our dorm kitchen. We'd all be going hungry by now if not for

Lila's weird obsession for buying in bulk at Costco.

The three of us creep into the dorm. Blood is smeared all over the floor and across one wall. In the kitchen lies a body, most of it eaten down to the bone. I cover my mouth and nose with one hand, trying not to be sick.

Carter squeezes my shoulder before leading us the rest of the way inside. A quick search of the rooms and closets shows the place to be deserted. I even check under the sink for good measure. We found Johnny hiding under the sink of our room after we cleared it.

"You go help your boyfriend," Eric says, opening the cupboards. "I'm on brownie mix patrol."

"Pull out everything you find that's edible," I reply. "We're going to need the food."

Eric replies with a noncommittal "Uh-huh" as he rifles through cupboards. I purse my lips in frustration and head off in search of Carter.

I find him digging through a closet in one of the bedrooms. I opt to search underneath the bunk bed. I don't even know if this was Kevin's room, but it seems like a good place to store supplies.

I don't find any medical supplies, but I do find a case of unopened Clif bars. Score. I pull it out and deposit it on the desk near the window.

The blinds are open, giving me a full view of the parking lot below. Flies gather on the pile of bodies off to one side, a black amoebic mass that shifts and roils. At least two dozen vultures hop around on the bodies, pecking at eyes and tearing off strips of flesh with their beaks.

"Vultures have an amazing biological design." I make my voice light, trying to ignore the sick feeling I experience every time to see all the bodies.

"How so?" Carter joins me at the window.

"Look at their heads. No feathers, just that rubbery skin. Perfect for sticking inside dead things to eat." I sigh.

"Maybe humanity will evolve like that in another hundred years."

"I just had a disturbing mental image of hairless humans with rubbery red heads." Carter wrinkles his nose. "Thank God this will all be a bad memory in the history books before that happens."

I give him what I hope is an agreeable smile, even if I don't agree. Everyone except me seems to think this is a storm we have to ride out until the government gets its shit together and cleans up things—I'm not convinced—but it's not worth arguing about. There's enough arguing in the house about pot and video games. Throwing the future of humanity into the mix will only give me a headache.

My gaze twitches back to the flies, the vultures, and the dead. Carter and I could have easily been among the pile if not for sheer dumb luck. Dumb luck, and Carter's clear thinking in a moment of crisis.

*

Automatic rifle fire. Screams.

Carter and I, holed up in a tiny dorm room, peered through the window. Hummers and a military tank rolled down Granite Avenue. We barely escaped my infected roommate when she attacked and tried to bite us. Now we hunkered down in the suite next door. Eric and Reed, two of the guys who lived in Creekside, were with us. Also with us was Lila, whom we'd found running hysterically through the hallway.

"What are they doing?" I whispered. "Why would they bring a tank onto campus?"

"Some of the worst outbreaks were at College Creek apartments on the other side of the school." Eric puffed on a joint, taking long, desperate drags. The glowing tip was the only light in the stuffy room.

"My point exactly," I said. "Shouldn't soldiers be

helping anyone who's not infected? Like, helping us evacuate? They don't need tanks for that."

"Maybe it's standard protocol." Reed snagged the joint from Eric, taking his own desperate drag. "You know, when going into an area hit with a biological disaster."

A bad feeling settled in my gut. I pulled out my phone and called my mom.

As the call connected, I heard muffled music in the background. "Mom? Are you guys okay? Are Rachel and Lisa with you?"

"Hey, weirdo." Rachel's voice came over the line. My little sister, though only fifteen, managed to speak with an air of authority that comes from a lifetime of getting what she wants.

When she was little, it was because she had a mop of blond curls and big, innocent blue eyes. By the time she was thirteen, she had the figure of an adolescent supermodel and wasn't above flashing a smile or her cleavage to get what she wanted. Mom always said I could learn a lot from my little sister.

"Rachel, put Mom on," I said. "There is some crazy stuff going on up here. I don't know how widespread it is, but you guys should load up on supplies and get out to the cabin, just in case. Stay there for a week or so until all this blows over."

Rachel makes a sound of disgust into the receiver. "Look, I know you have a lot of crazy non-conformists and sweat lodges up in hippie-ville, but don't get your panties in a twist. Police and military are keeping the streets safe around here. There's a curfew in place, which makes it hard to hang out with friends, but—"

"Rachel!" It's all I could do not to shout into the phone. "We have armed soldiers with guns on campus. I think things are more serious than we've been led to believe."

This earned another grunt of disgust from my little

sister. "This is what you get for picking that stupid school. You had a scholarship to Loyola, Jen. None of us knows what you were thinking. And don't get me started on that hairy boyfriend of yours."

The sound of gunfire makes us all jump. I drop the phone, crowding around the window with my companions.

"Jen? Jen, what the hell?" Rachel's voice carried from the dropped phone, but I barely registered her words. "Whatever. Call us back when you're done being a freak."

The Hummers disgorged dozens of soldiers, all of them in full battle armor. Even more flowed out of the tank. Everyone was armed. They spread out down the street, machine guns poised to fire. They looked like they were headed into a Middle Eastern war zone, not a tiny college campus in sleepy northern California.

"Oh, shit." Carter pressed his index finger against the glass. "Look."

Coming up the road was a cluster of white-eyed, loping students. They were bloodied and wounded, some more grisly than others. Some had nothing more than a bloody arm or leg, while others had gaping necks and deep cavity gouges.

"That's why they're here," Lila announced, voice shrill with anxiety. "The soldiers are protecting us."

My hands grew clammy as I watched the white-eyed students surge up the road.

Zombies.

The word was impossible. Or so it had seemed only a few days ago. But I'd seen enough to know exactly what those white-eyed people were. Carter and I had seen them tear into fellow students too many times to count.

Maybe they're rounding up the kids for the CDC. The CDC tents on the outskirts of town had been here for over two weeks.

Were they going to round up the sick, carnivorous kids? Put them in holding cells while the CDC worked on a cure? Worse, would they put them in a concentration camp? There were so many of them, and it wasn't just students who were infected. All over the small town of Arcata, people were attacking and biting other people.

Fire leaped from the tips of the machine guns, launching a barrage of lead into the oncoming students.

I screamed. Carter grabbed me, holding me close, but I couldn't peel my eyes away from the horror. As bullets flew from the machine guns, students collapsed to the ground, felled by headshots.

"They can't do that," Reed whispered, glued to the window beside us. "They can't just kill people."

"They're sick." Eric's voice cracked with emotion. "They need help."

Then one of the soldiers turned his weapon on a nearby dorm. Perhaps he saw a sick kid in the doorway. Who knows? Whatever the reason, he opened fire.

What happened next was nothing short of a stampede. Screaming students poured out of the dorm. Some scrambled out windows and tried to scale down balconies. Others tried to barrel out the front door.

Some were sick. I saw blood-smeared bodies and white eyes that almost seemed to glow in slack faces. But there were more healthy students than sick ones.

And then all the dorms seemed to open and spill forth students. We even saw people from Creekside flooding out the front doors. My muscles twitched, the sight of so many fleeing students making me want to flee, too.

"Dudes, we gotta go." Reed shifted, body angled toward the door.

"No way." Carter grabbed him, pulling him back. "We're not running toward the men with guns. That's just stupid."

"But what if we get stuck here?" Eric asked. "What if—?"

The soldiers turned toward the mass of kids

descending on them. They never once let up on the triggers. Bullets sprayed fire and death. Students—both dead and alive—fell.

There was only one explanation for the carnage: The government was doing damage control. They didn't have a cure. They were trying to contain the zombie outbreak, to keep it from spreading.

*

The military opened fire on everything and anything that moved on Granite Avenue. Following Carter's instinct to hunker down and stay put in the dorm room had saved us.

I try to block out the memory of the slaughter. There is no other word to describe what happened.

"I'm pretending I'm making a supply run for mom at an ultra," Carter says, turning away from the window. "Dad and I always used to run to the local drug store to get her stuff during races." His voice drops. "Except this is the first time I've ever had to deal with a bullet wound."

"She's going to be okay," I say, giving his hand a squeeze. "We'll get her the things she needs."

We finish searching the room. We find a half-used tube of Neosporin in a desk drawer—which Carter pockets—but no other first aid supplies.

"I don't think this is Kevin's room," Carter says.

"We'll find it," I reply. "Let's go search the others."

As we cross the hall to the next bedroom, we hear a shout of glee from the kitchen.

"Ghirardelli brownies," Eric crows. "These things are the best!"

Carter rolls his eyes as he enters the next room. I spot a stack of textbooks on the floor.

"Carter, look at these." I spread the books out on the desk so we can read the titles. *Emergency Response Guidebook. Paramedic: On The Front Lines Of Medicine.*

Paramedics Care: Principles and Practice.

"This must be Kevin's room." Carter hurries to the closet.

I yank open desk drawers. I find two more books and add them to the ones on the desk; those could come in handy. Just as I head to search under the bed, Carter lets out a yell of triumph.

"First aid kit!" He emerges from the closet, beaming. Clutched in his hands is a red canvas first aid kit. The price tag still dangles from the zipper.

"It doesn't look like it's ever been opened," I say, returning his grin.

Carter unzips the kit, laying it open on the bed. He pulls out a folded inventory list tucked inside the interior pocket.

"Everything we need is in here," he says, scanning the list.

"Looks like you guys scored." Eric wanders in with two boxes of brownie mix under one arm. "Mrs. S. will be patched up in no time."

"Did you find anything else useful in the kitchen?" I ask.

Eric shrugs. "There's food and stuff."

Food and stuff. I check a sigh, making a mental note to come back later to organize and inventory things.

"We should clear out these bodies," Carter says, zipping shut the first aid kit. "Take them outside with the rest."

Outside in the hallway, we each grab a body by the ankles and drag them toward the stairwell. I grimace at the blood we smear across the floor. It joins several other smears, leftover from the zombies we cleared out of our current residence earlier this week.

I make it a point not to look directly into the ruined face of Jennifer, who had once been a living, breathing person. Spear-wielding Jenna doesn't let herself get caught up in memories of the dead.

3
Disposal

JENNA

The head of the dead thump against the stairs, filling the air like discordant drumbeats. My hands, gripping the dead girl's ankles, are slick with sweat.

I have dragged exactly four bodies out of Creekside. I helped kill more than that, but I only had to dispose of four. How many more will I have to drag out before I get used to the heavy weight of a dead body?

We reach the lounge on the first floor. I pause just inside to catch my breath as Eric and Carter drag their burdens toward the exit.

"Where's Reed?" I ask, realizing the lounge is empty except for the three of us.

Carter frowns, scanning the room. "Do you think he went outside?"

"Why would he go outside?" Eric asks, wrinkling his nose. Except to get rid of bodies, no one in Creekside has gone outside since the military slaughter.

"He went down the stairs," I reply. "We all saw him and he's not here."

"We'll look for him," Carter says. "He couldn't have gone far. Maybe he just needed some fresh air."

The swinging glass front door of Creekside is mostly intact. There's a jagged hole near the bottom corner, but overall, it came through the military attack in better shape than any other dorm entrances I've seen.

Outside, Humboldt University campus is eerily quiet. Between the students that evacuated before the quarantine went into effect, the hundreds that were turned into zombies, and those slaughtered by the military during the riot, we have yet to see other humans around here.

The bodies left to rot all along the street are an inescapable memory. The smell is almost enough to knock me over. It's worse than a gym locker room, worse than the dump, worse than the time my childhood cat left a dead squirrel under our house. It's like all three smells combined, then magnified.

I'm not sure whether to breathe through my nose or mouth. I should have thought to bring a handkerchief. I pull up the collar of my T-shirt, covering my nose.

I glance over at Carter to see how this is affecting him. His mouth is set in a hard line, the skin around his eyes pinched.

I try not to look at the bodies, but it's impossible. I recognize some of them.

Darren from Chemistry 101. Laura from Spanish 2. Clinton from Creekside.

All killed. All gunned down.

There are soldiers mixed with the students. Some of the soldiers fell from zombies, but others were taken down by students. In the panic of the shooting, some students seized weapons from fallen soldiers. Others attacked with bats, kitchen knives, whatever they had on hand. Someone fired a rocket launcher at one of the dorm buildings, leaving half of it collapsed.

I swallow, letting myself succumb to the memories. There's no blocking out the horror of that day. What did Carter's mom think when she saw the carnage?

I don't see any sign of Reed. Where could he have gone?

We add the bodies to the growing pile in the far corner of the parking lot near a gazebo, sending a dozen vultures into the sky. I avert my eyes, even though it's impossible not to see the writhing maggots in the bodies. Sooner or later, we're going to have to figure out what to do with all the dead, especially if we plan to stay in Creekside for the long term.

"Have you guys noticed there aren't any guns?" Eric asks.

"What?" I frown at him.

"With the bodies," he replies. "There are lots of dead soldiers, but no guns."

I hadn't noticed. I glance at the nearby pile of dead on the road. It's a jumble of soldiers and students.

Eric is right. There are no weapons.

"You think someone came through and rounded them up?" Carter asks.

"Yeah." Eric nods. "It's what I would do. Maybe the military did it before they pulled out."

"Maybe." I try to pretend it's no big deal, even though the absence of the weapons leaves me uneasy. Where could they have gone?

Two gunshots split the air, sending a jolt of fear through me.

Reed comes tearing around the side of a nearby dorm. "Hide!" he hisses. "We have to hide!" His eyes are wide with terror, the whites showing all the way around his irises. His skin is pale with fear. Reed sprints into the darkened alcove of Willow, a dorm in the same cluster of buildings as Creekside.

Carter grabs my hand, pulling me after Reed. Eric is right behind us.

Reed darts through the jagged opening of Willow's front door, which was shot to pieces with bullets. He catches his shoulder on a glass shard. He never even slows, tearing his shirt free and disappearing into the darkness beyond.

Shit. There could be more zombies inside. Or possibly other people. What the hell is going on?

I hesitate outside of Willow, my eyes sweep the buildings and parking lot, looking for the source of the gunshots. All I see are bodies and abandoned cars. The only thing that moves is a paper Starbucks cup, pushed across the blacktop by an invisible wind.

"We should get inside," Carter says. "Someone shot at Reed."

I want to go back to Creekside, but it didn't miss my notice that Reed ran away from our dorm, not toward it. I nod in reluctant agreement and duck into the dark building with Carter and Eric. Inside are bodies, blood, and overturned furniture.

"Back here!" Reed gestures to us from behind an overturned sofa.

We obey, hurrying to the blood-smeared sofa. I grab Carter's hand. He flattens himself in beside me, putting his free hand around my waist. I rest my head against his chest, breathing hard.

Eric turns toward Reed, mouth opening in question. Reed shakes his head emphatically back and forth, his message clear: *be quiet.*

We wait in silence. Reed's eyes are wild, his usually perfect afro in disarray.

Seconds tick by. They stretch into minutes. When fifteen minutes has passed, I gesture to get Reed's attention. *Is it safe to move yet?*

Reed hesitates.

Then I hear it. The voice.

"Where the fuck did that little weasel go?"

"I saw the others in the parking lot. He must be around here somewhere," says a second voice.

"They could be hiding in any of these buildings."

The two people don't speak loudly, but in the dead quiet of Humboldt University, they may as well be shouting through a megaphone.

"Mr. Rosario will be pissed if he gets away. You know how she feels about thieves."

"We'll find him."

The voices fade as the two people move away. The four of us wait in silence.

When several minutes have passed, Reed peeks over the sofa. "Out the back," he whispers.

"There are no doors in the back," Carter points out.

Reed shakes his head. "We have to use a window. Too risky to go out front. They could find us."

"Who are they?" I ask. What has Reed gotten us into? He shakes his head. "I'll tell you later."

We follow Reed to the back of the downstairs dorm lounge. Even though I'm pissed that he put us all in danger, I don't want to compound the situation by arguing with him now. The darkness is thick, but the smell of death is unmistakable. We find three bodies near the bathroom, all with headshots. Bullet casings crunch underfoot. From the grisly wounds on their bodies, they look to have been zombies when they were executed. I hope so.

Carter opens a busted window. Pieces of glass shake free. We slip outside.

"We have to get back to Creekside, but we have to stay out of sight," Reed tells us, voice compressed with fear. "We don't want those guys to know where we live. Come on."

His fear is contagious. My skin crawls. I glance up at the dark, empty windows of Willow dorm, feeling like we're being watched. Carter grabs my hand and squeezes it, giving me a reassuring smile.

The dorm buildings sit in a loose circle, broken up by chunks of land crowded with redwood trees. Following Reed's lead, we race along the back of the dorms and dart through the forested areas.

The wooded parts leave me feeling exposed and vulnerable. I wish I'd brought my spear outside. I make a silent vow never again to leave Creekside without some sort of weapon, not even for a minute.

We sprint as fast as we can, making as little noise as possible. Only when we reach the back of Creekside do we double over to catch our breaths.

This short little run makes me see how out of shape I am. I vow to do something about that, too.

I glance at the minivan parked under the trees behind the dorm. Carter and I bought that van together a few months ago and named it Skip. It's covered in a layer of grime, looking as sad and ruined as everything else out here.

"You owe us an explanation," Carter tells Reed. "What's going on?"

"Inside first," Reed says. "I'll explain after that, I promise." He reaches for the nearest window, his hand and wrist snaking through the shattered opening.

The loud click of a gun's safety sends a jolt of panic through me. Carter leaps forward, pressing me back against the wall as two figures emerge around the building.

"There you are," says the foremost of the two men, leveling his gun at us. "You should have known better than to run from us."

4
Awake

KATE

My eyes snap open from a black, dreamless sleep. I stare at the white popcorn ceiling above me, trying to figure out where I am.

Pain hits me with the force of a swinging socket wrench. It's a head-to-toe, all-consuming ache.

There is only one thing that can make me hurt this much, and it's not childbirth. In comparison, childbirth had been a cakewalk for me.

Running. Only a long, brutal ultramarathon can leave me feeling like I've been run over by a truck. Or in this case, chased by zombies and shot by my best friend.

With a soft groan, I ease myself into a sitting position. Thinking of the bullet wound on my arm makes me think of Frederico, my best friend. He died on our two-hundred-mile run from our home to Humboldt University. He died so I could reunite with my son.

Where is Carter? I look around the room. Blue curtains cover the windows. Gray carpet, spotted with lopsided stains, sits beneath my bare feet. On the other side of the small room is a six-person table and kitchenette.

Dorm room. I'm in a dorm apartment on the second floor of Creekside. I vaguely remember tottering up the stairs as Carter told me how he and his companions had cleared one of the suites and taken up residence there.

Sitting at the table, hand poised above a note pad, is a young man. He's a handsome kid if you can see past the huge, ridiculous sideburns that conceal half his face. A joint dangles in one hand, which he stubs out when he catches me looking at it.

"Sorry, Mrs. S." He gestures to the joint. "I only use it to stimulate my creativity. I'm not a pothead or anything." He crosses the room, holding out a hand in introduction. "My name is Johnny. I was hiding under the kitchen sink until Carter and the others cleared this dorm room after theirs caught fire."

I shake his hand, trying to imagine this young man folded into the cabinet beneath the kitchen sink. I can't fathom how he fit, but I'm glad he's alive.

"You can call me Kate," I say. "Nice to meet you, Johnny."

He plops down on the coffee table across from me, eyes intent as he rests his elbows on his knees. The way he stares at me is unnerving. I feel like a bug under a microscope.

"Mrs. S.—Kate—I'm a writer. Carter told me a little bit about your running. I want to write your story. Will you tell me about your run to Arcata?"

This kid is intense. I rise, stifling a groan as I head toward the kitchenette for a drink of water. *Stiff* does not begin to cover how I feel. I'm pain on two legs.

Moving is good, I remind myself, focusing on the sink piled high with dirty dishes. Moving will loosen up muscles and speed up the recovery process.

Except that my rolled ankle throbs, which moving hurt that much more. What I wouldn't give for an Epsom salt bath right now.

"Kate?" Johnny trails after me.

"I need some water." And perhaps a table to put between me and this intense kid. "Where's Carter?"

"He's out getting first aid supplies for you."

I pause mid-stride, turning around to look at Johnny. "What?"

"Carter wanted to get first aid supplies for you. Don't worry, he's in the building. A few of our friends are with him. They should be back anytime now."

Panic constricts my throat. I fight against it, reminding myself Carter and his friends are capable of watching each other's backs. They survived together, cleared this dorm room, and even cleared the downstairs lounge.

"How long have they been gone?" I ask.

"Forty-five minutes or so. They should be back any minute. Don't worry."

I turn away, attempting to calm the unreasonable panic clenching my chest. This, unfortunately, gives me a close-up view of the sink. Not only is it piled high with dirty dishes, but there are ants crawling on the hardened lumps of food stuck to the plates and silverware.

The crowning glory is the cast iron skillet sitting on top of the pile. It looks like someone cooked chili in it. The ants are in a full frenzy on the congealed food.

The sight of the ants makes my skin itch. I hate the insidious little fuckers. Even in a world where shit's gone sideways, I still have the energy to hate ants.

As I focus on my surroundings, I realize the mess doesn't stop at the sink. The trash can overflows. I count three garbage bags mounded next to it, a trail of ants going into each of them.

Just because the world has ended doesn't mean young adults have become any better at cleaning up after themselves. Apparently, I've left zombie-infested road-ways and entered a pigsty.

I hurt way too much to form a coherent plan to deal with the disgusting mess. There has got to be a clean water glass around here somewhere.

I open a few cupboards and find a pint glass printed

with the backside of a naked lady. The text across the top reads *Bottoms Up*.

Yep. I'm in a pigsty. A pigsty populated with college kids.

Stacked along the countertop are all matter of containers, every last one of them filled with water. Larger containers are on the floor, also filled with water.

I take a long drink, then refill the glass and take a second one. "No more running water?" I ask, gesturing to the various containers. It takes every scrap of will-power not to comment on the ants.

Johnny shakes his head. "We lost power a few days ago. We knew it was going to happen, so we filled up everything we could with water. There's also the water heater. We've been using that for the toilet. We should be set until help comes." His eyes dart at this last statement, communicating his discomfort.

Until help comes. I consider my words carefully, not sure how well the young man in front of me has adjusted to this new world. "How secure is this building?"

He shifts, eyes once again darting away. "We haven't cleared any other rooms, but we did the lounge on the bottom floor. That gave us a way in and out of the building."

Apparently, they half-ass survival the same way they half-ass dish duty. This does nothing to calm my nerves.

A pretty Asian girl enters the common room, eyes widening at the sight of me.

"Mrs. S.," she exclaims. "You're awake! I didn't think you'd be up for another two days."

I half smile, half frown at the odd statement. "Why would you think that?"

"Carter said you always sleep a day or two after a one-hundred-miler. Since you ran two hundred miles to get here, we figured you'd need four days of sleep." She speaks fast, her eyes never leaving my face.

"This is Lila, by the way," Johnny says.

Lila and Johnny both stare at me like I'm some sort of strange, unexpected wild animal in their midst. It's unnerving, only reinforcing the uncomfortable feeling of being under a microscope.

"How long have I been asleep?" I ask.

"Almost two days," Johnny replies. "You didn't even get up to pee."

I can tell by my dry mouth that I'm dehydrated, which isn't surprising considering how far I went on foot. It's not unusual to be dehydrated after an ultra. It can be challenging to replenish water as quickly as it sweats out. Or, in my most recent case, it can be challenging just to find water.

"Are you sore?" Lila asks.

"Don't be stupid," Johnny says. "She just ran two hundred miles. Of course, she's sore. Right, Mrs. S.?"

I wish he'd stop calling me that. It makes me feel old. I'm thirty-nine, not ninety-nine.

"Kate," I remind him. "Please, call me Kate. Yes, I'm a little sore." No need to tell them my body feels like it's been worked over with a baseball bat.

Lila's face brightens. "I have just the thing. Hold on."

She returns from her room carrying a small glass jar filled with a pale-yellow substance. It looks like a candle, but when she opens it, the unmistakable smell of marijuana wafts out.

"I'm developing a cannabis salve for athletes," she tells me. "This is a blend of coconut oil, beeswax, and cannabis oil. I also mixed in a little copaiba essential oil, which is great for reducing inflammation." She holds it out to me. "Here, try it."

Dubious, I take the jar. I don't really want to walk around smelling like a marijuana plant, but the girl's eyes are so earnest I don't have the heart to tell her no.

The balm inside has the consistency of soft wax. I sniff it again, holding back a grimace. I've never liked the smell of pot.

"I'm getting a degree in chemistry," she tells me. "I'm going to start my own cannabis company after I graduate."

"Lila is always working on different balms and stuff," Johnny says.

"Cannabis is good for so many things," Lila says. "Pain relief, stress relief, skin care, all kinds of things. It's not just for getting high." She says this in such a way that leads me to believe she spends a lot of time defending her chosen career plan.

I decide not to point out she needs to work out a way to eliminate the stinky odor of this stuff if she wants to have a chance in hell at selling it.

"Thanks. I'll try it." I scoop out a lump. After a moment's consideration, I decide to rub some on my swollen ankle. That particular part of my body can use all the help it can get. And it's the farthest away from my nose.

"I should take a picture of it," Lila says. "To track the recovery time as you use my salve." Her face falls. "Too bad my phone is out of batteries. The guys stole solar panels to run the Xbox and ham radio, but we don't have any other power. The solar panels don't last long anyway." She looks away, gaze shifting to her shoes. "Besides, until the government cleans up this mess, there's no one to call."

I note how both Lila and Johnny talk about our current state as if it's temporary. Like we've entered a dark tunnel but will find our way back out in a few weeks.

How much have they seen? How much do they know about what's happening?

I think back on my journey here, of all the death and desolation I encountered over the two hundred miles. The world I passed through isn't one that will heal quickly.

I don't say this. There's no reason to upset these kids right now.

A weight settles on my shoulders as I think of Carter. I want my son here, with me, so I can see he is whole and in one piece.

"I'm going to go find Carter," I say. "Do you know which floor he's on?"

"I just saw him, Eric, and Jenna out the window," Lila says. "They were hauling some bodies outside. They must have killed a few on their supply search."

Jenna. Carter's girlfriend. The one he never told me about. I stifle my irritation. It would have been nice to know my son had someone special in his life.

Johnny, watching my face, says, "Don't worry. The army wiped out just about everything and everyone around here. It's pretty safe out there."

If his intent was to comfort a fretting mother, he failed. "What do you mean, the army wiped out everything?" I ask, voice sharp.

Johnny and Lila shift, exchanging glances. I can't discern their expressions.

"Arcata was under martial law for a few days," Johnny says at last. "Things . . . got out of hand. They opened fire on everything. And everyone."

I recall the carnage I saw on Granite Avenue, the long road leading to Creekside dorm where I am now. All the dead kids, many of them murdered with guns. The dead soldiers littered among them. The burned buildings. *Out of hand* doesn't begin to cover what I saw. From the uncomfortable look on Johnny's face and the way he avoids my gaze, I can tell he doesn't want to talk about it.

Lila busies herself in the kitchenette, rifling through the cabinets. "Are you hungry?" she asks with forced cheer. "We have SpaghettiOs."

My mind is sucked down a tunnel to the last time I ate SpaghettiOs. It had only been a few days ago. Frederico had still been alive. Exhausted, hungry, and desperate, we raided an RV for supplies after we killed the family of seven zombies inside.

I would prefer never to eat SpaghettiOs again. I wish Frederico was still here. A wave of sadness passes through me at his loss.

"No, thanks," I say. "I'm going to go find Carter. I—"

Several gunshots sound from outside. I fly to my feet and half run, half limp to the balcony. I throw open the door just in time to see Carter, Jenna, and another boy disappear into a nearby dorm building across the way.

Carter!

His name leaps to my throat, but I swallow it back. I limp onto the balcony and crouch behind the railing, peering into the parking lot.

Two men run into view, guns in hand. They look like homeless vagabonds, the sort that live throughout northern California. Their clothes are faded and stained. They have sun-darkened faces and permanent dirt in the grooves of their knuckles and necks.

Anger rockets through my bloodstream. How dare these fuckers aim weapons at my son?

"Where the fuck did that little weasel go?" says one.

"I saw the others in the parking lot. He must be around here somewhere," says the second man.

"They could be hiding in any of these buildings."

"Mr. Rosario will be pissed if he gets away. You know how she feels about thieves."

Mr. Rosario.

My anger intensifies, a hot coal in my belly. I've met Mr. Rosario. Why the plump, overweight woman goes by a man's name is still a mystery to me. Some of her people found me and Frederico on our journey here. They held us at gunpoint, tied us up like prisoners, and carted us off to a remote, off-the-grid camp run by the drug dealer. We barely made it out of there alive. In fact, Mr. Rosario had done her best to kill us.

And now her people are downstairs, threatening my son and his friends.

To hell with that.

I snatch the disgusting wrought iron skillet out of the sink and march straight to the door in my bare feet. Well, I try to march. It's more of a determined limp. Every nerve ending in my body complains and begs me to sit back down. I relegate the pain to a distant part of my brain and shove my way out the door.

"Kate, where are you going?" Johnny says.

"You can't go out there," Lila adds. "It's dangerous!"

I leave them behind and head toward the stairwell. I didn't run two hundred miles and lose my best friend to let that bitch's goons kill my son.

5
First Kill

JENNA

Carter has me sandwiched between his back and the wall of Creekside. My scalp prickles with fear, and even though I want to shove him out of the way, I'm afraid any small movement may escalate the situation.

"I'll give it back." Reed reaches into his hair. He plucks out a small package with several clear plastic eyedroppers inside, looking chagrined as he tosses it at the feet of the men.

This isn't the first time we've seen Reed hide drugs in his hair. It was a well-known phenomenon throughout the dorm. Reed's eight-inch afro is infamous for a variety of things, but chief among them is its ability to conceal drugs.

It was funny before the zombie outbreak.

It was funny before drug dealers came after us.

Anger crests inside of me as I glare at the droppers of acid. I struggle to hold back my rage, knowing it has no place in our current situation.

Eric doesn't have the same self-restraint. "You fucking idiot," he bursts out. "You risked all our lives so you can get high?"

"I'm sorry," Reed says. "I was being stupid. I didn't think—"

"Yeah, you didn't think," says the tall man. "Where's the rest of it?"

Rest of it?

I want to scream as Reed reaches into one of his large cargo pockets and disgorges another dozen baggies. Inside each one are more plastic eyedroppers filled with acid.

"How did you know where the stuff was?" asks one man. He's the shorter of the two, with a scruffy beard and a black hoodie with a peeling Nike logo.

"Word gets around," Reed says. "I overheard Jay talking to some guys at a party last week. I knew he kept stuff in his car. The way things are now, I didn't think anyone would be coming for his stash."

The pieces click together. Reed broke into one of the abandoned cars to get drugs and got caught by these assholes.

"The way things are now," the shorter man drawls. "Just because we're in the middle of the fucking zombie apocalypse doesn't mean Mr. Rosario's men let Granjero's men steal from us."

Reed pales, his expression bringing a feral smile to both of the gun-wielding vagabonds. "How did you know I worked for Granjero?" he asks.

"We didn't," says the second hobo. He wears fraying cargo pants and a rumpled peacoat. "It was just a guess."

"A guess you just confirmed," says the other man.

I have no idea what any of this means, though I can hazard a guess. Reed must have been selling drugs on the side.

"Let my friends go," Reed says. "They haven't done anything."

"Sorry," says the taller man, though he doesn't sound sorry. "Mr. Rosario says anyone who works for Granjero has to be eliminated. Anyone associated with—"

Someone leaps around the side of the building, wielding a large cast iron skillet. The skillet connects with the man's head with a dull, wet *thunk*. He drops without a sound.

The shorter man whirls around. The gun cracks once, the sound making me jump.

The person with the skillet is faster. She swings it, knocking the gun from the man's hand. Then, like a pro tennis player, she backhands the guy with the cast iron pan. The side of the guy's face is crushed.

The world stills, quiets. The woman standing with the food-encrusted skillet is Carter's mom. Her eyes are fierce, her face blazing with fury and retribution as she gazes at the two men lying before her bare, battered feet.

Both men are still and unmoving. Blood gushes from the face of the man she backhanded with the skillet. A slow seepage of blood flows from the skull of the first man she hit. Behind her, crouched at the corner of the building, are Johnny and Lila. Their mouths hang open, eyes wide as they take in the two bodies. Reed and Eric stare at the scene, agape.

I blink, trying to reconcile the woman in front of me with the skinny woman who limped into the dorm parking lot two days ago looking like she'd been dragged across the grill of a semi. I can't align this hard woman with the broken woman Carter described, a woman crushed by grief after her husband died. I can't align her with the image of a loving and slightly exasperated mother who ordered hops for my boyfriend off the Internet before he was old enough to drink.

From the look on Carter's face, I can guess he's having similar struggles. The woman in front of us is strong and, if I'm being honest, a tad scary. Maybe a lot scary.

Carter's mom looks at him, eyes hard and un-apologetic. "Sorry you had to see that, baby," she says. "These men would have killed you. All of you." Her eyes take in the rest of us. "Frederico and I had a run-in with Mr. Rosario. She tried to kill us. We barely escaped."

"Mom," Carter blurts, "you killed them."

She sighs, her face taking on the look of an overly patient parent who doesn't have the energy to explain a universal truth to a child.

"Go inside, sweetie," she says. "I'll be there in a minute."

She sets the skillet on the ground, pausing to flick ants off her hands and arms with a grimace. Then she picks up the legs of one dead man. She drags him around the building and disappears from sight. Reed picks up the legs of the second guy, eyes still wide. He trails Carter's mom around Creekside.

The rest of us follow the procession. A few of the vultures spring in the air when Reed and Carter's mom get too close, flapping and squawking. A swarm of flies buzz upward in a cloud, disturbed by the movement.

From the edge of the parking lot, we watch Reed and Carter's mom deposit the bodies in a pile. I see Reed exchange a few words with her, but they're too far away to hear. When Reed wipes at his face, she puts an arm around him.

"She killed them," Carter whispers, still sounding stunned.

"I know." I don't know whether to feel relieved or disturbed or terrified. I decide that it's okay to feel all three.

"They would have killed us," Eric says, licking his lips as he stares across the lot. Carter's mom still stands with her arm around Reed's shoulder, talking to him.

On a fundamental level, I understand she just saved our lives. Those guys would have killed us. But knowing this doesn't reconcile the fact that I just watched my boyfriend's mom kill two people with cold, lightning fast efficiency.

My mother won't even kill a spider; she makes us do that for her or, if she sees more than a few in the house, she goes to the nail salon and calls an exterminator. But

Carter's mom killed those two men as easily as all of us kill zombies.

That hadn't been easy at first, either, I remind myself.

*

Carter and I remained barricaded in the dorm room with Reed, Eric, and Lila long after the soldiers had left. Long after the slaughter ended. The sound of gunfire continued off in the distance, either in town or on other parts of campus, but they weren't at the dorms anymore.

We watched survivors creep out of nearby dorms and flee. Some went on foot, some took cars. Those that took cars attracted herds of zombies, but they disappeared from sight before we could see what happened to them.

We stayed where we were because we were too scared to move. Too scared to do anything except sit around and be afraid together.

It didn't help that outside the barricaded door came the soft moans of Jake and Chris. They were two guys who'd been passed out on the living room floor when we made our way here. Having seen bite marks on them, we left them where they were.

Now they were back, undead and hunting for us. The door vibrated from their scratching and pounding.

"What are we going to do?" Reed hissed. "If we go out there, one of us could get bitten."

No one answered him. None of us wanted to be the one to say what we were all thinking: To get past Chris and Jake, we had to kill them. Really kill them.

We saw the soldiers drop zombies with headshots. We knew the stories. It should have been fiction, yet somehow it had become our reality. The only way to stop the monsters on the other side of the door was to bash in their heads.

Even though we knew this, none of us wanted to be the first to say it. None of us wanted to be the one to do it. Chris and Jake were our friends. Our dorm mates. The idea of puncturing their skulls with a sharp object wasn't right.

So we sat in quiet, pensive silence, hoping they would go away.

They didn't.

The frantic pounding died away, but they remained outside the door, moaning and scratching at the wood.

I eventually forced myself to move. I dug around under the beds and in the closets. To my relief, I unearthed a good supply of snacks. There were granola bars and bottled water. Carter even found a case of mashed potato cups on the top shelf in the closet, which we mixed with lukewarm water from plastic bottles.

After nearly eight hours, all of us had to pee. Really bad. Reed suggested opening the window and whizzing out on to the roof, but none of us was brave enough to actually do it. Eric came up with the idea of peeing in the empty water bottles after we made the mashed potatoes.

None of this helped Lila and me. Reed was the one who suggested we relieve ourselves in the potato cups. After we ate the mashed potatoes, of course.

The room was sticky hot from all the bodies crammed inside. Even so, no one suggested opening the window to let in fresh air.

Sporadic gunfire continued outside. We tried to figure out where the soldiers were as time passed, but it was difficult to pinpoint. We concluded they were moving around, possibly rounding up the pods of kids who had turned. I cringed to think of the soldiers killing them.

As I squatted in the corner, peeing in my mashed potato cup, I saw Carter watching me. His jaw was clenched, his eyes hard.

"We can't sit around and wait for things to get better on their own," he said. "We don't have enough water bottles and mashed potato cups to go another eight hours. If we want out of here, we have to do something."

"Duh," Eric said. "We know that." At Carter's glare, he added, "I just don't know what we're supposed to do."

Carter stalked across the small space. "Move," he said to Reed, who sat in one of the desk chairs.

Reed moved without a word.

Carter turned the wooden chair on its side, studying it. The legs were made of six pieces of wood that formed a square base.

"What are you doing?" Lila asked.

"Making weapons," Carter replied.

He brought his foot down on the chair. It took a few tries, but he managed to snap it off from the base. Propping the base on the edge of the bed, he used his foot to snap it into six separate pieces. Then he took a pocketknife from his jeans and set it against the end of a chair leg.

The noise he made from breaking the chair set off Jake and Chris. One of them keened outside the door, nails grating along the door.

We all watched Carter in silence, transfixed on the sure movements of his hands, and he began to whittle the end into a sharp point.

We all jumped when my phone rang. This only increased Jake and Chris's agitation.

I hurried into the closet, muffling my voice in the hanging clothes.

"Mom! Are you guys——?"

"Jenna, where have you been?" My mother's annoyed voice carried over the line. "I've been trying to get in touch with you since you called earlier. Rachel said you were hysterical."

Annoyance pricked at me, but I did my best to ignore it. Arguing with my mom never got me anywhere. "I've had my phone with me the whole time, but it hasn't rung," I tried to explain. "Everyone's cell service has become intermittent since all this . . . *stuff* started."

"The authorities just sent out a non-mandatory

evacuation notice," Mom replied.

"What does that mean?"

"It means they're suggesting we evacuate, but it's not mandatory. I talked with your sisters and we decided we're going to go up to the cabin for a few days. The weather is supposed to be clear, so we can lie out on the deck. It'll give us a chance to work on our base tans before summer comes."

Only my mother would consider the state of her base tan at a time like this. Ever since my dad left her for a younger woman, she spends more and more time obsessing over the way she looks. I wouldn't care so much if that obsession didn't carry over to my sisters and me. She's always cared more about my clothes than my grades.

All this went through my head, but all I said was, "That's a good idea. You guys should go up there and relax for a few days."

"Why don't you and that hairy boyfriend of yours come and join us?"

This sentence both irritated and pleased me. It irritated me that she'd never once called Carter by his first name, but it pleased me to hear annoyance and dis-approval in her voice. Her disapproval of Carter was just further confirmation that I'd managed to land a good one. The guys my mother wanted me to date in high school were all rich, good-looking, grade-A assholes.

"We'll try, Mom," I said, even though I knew there's no way in hell we'd make it to the cabin even if I wanted to go there.

"Damn it, my battery is running out," Mom said. "Can we Skype before I lose all reception? We all want to see you with our own eyes and make sure you're okay. Rachel did say you were hysterical."

I didn't really want to Skype with her. There is never a Skype conversation that transpires without some sort of negative comment about me. The color of my hair, the shirt I'm wearing, the condition of my skin—my mother misses nothing, especially an opportunity to point out areas of improvement.

Still, who knew when I'd get a chance to see her again? Her cell phone wasn't the only one running low on battery. There was no telling how long cell phones would work considering the downward spiral of things.

"Yeah, okay." I leaned out of the closet, giving Carter a questioning look. He stopped his whittling and joined me in the closet. There wasn't much light, but there was enough for the phone camera to register our faces.

"We're going to try and Skype with my mom," I said. "She and my sisters are going to our family's cabin in Big Bear. I told her we might try to join them."

Carter nodded, understanding what I wasn't saying. That Mom didn't know how bad things were in Arcata and that he wasn't supposed to tell her. Carter got my fucked-up relationship with my mother.

My hands moved of their own accord, mussing up his beard to make him look bedraggled. Carter disentangled my hand from his beard, frowning at me.

I felt like an idiot as soon as I realized I was subconsciously trying to rile up my mother. I didn't need to do that right now.

I took a deep breath and hit the Skype button. When my mom and sisters filled the screen, I waved to them.

Waving back at me was a woman with large breast implants, BOTOX lips, and chemically induced blond hair. My mom had a lot of work done even before my dad—her cosmetic surgeon—left her for his yoga instructor.

On either side of my mom were my two sisters. Lisa, the older sister, fights her full figure with strict adherence to CrossFit and the Paleo diet. Rachel, my younger sister, thought every article of clothing designed for the torso needed to have a plunging neckline. Today, she was in a snug velour sweat suit that barely covered her breasts. I don't know where she found this stuff, and I don't know how she had time to worry about her cleavage with all the shit going down.

"Jenna, please tell me you're going to let your hair grow back to its natural color when all this is over," said my mom, frowning critically at me.

"And if you're going to bring your lumberjack with you, please ask him to shave," said Rachel.

"Hi, Rachel," Carter said, ignoring the rude comment.

"Hi, Lumberjack," she replied, not even bothering to grace him with a fake smile like she usually did.

"Be nice to my boyfriend," I said, planting a full kiss on his lips. I feel like a jerk since that kiss was only for my family's benefit, not mine and Carter's.

"We'll charge our phones while we're driving, but there are reports of cell service being out all over the place," said Lisa. "Get out of there as soon as you can and come to Big Bear."

"I will." I give them my best fake smile, my throat tight. I might not like my family very much, but I still love them. I want them to get to safety.

"Don't let yourself go just because things might be rough for a while," Mom said. "Keep up your skin care routine. And don't forget to condition your hair."

Tears sprang to my eyes, a mix of indignation and despair roiling inside me.

"I will, Mom. Travel safe."

I let out a shuddering breath as the call was disconnected, unprepared for the sudden wave of emotion that hit me. This could be the last time I ever saw my mom and sisters.

When Carter put his arms around me, I buried my face in his shoulder. A few shuddering breaths left my body, but I managed to keep it together. I wiped my eyes dry on his shirt.

"I hope they make it," I whispered.

"They will," Carter said, voice strong and reassuring.

"Things aren't as bad in Southern California as they are here."

I nodded, releasing him to return to his project. I buried all thoughts of my mom and sisters, forcing my attention back to our current situation: that of Chris and Jake pounding on the bedroom door.

It took us another few hours, but soon Carter had sharpened spears for all of us. By that time, the stuffy heat of the room had grown unbearable. I wiped sweat from my eyes with the sleeve of my shirt. As much as I didn't want to confront Jake and Chris, I really, really wanted out of this room.

"Are we actually going to do this?" Eric asked as Carter passed out the homemade spears.

Bash in the heads of our former roommates? No one answered.

That's when we smelled it. Smoke.

"Oh, shit," Reed said. The wall between this bedroom and the room next door—the one shared by Reed and Eric—was smoking. Grayish white wisps curl into the air. With it came the distinct smell of pot.

"Dude, what did you do with that joint you were smoking?" Eric asked Reed.

"The joint *I* was smoking?" Reed demanded, offended. "That was *our* joint, dude. Not just mine."

"But you were smoking it last."

"That doesn't make it mine! Besides, that was hours ago. No way that joint could have started a fire now."

"It doesn't matter," I snapped. "What matters is that *something* in your room caught fire." No wonder it was so damn hot in here. I heft my makeshift spear. "We have to get out."

The first black tendrils curl around the wall, bits of it crumbling away to reveal insulation. Carter shoved the dresser away from the door. Jake and Chris both keened and snarled, bodily throwing themselves at it.

"Jenna," Carter said, "open the door on the count of

three."

I positioned myself beside the door that shook in its frame from the impact of those on the other side. Lila crouched behind me. She held her spear like a club, but from the look on her face, I wasn't confident she'd use it.

Reed, Eric, and Carter lined up on the other side, each brandishing their chair leg spears. I'd say they looked like warriors, except they were all too terrified to be mistaken for warriors.

Before I turned the doorknob, the door exploded inward. Jake's stocky frame tumbled through, covered in dried blood from a bad bite to the neck.

There were several seconds when all of us had the opportunity to lay into him with our spears. He was down, caught in the tangle of wood. But we stood there in frozen shock, staring at the blind, snarling thing that had once been our jovial friend. Flames of fire licked a widening hole in the wall.

Then Chris burst through, tripping and falling over Jake. He reached out with a bloody hand and grabbed my ankle.

In a state of panicked fear, I grasped my spear like a baseball bat. Screaming, I swung it at Chris's head. I struck him in the temple, but only hard enough to enrage him. As he turned toward me with a growl, my chest seized with fear.

Carter leaped forward, gripping his spear with both hands. He slammed it downward.

Warm blood sprayed out, soaking my pants. Chris collapsed and went still. His grasp on my ankle slackened. I scrambled backward, breathing with rapid panic.

Jake bucked, throwing off Chris and crawling free. He moved like an animal, charging on all fours straight at Reed.

This time, no one hesitated. Carter shattered the spell that rendered us motionless seconds before. All of us leaped at Jake with our spears. I drove mine through his back. I felt the bone of his spine crumple beneath the impact. The force traveled up both arms and rattled my teeth.

Eric shoved one through the base of his skull. Carter and Reed's pierced his neck and head.

Jake went still. The room fell silent, our harsh breathing mingling with the crackling flames.

Carter was the first of us to recover. He sprinted out of the room, heading toward the kitchen to retrieve the fire extinguisher.

When we had the fire out, we conducted a quick search of the remaining three bedrooms in the small apartment. Two were empty, but inside the third one we found someone. Or what was left of him. Craig had been almost completely eaten, his rib cage bulging upward from the floor. Torn pieces of his flannel shirt lay scattered around the room.

I clung to Carter, letting shock spread quietly through my body. I had just helped kill someone. Two someones. Arguably, both had already been dead, but did that excuse the act? I wasn't sure.

*

I swallow hard as I watch Carter's mom comfort Reed next to the pile of bodies we cleared out from the Creekside dorm. Our small group had killed many of them. Even Lila had pitched in. Most of them had been concentrated in front of our building. We had to use the Attack and Stack method to keep them from breaking through the front door and stampeding us.

Was what we did to clear the dorm and save ourselves any different from what Carter's mom had done? Somehow it seems different, killing real people versus zombies.

I resolve not to judge her. She saved us. I'll focus on that.

"We should get inside," she says as she and Reed cross the parking lot and return to us. To my shock, I see she has the guns from the men tucked into the waistband of her stretch pants. She sees me looking but doesn't attempt to explain. Instead, she leads us inside, limping on her bad ankle.

6
Ultra Brew

KATE

I search inside myself, trying to decide how I feel about the fact that I just murdered two men. Not zombies, but real, living people. I killed them in less time than it takes to drop a deuce.

I should feel bad, or dirty, or remorseful. At the very least, I should be worried about karma or an impending trip to hell.

But all I feel is relief. Relief that my son is alive, and those two scumbags are vulture food. If I was handed a do-over, I wouldn't change a thing.

I realize this says a lot about me and the person I've become over the last two hundred miles, but I don't have the energy to care. Carter is alive and safe. That's all that matters.

Anger hangs over the small group as I lead them through the lounge area. The comfy sofas and plush chairs I remember from my visits are still here, except now the room is adorned with bloodstains in several places. The fluorescent lights sit dormant, casting everything in a dark half-light.

Someone is handy with a screwdriver. The vending machines have all been dismantled, the big Plexiglas windows stacked against the far wall. The junk food has been raided. I notice a few of the healthier snacks—nuts and dried fruit—still stacked inside.

By the time we make it back to the dorm apartment on the second floor, the kids are ready to rip Reed a new asshole. Not that he doesn't deserve it for putting them all at risk. I'd seen true remorse in him when he helped me dispose of the bodies, which infinitesimally alleviates some of my anger.

"You fucking asshole." The boy named Eric, who has a fledgling potbelly, closes the apartment door. His voice is flat with rage. "What the fuck happened out there today?"

"I'll tell you later," Reed mumbles, heading toward the hall that leads to the bedrooms.

"No way." Jenna blocks the entrance. "You brought home men who wanted to kill us. You owe us the truth. The full truth."

I do my best to covertly study the tall girl with light brown hair who's dating my son. I like the way she stands up to Reed even as I struggle not to be offended by her existence in Carter's life.

"Later, I promise." Reed tries to push past her, but Jenna stands firm. Another point in her favor.

"Don't blow us off," Carter says. "Those men chased us and shot at us, but not just because you stole their drugs. You need to come clean with us right fucking now."

The severity in my son's voice grabs my attention. Sweet, easygoing Carter doesn't often lose his temper. Oddly, this sets me at ease. Hopefully, it means he isn't waiting for a magical rescue by government officials like Lila and Johnny.

Reed slumps onto the sofa, looking like a kicked dog. He runs his hands through his poufy hair.

"Look, I come from a poor family in Oakland, all right? My dad is a truck driver. My mom took off when I was a little kid. The only way I could go to college was if I took out loans that would take me fifty years to pay back. I didn't want to go into debt." He rests his elbows on his knees, refusing to look at any of us. "One day, the guy I bought pot from said he knew a guy. If I agreed to sell stuff for this guy, I could make enough to pay for college."

Reed continues to work his hands in his hair. Silence stretches. None of us offer comfort, even though his anguish is obvious.

When Reed speaks again, his voice is gruff. "The guy I work for is called Granjero. There's always been a turf war in Arcata between Granjero and Mr. Rosario."

"So, when most of the town was zombified, you decided it was okay to grab some of Mr. Rosario's stuff?" Jenna demands.

"I didn't figure anyone would ever know." Reed shrugs as he rises, giving us all a defensive glare. "How was I supposed to know a few of Mr. Rosario's guys were still around? Look, I fucked up, okay? I'm sorry. Now if you are all done glaring at me, I'm going to get high."

"Not so fast." I limp over to him. "Give me the drugs." Reed may have thought no one noticed him retrieve the bags of acid from the ground, but I'd seen him scoop them up during the confusion.

Reed opens his mouth. Before he speaks, I hold up a hand. "Don't try to bullshit me. I saw you take them. No one needs to be high on acid at a time like this." Some might argue the end of the world is a perfect time to be on acid, but that's not how I see it. "Now, Reed. Hand it over." I might not be this young man's mother, but if I talk like one, maybe he'll comply. He did, after all, shed a few tears of shame outside when he helped me dispose of the bodies.

The sullen glare Reed gives me isn't so different from the one Carter might give me. He slams the baggies of acid into my hand and slinks from the room. This time, Jenna doesn't block his way. The quiet that follows

Reed's exit is thunderous.

"Kate," Eric says, voice wavering in a brave attempt to dispel the tension, "you're not by any chance covered in Lila's weed balm, are you?"

"It's athlete's balm," Lila says. She rises so easily to the bait, I get the impression that she and Eric go at each other on a regular basis. "And yes, she has some on her ankle. She's helping me test my product."

Eric snorts. "I'll make you the best pot brownies you've ever had," he says to me. "*That* will cure all your aches and pains."

"She wants pain relief, Eric," Lila says. "She doesn't want to get stoned." She hesitates, looking at me. "You don't want to get stoned, do you?"

Eric doesn't give me a chance to answer. "You can answer that question *after* you try one of my brownies. Besides, we need to celebrate not dying. Brownies are perfect for that. If you knew how many people lined up to write term papers for me in exchange for brownies, you'd be impressed."

He and Lila continue bickering. I watch them, refusing to take sides, although I do not intend to eat the brownies.

Carter pushes off from the wall and stalks to the door. Tension makes the tendons in his neck stand up. He clenches his jaw so tightly his teeth grind.

Jenna straightens, eyes filling with concern as she takes in Carter's stance. "Where are you going?" she asks.

"I'm going to work on Skip," he replies.

I follow him out the door, limping on my bad ankle. I expect Jenna to come, too. She takes a few steps, sees me, and then falls back. I don't know if this is because she's uncomfortable around me, or if she's trying to give us some privacy. Whatever the case, I'm grateful. I still haven't adjusted to this new reality where zombies walk the earth and my son has a girlfriend.

"You should stay inside and rest your ankle," Carter

tells me. "We got you first aid supplies."

"I'm okay."

"I've heard that before. Usually it means you hurt like hell."

I shrug, not bothering to deny it.

"Aren't you going to put shoes on?"

"No."

We both look down at my wrecked feet. It's obvious they're too swollen and fucked up for shoes right now.

Carter gives me a disgusted look that says, *Whatever, Mom,* then stomps down the hallway to the stairs. He pauses at the front glass doors to scan the area outside. Nothing moves besides the vultures and the flies. When he determines the way is safe, he pushes out the front door.

I follow him around the building to a small clearing of redwoods, stopping to survey the beat-up blue Dodge Caravan that sits beneath the trees. The hood is faded. Paint around the doors is starting to curl up, exposing the raw fiberglass underneath. The passenger side window is missing.

Carter stops in front of the busted van, glaring at the world at large. Then he spins around, focusing that glare on me.

I set my shoulders, meeting his angry eyes. "Just say it."

"You killed those men!" The words burst from his throat. "Mom, you *killed* them!"

Anger and fear war in his features. I want to hug him, to comfort him like I did when he was a little kid. But a hug won't fix what I've done.

"I did what I had to do to save you," I reply. "I wish it could have been different."

"What if someone finds out?" he bellows.

I'm not sure how to respond to this. "It's not exactly a secret, Carter. Your roommates all saw it."

"I'm not talking about them!" He swallows, gathering

self-control. His voice drops to a whisper. "Mom, what if you go to jail?"

His question takes me by surprise. I absorb his features, taking in the fear in his eyes. I realize belatedly that he's not angry at me for killing Mr. Rosario's men. He's afraid I'll be caught and punished for it.

The idea of a surviving police officer coming to arrest me is laughable, but I do my best to digest Carter's concern and address it.

"Sweetie, there's no one around to arrest me. The only way to survive is to kill people. You told me yourself you've killed zombies."

"That's not the same thing. They're already dead. You killed real people. What if someone finds out when this mess is cleared up?"

I finally understand what has him so upset. Like Johnny and Lila, he thinks our current state is temporary. He's in full-fledged denial.

"If police come for me," I say at last, "I'll deal with it."

His mouth twists. "That's all you have to say? You'll *deal with it?*"

"What else can I say? I'm not sorry. I didn't run two hundred miles and lose Frederico to watch some dickheads kill my son in front of me. No fucking way." My words come out too hard and blunt. I wish I could take them back, mash them up and soften them, but that's not in the cards today. I'm too tired and too achy to find soft words.

Carter's shoulders sag. "I just don't want anything to happen to you," he mutters, looking at the ground.

My irritation dissipates. My insides soften with love for my son. "It's okay, baby. Thanks for caring." I reach out and squeeze his shoulder. "We haven't had a chance to catch up since I got here. Tell me how you're doing."

"I'm fine, all things considered." He cocks his head at me, all remaining tension draining away. "You wanna meet Skip?"

"Skip?" I shrug, thinking he has another roommate. "Sure. Where is he?"

To my surprise, Carter gestures to the deplorable transportation specimen behind him.

"Mom, meet Skip. Reed calls it our soccer-mom-mobile."

I take in the battered state of the minivan. "Why Skip?" I ask.

"Because Jenna and I are going to use it to skip from town to town when this semi-apocalypse blows over." He opens the side door, revealing an interior stripped of seats and carpet.

Semi-apocalypse. I do my best to swallow the uneasiness summoned by that word, studying the interior of the van. The bare metal floor is exposed. Up against the passenger sidewall are three beer kegs. They sit inside a plywood holder bolted to the side of Skip.

"I paid a few guys to make these keg holders in the woodshop," Carter says. "I'm going to drill holes and mount taps in the side of the van. Jenna and I are going to travel all over the country and sell beer at ultramarathon races."

I nod, sitting on the lip of the open sliding door. "How long have you been dating Jenna?" I prop my bad foot up inside the van. It hurts like a son of a bitch.

"Six months."

"Six *months*? You didn't say anything about her the last time I was up here to visit."

"Jenna was down in Southern California for her sister's birthday," he says with a shrug. "She didn't come up in our conversations."

"Carter." He's bullshitting me, and we both know it.

"Look, I knew you'd have a hard time with it, okay? It was hard on you when Dad died. It was hard on me and Uncle Rico, too, but the three of us found a way through it. I knew introducing someone new into our family would throw you off."

He watches me warily. I swallow, waging a silent, inner battle. Everything he says is true, even if I want to deny it.

"You're right," I say stiffly. "I'm having a hard time with it. It's my issue, though. I promise to try and get over myself, okay? If this girl is special to you, I want to get to know her." That sounded okay. Now I just have to work myself into believing those words. "Tell me how you guys met."

He sits next to me in the van. "We met one night at a dorm mixer in the lounge downstairs. I wasn't really into the party. I was reading one of my beer-making books on the couch. She came and sat next to me and started asking a bunch of questions. Turns out she had an interest in learning to make beer." A goofy smile spreads across his face.

In that single smile, I see how head-over-heels he is for this girl. I keep quiet, wrestling with churning emotions. I should be happy for Carter. I *need* to be happy for him.

"Anyway, we talked for hours. I agreed to let her help me make some beer." He gestures at the three kegs behind us. "These are our brews. We call them Ultra Brews." He grins at my lifted eyebrows. "Named after ultramarathons, of course. This is the DNF. It's an IPA." He taps the first keg. DNF stands for *Did Not Finish*, a racing term used by ultrarunners when they fail to complete a race. "This is the Vert, for the vertical gain of ultramarathons. It's a stout. And this is the Finisher, a pilsner. Look, Jenna already has some labels designed."

He pulls out a binder stashed between two of the kegs. Inside are dozens of pages, each filled with different label ideas for each of the beers.

"Jenna is an artist. She likes to draw," he explains.

The girl has a gift. That much is evident from the first page. Her lines are strong and sure. She's either spent a lot of time at races or a lot of time talking with Carter about them, because every one of them captures the spirit of an ultra. From steep mountain trails to a finish line ribbon, it's all there.

"And look at these." Carter's voice lifts with excitement and pride. "There's even a few ideas for our Ultra Brew logo. Once we settle on one, we're going to have the graphics painted on the outside of Skip."

"I love her work," I say, flipping through the binder. It's a relief to have something positive to say about his girlfriend.

"Jenna is double majoring in business and art. We were in the process of working up a financial plan for Ultra Brew when the outbreak happened. Maybe we'll have time to finish everything while we wait for all this to clear up and return to normal."

"You think everything is going to return to normal?" I ask.

"Our country has more resources than any other in the world," he says with a shrug. "Things might be bad for six months or so, but it can't stay this way."

I look away, staring at the back of Creekside. The wood siding, painted to match the redwood trees of the campus, looms over us in big silence.

"Don't you think it will clear up?" Carter frowns at me.

"I hope so, baby." I smile at him. "I love everything you and Jenna have dreamed up together. I look forward to getting to know her."

"She's great. I know you guys will get along. She likes running. She used to run track."

I hate the fact that this bit of information melts something inside me. I shouldn't soften to someone because she likes running, but I can't help it.

"I have some paint remover," Carter says. "I'm going to start removing the bad paint, so Jenna and I have a clean canvas to work on." He grabs one of the cans of turpentine from the back of the van, along with some old rags.

I join him, grateful to have something mindless to occupy my brain. I don't have to think about Jenna, or Carter's state of denial, or how we're going to survive the next week, or the fact that my bullet wound hurts like a motherfucker. All I have to do is strip some paint.

It's almost as blissful as running.

Almost.

*

It's dusk by the time Carter and I return to the dorm apartment. The air has cleared of the earlier argument. Eric and Reed are eating brownies baked on the barbecue. Jenna and Lila are giving one another pedicures. Johnny sits at the kitchen table talking to someone over a ham radio.

The living room is a mess. Discarded pieces of clothing, mostly jackets, shoes, and socks, are scattered around the room and draped over various pieces of furniture. A mixing bowl and spoon have been added to the precarious pile in the sink.

It's all eerily normal. Like a slice of old-world reality has been preserved in the delicate bubble of this apartment. You wouldn't know several of the residents had been held at gunpoint. You wouldn't know they'd all seen me kill two men a few hours ago. You certainly wouldn't know the world had been turned upside down on its head by hordes of the undead.

"How does your ankle feel?" Lila asks. "Do you want some more athlete's balm?"

Eric snorts. "Lila thinks she's going to make millions on her pot lotion."

Lila rolls her eyes. "Eric thinks he can scrape through life by trading pot brownies for term papers."

"I'll take some more of the balm." I might not like

smelling like a bong, but I have to admit it feels a little better than it did a few hours ago.

"What did you think of Skip?" Jenna asks, looking up from her pedicure. The smile she gives me is tentative.

"It's the soccer-mom-mobile," Reed quips.

"It's great," I say to Jenna, ignoring Reed. Now is as good a time as any to support my son in his relationship. "I think you guys have a great idea with your Ultra Brew concept." I don't mention there won't be any more ultras.

"Here." Carter hands me a first aid kit. "We got this from a guy studying to be a medic. You should go take care of yourself."

"Thanks, sweetie." My throat tightens as I consider the danger he placed himself in to get these things for me. "Next time, I'll make do with whatever you have on hand, okay? You don't need to put yourself at risk for me."

He looks pointedly at my feet. "You have blisters the size of turnips. Were you planning to lance those with a kitchen knife?"

Johnny pauses in his conversation on the ham radio. "You lance your own blisters?"

I don't bother trying to explain how painful and uncomfortable it is to walk on feet covered in blisters. "I'll just go clean up in the bathroom."

As I head down the hall, I swallow against a growing knot of anxiety in my gut. These kids, with their pot brownies and pedicures and beer, haven't fully made the transition into the new world. It doesn't take a genius to see they're all sitting around waiting for things to get flipped right side up. If they can't accept the new reality, they won't survive.

7
Darkness

JENNA

That night I go to bed without dinner.

I tried to pretend everything was normal, that we hadn't been held at gunpoint. I tried to pretend it didn't bother me when Carter stalked out of the apartment without so much as a backward glance at me. I tried to pretend his mom hadn't cut me off when I tried to go after him.

Giving myself a pedicure hadn't fixed anything. Neither had the useless banter I tossed about with Reed and Eric while they made brownies on the barbecue.

All in all, the day left me feeling like I'd been fed to a wood chipper. Tired of pretending, I went to bed after Carter and his mom got back from working on Skip. Kate kept sneaking glances at me, but looked away anytime I caught her looking.

I always marveled at the way Carter talked about his mom. It was evident they got along and had a good relationship, even if she had gone over the deep end when his dad died. I can't fathom getting along with my mom, even though I secretly miss her and my sisters. I hope they're safe.

I lie in bed, staring up at the dark ceiling. With the streetlights outside having gone out when we lost electricity, there's little ambient light in the room. The blackness suits my mood.

When the door opens, I spot the tall, unmistakable silhouette of Carter. He's a lean smudge against the surrounding gloom of the tiny room.

"Hey, babe," he says quietly.

I don't answer right away, trying to decide if I want to pretend to be asleep.

"Hey," I say at last.

The side of the bed dips as he sits down next to me. "Sorry I stormed out earlier."

His apology chips away at the resentment that's built in me all evening. "You okay?" I ask. "What your mom did . . . I know it upset you."

His laugh is toneless. "It's not every day you see your mom kill two men in front of you."

"It's not every day you're held at gunpoint by drug dealers during a zombie apocalypse."

His hand, warm and strong, finds mine. "We've all been through a lot today. I shouldn't have stormed off and left you. I'm sorry."

And just like that, all my resentment slides away. I lace my fingers through his. "It's okay."

When he leans down to press a kiss to my lips, I wrap my arms around his neck and pull him down. He sinks onto the bed beside me, pulling me tight against him. I burrow my head against his chest, feeling better than I've felt all day.

"How did things go with your mom?"

He doesn't answer right away. "She's different," he says at last. "She was so . . . fragile after Dad died. She isn't fragile anymore."

The woman I saw outside today is definitely not fragile. Scary, yes. Tough, yes. Crazy, most definitely. But not fragile.

"I told her I was worried about her getting arrested when the dust settles," Carter continues. "She shrugged it

---

off and said she'd deal with it when the time came."

Once again, I find myself at a crossroads with Carter. He thinks the world is going to fix itself. Even with evidence to the contrary all around us—not the least being our experience today—he keeps burying his head in the sand.

A knot of frustration forms in my chest. I do my best to ignore it, not wanting to fight. Instead, I concentrate on the comforting feel of his arms around me.

"Sounds like a reasonable plan to me," I say. "There's plenty of other things to worry about right now." Like clearing all the other rooms in Creekside and organizing the food, but I don't say this to Carter.

He sighs. "You're right. We can worry about it if it happens."

I don't want to think about tomorrow or the future. I don't want to think about today. All I want is Carter.

Instead of answering, I twist my head, find his mouth, and kiss him. His warm hand slips beneath the hem of my shirt and grips my waist. I don't resist when he pulls off my shirt and unclips my bra.

There's barely any light, but even so, I feel his eyes rove over me. I know all too well what he sees. Large breasts. A trim waist, flat stomach, and round hips. They're the parts most boys see when they look at me. Combined with my long legs, I've been compared to a Victoria's Secret model since I was fourteen years old.

"You're so gorgeous," he murmurs against my skin.

When he touches me, I feel cherished. Carter's the only boy who doesn't treat me like an object or a trophy. Even so, the compliment makes me stiffen. A lifetime of programming can't be wiped away, not even in six blissful months of dating the sweetest guy on the planet.

He absorbs my silence like he always does. I sense the conflict it stirs within him and wish I could get my ass in line and act like a normal girl. I should say thanks. I should tell him how much I love his blue eyes and his smile. Returning a compliment is normal couple stuff.

Words refuse to form on my tongue, lodging instead in my throat.

"I have something from our scavenging mission today." I feel his grin against my face. He's trying to lighten the mood for my sake.

I nip playfully at his ear, grateful for his understanding. "What do you have?"

He reaches into his pocket and tosses a few crinkly wrappers between us. I laugh as pale green squares materialize in front of me, their shape unmistakable.

"Really?" I ask. "You got glow-in-the-dark condoms?"

"It's not like we have television anymore," he replies. "We need something to entertain us."

I fall laughing in his arms. "You, Carter Stephenson, were always more entertaining than television."

Someday, I have to tell him how much I care about him. Someday.

But not tonight.

8
Stairwell

KATE

The next morning, I wake early. Dressed in the capri stretch pants and plain T-shirt given to me by Lila and Jenna when I first arrived, I rise from my bed on the sofa and head to the stairwell. Running always helps me clear my head. Since it isn't exactly safe to go out for a run, the stairwell is the next best thing.

My muscles are full of protest. The night of sleep and inactivity gave them an excuse to stiffen. My legs scream with every step. My back, arms, and stomach are sore. My gunshot wound throbs. Worst of all is the swollen ankle and poison oak crawling up my arms. Bits of it have seeped onto my neck. I'm an achy, itchy mess.

All the more reason to tackle the stairs.

But my achy body isn't the main reason I head for the stairs when the sun is barely up. I need to think. I need to come up with a plan to keep Carter and his friends safe. To drag their brains into the new reality.

To my surprise, when I swing open the door, I find someone else already there. Jenna, sweat dripping down her temples, pauses on the landing when she sees me. The flashlight in her hand illuminates the cement floor between us.

We stare at each other in surprise, unspoken

awkwardness ramping up with each passing second. I should say something, make an effort at friendliness with my son's girlfriend. Truth be told, she's the last person I want to share this stairwell with.

"Hey, Mrs. S.," she says, the first to break the silence.

I attempt a friendly smile, hoping it doesn't look like a grimace. "Hey, Jenna. Please, call me Kate. What are you doing here?" I try to make this last question casual, but it comes out sounding more like a demand.

She doesn't react to my tone, instead plastering on her own forced smile. "I used to run track. I fell out of the habit when I got to college. Yesterday, when those guys came after us, we had to take the long way around to get back to Creekside. We didn't run far, but it made me realize I'm really out of shape. I want to start exercising again."

This is the first practical thing I've heard anyone say since arriving here. It makes me reluctantly warm to Jenna.

"What were your distances in track?" I ask, intrigued despite myself.

"I did hurdles and the mile. I originally signed up for track to get back at my mom for trying to make me into a cheerleader, but I ended up really liking it."

"Maybe you should give us all hurdle lessons," I say. "That could come in handy if we need to make a run for it and jump over zombies."

Her answering grin is tentative. "Maybe I should. I could set up a course in the hallway."

I raise a brow. "Coffee tables for obstacles?"

"No, too wide. Maybe some pillows. They would be about the right size."

The mental image of the hallway lined with pillows, coupled with the idea of making Carter, Reed, and the others leap over them, brings a laugh bubbling up. Jenna laughs, too.

It's a nice moment. I let it stretch out, enjoying the

sensation of sharing a chuckle with Carter's girlfriend. Maybe this won't be as awkward as I'd feared. Maybe I won't completely mess it up.

"Should you be moving on that ankle?" she asks.

"A normal doctor would tell me to ice it, elevate it, and stay on my backside for a week or two," I reply. "But it will loosen up and heal faster if I move it gently."

Jenna frowns. "No offense, Mrs. S.—Kate—but I don't know if walking up and down the stairs is considered gentle."

"It's gentler than running up and down the stairs."

A crease dents her brow. "Do you run up and down a lot of stairs?"

"There's an ultramarathon called the Quad Dipsea. It's twenty-eight miles of stairs."

"Twenty-eight *miles* of stairs?"

"Yeah. They go up one side of a mountain and down the other side. You run them four times in the race. There's over nine-thousand feet of vertical climbing."

Jenna digests this. "You know," she says after a minute, "that sort of sounds fun. If you had time to train for it."

I look at her askance, trying to discern if she's being sincere or sarcastic. As far as I can tell, she looks sincere. "It is fun."

"I'd say maybe I'd run it sometime, but I doubt there will be any ultramarathons in the near future."

Her words surprise me. "Why do you say that?"

"The world as we knew it is over," she says. "I know it's gone, even if everyone else is in denial."

"I noticed." It's a huge relief to know someone else sees the true state of the world. I thaw a bit more toward her. "Can I join you?" I gesture to the stairs.

This time, her smile is less forced. "Yeah, okay. Honestly, it would be nice to have company. The stairwell is kind of creepy."

I hadn't thought of it that way. After being out on the

open road, the stairwell seems like a safe container.

We tread up to the third floor in silence. When we reach the landing, we turn around and go back down. My bare feet are soundless on the concrete steps. Jenna, in her workout shoes, keeps her steps light.

I attempt to make conversation. "Has anyone, ah, noticed that there's an ant problem in the kitchen?"

Her grimace tells me she's well aware of the disgusting state of things. "Things pretty much went to shit when the power went out. We have water for drinking and keeping the toilets full, but no one wants to go to the creek to get water for washing dishes. We all talk about how great it is to have a nearby water source, but no one has used it yet."

I glance at Jenna through my periphery, an idea forming in my mind. "Any chance you're up for a mission?"

"You mean go to the creek for water?" Her eyes widen.

"There's two of us," I reply. "As far as I can tell, the immediate area around here is pretty clear. We can watch each other's backs." It wouldn't be a bad idea for the two of us to spend time together. What better way to get to know one another? I'm sure Carter would approve.

"What do you say?" I ask.

9

Water Run

KATE

Armed with my screwdriver, Jenna's wooden spear, and good intentions, we head to the first floor. Except for Johnny, who's up talking on his ham radio, everyone else in the dorm is still asleep, even though it's almost nine in the morning. I forget how much kids in their late teens and early twenties like to sleep.

When we told Johnny our plan, he didn't offer to help. He was too absorbed in a conversation with some guy named Foot Soldier on the other end of the ham. It's nice to know he has his priorities straight.

My battered feet are encased in my trashed running shoes, the same ones I wore all the way here. It was too painful to put on socks. As much as I prefer to be barefoot right now, going into the woods without shoes is plain dumb. The laces are loose, just tight enough to keep the shoes on my feet, but not so tight as to pinch the various blisters and other pain points.

Between me and Jenna is a large plastic tote we pulled from the hall closet. It had been filled with someone's shoes until we dumped them out.

"If you told me two weeks ago that I'd be filling someone's shoe tub with drinking water, I'd have rolled my eyes," Jenna says.

"Dish water," I remind her. "We're getting water to wash the dishes."

"I know, but if there's any leftover there's a good chance we'll use it for cooking or drinking."

"True." Another thought occurs to me. "What are you guys doing with dirty clothes?"

The look she gives me is one I know all too well. It's a sheepish grimace that tells me I've asked the very question she doesn't want to answer.

"Um, we sort of toss them into the dorm next door."

Well, at least they're not letting dirty clothes *and* dirty dishes pile up in their dorm.

"I know it's not a long-term solution," Jenna continues. "To be honest, I'm not looking forward to washing clothes by hand."

"Understandable. Doesn't sound fun."

We stand at the double glass door entryway of Creekside, peering out into the parking lot. The sky is overcast, the air foggy. The vultures and flies are the only things moving.

"Come on," I say, taking the lead. "Let's go."

I step out into the parking lot, holding my screwdriver at the ready.

I considered bringing one of the guns from the drug dealers but ruled it out. Firearms make my skin crawl, and not just because I don't know how to use them. Accidental deaths are too likely with guns in the hands of rookies.

I left them wrapped in a towel with Reed's acid underneath the living room couch. Gauging by the other odds and ends under the sofa—a pair of underwear, a shoe, and a spatula—I'm not worried about anyone poking around and finding them.

Also under the sofa is my railroad spike, the only remnant from my journey to Arcata. The sight of it fills me with a montage of nightmares I'd rather not think about. Tucking it away is the easiest way to keep the memories at bay.

Jenna and I hold the big plastic tub between us. We also each wear a backpack filled with empty water bottles.

I pause as we step outside, once again scanning the parking lot. I strain my ears, listening for the telltale moans. I also listen for voices or any signs of people. To be honest, I'm more wary of people. Zombies I can handle.

"Looks clear," Jenna whispers.

I nod in agreement. We head around to the back of the dorm where Skip is parked.

"Carter told me about your plans to start a business together." I scan our surroundings, never resting my gaze in one place for long. "I like the beer labels you designed."

"Really?" Her back straightens, eyes brightening.

"Yeah. You did a great job capturing the ultra experience in your art. My favorite is the Vert."

"Thanks, Kate." Emotion swims behind her eyes. She looks both pleased and upset at the same time.

"Did I say something wrong?" It seemed like we were getting off on the right foot, despite my issues. I don't want to ruin it.

Jenna shakes her head. "I was just thinking about my mom. She thought my art was a waste of time. She thought everything that didn't involve snagging a rich boyfriend was a waste of time." She looks away. "I know it's dumb, but I wouldn't mind hearing her insult my art right now."

My throat tightens in empathy. All of Carter's companions are separated from their parents and families, both physically and electronically. Not knowing if they're safe or dead can't be easy on any of them.

"When was the last time you spoke to her?" I ask.

"A few days ago. She and my sisters live in Southern California. They were heading out to our family's cabin in Big Bear." Her voice drops, thick with emotion. "I hope they made it."

I struggle to find the right words. Jenna deserves more than empty assurances. "I hope so, too," I say at last.

This gets me a weak smile. We pass Skip and head into the redwood forest that grows behind the dorms. Carter and I used to take walks through these trees when I came to visit him. There are numerous footpaths, as well as a Frisbee golf course.

Morning fog sits on the ground, lowering visibility in the trees to a twenty-five-yard radius. This makes my shoulders itch. Mouth dry, I press forward, keeping my ears peeled for sound. I do my best not to limp on my injured ankle, to move as quietly as possible over a forest floor covered with pine needles.

It takes us five minutes to reach the small creek. Due to the fog, I hear the soft tinkle of flowing water before I see it.

I pause, looking around and listening. Jenna does the same. I can't help but approve of her caution. Of everything about her so far. My son snagged himself a girl with a good head on her shoulders.

"Looks clear," Jenna murmurs.

I nod in agreement. We drop our backpacks on the bank. Staying silent, we fill the bottles in our packs. Anything used for drinking will need to be boiled first. Even better would be water purification tablets.

There's an outdoors store in downtown Arcata. I make a mental note to plan a trip there in the next few days. Water purification tablets aren't the only things we could use. General camping and survival supplies would be handy.

They also have running shoes. I most definitely need a new pair. Come to think of it, all the kids could use a decent pair of shoes. Being able to move fast on foot is essential.

Beside me, Jenna stiffens. I sweep my gaze across the forest in response, looking for whatever caught her attention. All I see is redwoods, ferns, and fog. The sound of running water is the only thing I hear.

Jenna's hand lifts, finger pointing. I study the spot she indicates, searching for movement.

A deer emerges from the fog, ears flicked forward as she stares at us. We could be staring at our next meal if either of us knew how to hunt. Or shoot a gun. Or had a gun with us, for that matter.

Even if I did have a gun with me, the only thing I might succeed in doing is drawing attention of anyone or anything that's nearby. Nope, better to coexist with the pretty deer.

The doe continues to stare at us as we fill our bottles. Her ears swivel, flicking first in our direction, then rotating away to the rest of the forest. What I wouldn't give for rotating ears.

Jenna and I finish with the bottles and move onto the tote. The deer bounds away.

We shift, tipping the tote into the water. Something stirs on the edge of the fog again. I look up as two zombies lumber into view.

They're students, each of them dressed in jeans and sweat jackets. They move without sound, lifting their noses to scent the air.

My wrist locks around Jenna's arm, freezing us in place. I gesture ever so slightly with my chin, bringing her attention to the two zombies standing where the deer had been.

Jenna and I exchange looks. Do we dispatch the zombies, or ignore them and hope they go away?

The tote, half filled with water, gives me my answer. We can't hope to lug the tote away if the zombies are still alive. We'll make too much noise and draw their attention.

When Jenna's hand snakes to her wooden spear on the ground, I know she's reached the same conclusion. I nod to tell her I'm on the same page, drawing my screwdriver from my belt.

The creek lies between the zombies and us. I step carefully into the water, ignoring the cold bite as the current laps up to my ankle. Normally I would try to step on rocks to keep my feet dry, but I can't risk any of them shifting under my feet and making noise. Or, even worse, slipping and causing me to stumble. Stealth is our best friend right now, which means walking through the creek bed.

Jenna follows me without protest. When we exit the water, the zombies sniff the air. One of them grunts. The other lets out a soft moan in response.

I make eye contact with Jenna, holding up three fingers. She nods in understanding.

I count down, dropping a finger each time. Three. Two. One.

We charge forward, weapons raised.

It's impossible to move silently. Our shoes scuff against the pine needles and dirt, bringing both zombies' heads whipping around in our direction.

We're on them before they can do anything more than let out dual moans. Jenna strikes first, the length of her spear giving her an advantage. She jams it straight into the eye socket of the first zombie, driving the beast to the ground under the force of the impact.

I'm a heartbeat behind her. My screwdriver forces me into close quarters with the remaining zombie. His nails scrabble at me, his jaw unhinging as he lunges forward.

My screwdriver hits him in the nose. It drives through the soft cartilage and up into the brain. Thick, dark blood squirts onto my hand and wrist.

I leap sideways, letting the body *thunk* to the ground. My harsh breathing fogs the air in front of my face.

My eyes find Jenna's. We grin at each other, sharing a moment of silent triumph.

And then a grayish hand reaches out of the gloom, latching around my injured ankle. I yelp as I'm pulled backward.

10
First Fight

JENNA

Kate goes down, her ankle snagged by a zombie that crawls out of a cluster of ferns. Its back legs are ruined, forcing it to pull itself forward like a seal.

Jason. The name flashes through my head. That was the name of the boy before he became a zombie. I had a class with him, though I can't recall which one. *Jason.*

He has Carter's mom.

Kate flips around and delivers a vicious kick to Jason's head. Her legs are bare between her shoes and her capris pants. Jason snarls, but doesn't release his hold. He drags himself forward, jaws yawning. The bare skin of Kate's leg is only a few inches from his teeth.

I leap forward, bringing my spear down like a club. I smack it as hard as I can into the back of Jason's skull.

The soft *thunk* of wood hitting bone sends a chill up my spine, but I don't let up. I bring the spear back up and deliver a second blow. This time, the spear sinks all the way into his skull.

The creature that used to be Jason rolls sideways. Viscous blood seeps out of his head.

"Thanks." Kate gulps in air as she extracts her leg.

I offer her a hand up. She takes it, stumbling as she puts weight on her bad ankle.

"You okay?" I ask.

"I'm good." Kate retrieves her screwdriver out of the zombie she killed. "Thanks for having my back."

"What are you guys doing out here?" demands a new voice.

We spin around to see Carter emerge from the fog. His beard and hair are in disarray, eyes wide with fear and concern. There's something else there, too, something I don't see often in my boyfriend: anger.

"Hey, babe," I say softly, putting on my best smile to assure him we're okay. I leave my spear in the skull of Jason for the moment, thinking it better not to draw attention to it.

"We were just getting water," Kate says.

Carter's jaw sags open. "You were getting *water*? Why?"

"Why?" Kate echoes. "Carter, have you had a look at your dorm lately? It's overrun with ants. We need to clean it up." Kate gives me an approving smile. "You missed seeing your girlfriend take out two zombies. She's good with that spear."

A warm rush of pleasure flows through me at her words. I want Carter's mom to like me. If that means I have to be good at killing zombies, I'm happy to show her I can hold my own.

Carter's eyes travel from the three dead zombies to our bloody weapons. "You can't come out here alone!" His voice is nearly a shout.

Kate blinks at him. "We weren't alone, honey," she replies. "We were watching each other's back."

His gaze swings between us. Can he see we're getting along? I want him to see that. I know he put off introducing us. I know he was afraid Kate wouldn't like me.

"You guys scared me. Did it occur to either of you to leave a note so I would know where you are?"

"We told Johnny," Kate replies.

"All he told me was that you guys went outside. He didn't know where you went, or why."

"He must have been distracted," I say, trying to explain. "He was talking on his ham."

Carter's face darkens.

"Let's start over," Kate says. "Jenna and I both noticed the ant problem in the kitchen. We came out here to get water, so we could clean up."

"Why didn't either of you wake me? I would have come with you."

"You were asleep," Kate says. "Besides, Jenna and I were fine. See?" She gestures to the dead zombies.

Carter sags, the fight leaving him. "Next time you want to come out, promise you'll come get me."

I nod, eager to move past the awkward moment. Retrieving my spear, I cross the creek to where Carter stands. I give him a quick kiss on the lips.

Kate joins us. We gather up the filled water bottles. As we lever up the heavy tote now filled with water, Carter makes a face.

"How long do you think we're going to have to live like this?" he asks. "You know, before the dust clears?"

I frown, not sure how to answer that. Kate and I exchange a look. Carter, seeing it, stiffens.

"What?" he demands.

Neither of us answers. After a moment, Kate says, "Let's just get the water back to Creekside. I didn't run two hundred miles to live in an ant's nest."

Carter frowns. "Don't blow me off, Mom."

"Babe," I say, steeling myself for the words that need to be said, "the world is over. As in, *over* over. The dust isn't going to settle."

"What are you talking about?" His frown shifts to me. "This is the modern era. We live in the United States. You're talking as if we've been thrown back into the Stone Age."

"Babe, that's exactly what I'm saying."

He steps away from me as if stung. "What about Skip?"

"What about the van?" I ask, confused by the turn of conversation.

"That's our dream. Our future. Our beer company. I thought you wanted Ultra Brew with me."

"Of course, I want that with you," I say. "It's just not realistic anymore."

So many emotions storm across his face that I can't read them. As he stares at me, his face reddens.

"Just break up with me," he says angrily.

His words are like a slap in the face. "What? Carter, that's not what I'm saying."

"I'm just a way for you to get back at your mom for all the fucked-up things she did to you," he says. "We both know it's true. The beer company was all a part of that."

"No, it's not—"

He raises his eyes to my face. My voice dries up at his expression.

"The last time we talked to your family, you made it a point to mess up my beard and hair, so I would look even more rumpled than usual. Even in the middle of all the shit going on around us, you still made it a point to flaunt your granola boyfriend in front of them."

Self-loathing expands in my chest. "Carter, I'm sorry, I—"

"I only put up with it because I'm crazy about you," he says.

Tears well up in my eyes. Carter is, hands down, the most amazing boyfriend I've ever had.

This is my fault. I haven't told him how I feel. I haven't told him how much he means to me.

"Carter—"

"If the world is really over, you don't need me anymore," he says. "You'll never see your family again. They're probably dead anyway."

He spins on his heel and storms away. The sting of his words makes me hurt all over. I stare after him, heart aching, wondering how I managed to fuck things up so completely.

*

Other than to work out the logistics of the heavy water tote, Kate and I don't speak as we return to Creekside. I'm so ashamed, all I want to do is crawl under my bed and die.

So much for making a good impression with my boyfriend's mother. What must she think of me?

When we get back to the dorm, everyone is up. Johnny is still talking on his ham radio; Eric is still tinkering with his Xbox; Reed is eating a brownie over the mound of ant-infested plates in the sink; and Lila is flipping through a chemistry book.

Everyone looks our way as we enter, questions plain in their eyes. No one moves to help as we lug our burden into the room.

"Foot Soldier, I gotta go," Johnny says into his ham. "Talk to you later. Over and out." To us, he says, "Thank God you guys are all right. From the way Carter stormed back in here, we thought you two may have taken Skip for a joyride or something."

"Where is he?" I ask as Kate and I deposit the water tote in the kitchen.

"Bathroom," Lila says.

Everyone watches me as I head to the bathroom.

"I didn't think I'd ever see those two get in a fight," I hear Reed say in the kitchen.

I pretend not to hear him. Stopping in front of the bathroom door, I listen. The sound of an electric razor comes through the thin wood.

"Carter?" I tap lightly on the door.

No answer.

I try again. "Carter? It's me. Can we talk?"

All I get in response is the low hum of the razor.

Taking a deep breath, I try one more time. "Carter, look, I'm sorry. I'm really, really sorry. Can we talk?"

Again, no answer.

I decide to wait him out. I don't care if I look like a desperate idiot, or if everyone in the dorm hears us. Fuck pride. I can't lose Carter.

I pace up and down the short hallway, fidgeting with the hem of my shirt.

I'll just apologize, I tell myself. *I'll look him in the eye and make him see how sorry I am.* God, why had I been such a fucking idiot?

Because I had been. I treated Carter like an object, the thing I resented.

It was true that I took advantage of him to get back at my mom, but that wasn't the reason why I was with him. Far from it.

It can't be over between us. We didn't survive the outbreak of hell on earth just to break up now. I need him—want him—more than ever. He was the best thing in my life before everything went to shit. Now that everything has, literally, gone to shit, he's the only good thing left on the entire planet. I can't lose him.

The bathroom door bangs open. Carter fills the doorway.

I freeze mid-step, staring. Carter has shaved off every scrap of his beard. Gone are long, bushy strands that fell all the way to his chest. He's even cut off chunks of his longish hair.

The result is a shaggy-haired boy with a well-defined jaw, broad shoulders, and striking eyes.

He's fucking gorgeous.

Other than those times I rumpled him up to irritate my mother, I never thought much about Carter's looks one way or another. He could be green with purple polka dots and I'd still be crazy about him.

Seeing him this way dries up every word on my tongue. He's as hot as any high school football jock my mom ever pointed out to me. It's almost like seeing a stranger.

Blue eyes stare coldly at me, challenging.

"How do you like me now?" he growls. He stalks past me.

I stare after him, speechless.

11
Stripping Paint

KATE

When Carter emerges from the bathroom, clean shaven with hair cropped off his shoulders, words fail me.

Six months ago, I'd have rejoiced over his new look. Now, though, his bare face leaves his eyes exposed. He looks haunted.

Everyone stares at Carter, mouths agape.

"Dude," Eric says, the first to break the silence, "what's with the GQ look?"

Carter storms out of the dorm, slamming the door behind him.

Jenna hovers in the recess of the dark hallway, staring after him. She looks like she's been slapped.

I try to summon self-righteous motherhood but completely fail. I don't know the exact details of their fight, but I do know my son turned a state of the union talk into an argument about their relationship. He's obviously been carrying around the resentment for a while. His dad did the same thing.

One look at Jenna's face shows me nothing but regret. That's a point in her favor, even if what Carter accused her of is accurate.

I hesitate, wanting to give my son the privacy I know

he wants, but also wanting to know where he's going. It's not safe to be alone outside. And it's clear Jenna isn't moving.

I hurry out the door after Carter, stepping into the hall just in time to see him disappear into the stairwell. I follow him down to the ground level.

"Carter, you said yourself it's not safe outside."

He ignores me, pushing through the door and disappearing outside.

I find him behind the dorm with Skip. He has the can of turpentine out and is rubbing frantically at the paint. Turmoil lines every muscle of his body.

The last thing he wants is a lecture or a consoling mother. Sighing, I pick up a rag and a can of turpentine. Sliding on a pair of gloves, I join him in the arduous task of stripping paint. Carter slides a peripheral glance in my direction but doesn't speak.

I don't try to draw him out. That would be pointless.

I strip paint until the tips of my fingers burn. My back, shoulders, and arms ache from the repetitive exertion. My feet in particular scream at me, every part of me still sore from my journey here.

I ignore all the bodily gripes and keep working on the paint.

The sun creeps across the sky. Carter never says a word. I sigh inwardly, resigning myself to the role of silent companion.

It's nearly dinnertime when he finally speaks. "We were going to paint it blue."

I raise my eyes to look at him. "What?"

"We were going to paint the van blue. Jenna and I were still working out the details of the Ultra Brew logo, but we knew the background was going to be blue." He looks at me with devastated, red-rimmed eyes. "You know what, Mom? Fuck it. I'm not giving up on Ultra Brew. Just because she's decided she doesn't want to be a part of it doesn't mean I have to give it up."

I decide not to point out that Jenna never said she didn't want to be a part of the dream. The way I see it, Carter isn't ready to admit the world is in the shitter. Jenna is taking the brunt of that denial, even if Carter is also upset about something else that happened between them. He's always been slow to digest and express feelings. So was his father.

It's clear by Jenna's stricken reaction to Carter's words that she cares for him, but Carter is going to have to figure that out for himself. He doesn't need his mother to tell him his girlfriend wants to work things out. I would have thought that was obvious by the number of times she said sorry through the bathroom door, but apparently not so obvious to my son.

"Do you remember how hard things were right after Dad died?" Carter asks.

The turn in conversation catches me off guard. Those first days after Kyle died are not a bright spot in my memory. Not only had I lost my husband, but I fell into a deep dark hole out of which Carter and Frederico had to drag me.

"Hard to forget that," I reply. "Not my proudest moments."

Carter looks at me, a dent forming between his brows. "I always thought it was kind of beautiful."

"What was beautiful? My breakdown?" That doesn't make any sense.

"I remember thinking I wanted to find someone that I would love as much as you and Dad loved each other." He shrugs and starts dumping the paint in the mixing tray.

My mouth hangs open. That was Carter's takeaway from my ten days of dwelling in darkness without showering and eating? It takes me a moment to compose myself.

"What do you think Dad would say if he was still alive?" Carter asks.

It's my opening. I consider my words carefully, wanting to make my point without inciting another blow up with Carter.

"He would tell us to be prepared." For once, talking about my late husband doesn't make me feel like a crumpled ball of paper. I'm finally able to find happiness in my memories of him, rather than sink into despair over his loss. It's a good feeling. "Dad would tell us not to be caught out on the trail with only one shoe."

Carter chuckles, no doubt recalling the time I lost a shoe in a river during a one-hundred-mile race. The laugh exposes his Adam's apple and the ridges of his cheekbones, both of which have been covered in furry scruff for the last few years.

"I like the new look," I say.

"You always were after me to trim my beard and hair."

"I'm your mother. It's my job to nag you until you make yourself presentable."

"That's your job, huh?"

"Yep. And it was Dad's job—and yours—to take care of me at ultras. Remember how Dad always carried an extra pair of shoes for me after that race?"

"Yeah."

"It's just like—"

"Dude, check out Skip," says a new voice, interrupting my mom speech. I scowl at Eric, who waves down at us from the rooftop.

"That's an improvement!" he crows, fist pumping the air. "Nice job on the paint removal."

"How'd you get up there?" Carter asks.

Johnny appears beside Eric. "Roof access from the janitor's closet," he calls down. "We moved all the solar panels from the balcony to the rooftop. It should give me a few extra hours of time on my ham radio."

"More importantly," Eric says, "we should have Xbox action by tonight. You up for *God of War*?"

A smile splits Carter's face, the first I've seen all day. "Yeah. Sounds good."

Video games and ham radios. The kids are fucking around on the roof with solar panels so they can play with electronic toys. Talk about a waste of resources.

"Eric," I say, "do you think you could route power to a washing machine from the solar panels? Eventually, we're going to have to wash some clothes."

"Washing machine?" Eric scratches his chin. "I don't think the panels I have will be enough to power a washing machine. But it's a good idea. Let me think on it."

Thinking about it is better than blowing me off. I decide to take that for a win. Now, if only I can figure out a way to ease Carter into a new way of thinking.

Johnny and Eric disappear back inside. I formulate several more mom speeches in my head before absorbing Carter's bleak expression. In the end, I decide to keep my mouth shut and help with the van. The mom lecture designed to get my son's head out of his ass and on the road to reality can wait for another day.

He's on his own with his relationship.

12
Stairs

JENNA

I awake in an empty bed. Granted, it's a tiny twin-sized dorm bed, meaning it's far from empty with my body in it. But I'm used to sharing with Carter. The yawning space beside me feels like an empty football field.

A few feet away, Lila sleeps with a mask over her eyes. An essential oil book is upside down on her chest, her battery-powered reading light sticking up like an antenna. Her jars of essential oils are lined up on the desk, along with several baggies of marijuana buds. Lila must have been busy with her herbs last night. I was so drained from my fight with Carter that I didn't even wake up.

I consider staying in bed all day. It would be easy to cover up my head and hide from the world.

I give this serious contemplation for a full five minutes before discarding the idea. Hiding from Carter isn't going to fix things. Neither will pretending.

I've pretended long enough. I never challenged him when he talked about the world getting fixed. I never told him what I think. No, I played along, and now look where I am.

I'm not going to pretend anymore. The world is a shit

hole and we have to figure out how to survive.

First and foremost is food. We need to gather food. I'm talking about organized scavenging, complete with zombie clearance, comprehensive inventory, and supply room. A gathering of everything even remotely edible in the Creekside dorm building.

I rise, pulling on a pair of clean workout pants. I don a light sweatshirt and head into the sitting room in search of my tennis shoes. A good workout will clear my brain before I dig into my project.

Carter is sound asleep on the floor, one long arm thrown over his head. My heart constricts. I wish I could snuggle up with him, but what's the point? He's still mad at me, or else he wouldn't have slept out here on the floor.

As I grab my shoes and slip out into the hallway, I realize Kate isn't here. Her blankets are in a neat stack on the floor by the sofa, telling me she's already up.

I know where she is. She told me walking is important after an ultra. She'll be in the stairwell, which is exactly where I was headed.

Should I go back to my room? Go straight into one of the dorm kitchens and get to work?

"Don't be a wimp," I mutter to myself. I've promised to get myself in shape.

I'm also going to figure out a way to make things right with Carter. When that happens, I want to be on good terms with his mom. That won't happen if I avoid her. Besides, I kind of like her.

But does she like me? Maybe she thinks I'm total slime for treating Carter like shit.

Only one way to find out. And it's not by lurking in the hallway.

"Hey, Kate," I call, swinging open the stairwell door, going for my best chipper, friendly tone.

Her flashlight beam bounces off the wall as she climbs the stairs, smiling at me in greeting. "Morning,

Jenna," she replies. "I was hoping you'd join me for a workout."

Several layers of tension slough off me. "How long have you been out here?" I ask, falling into step with her as we climb the flight to the third floor.

"About fifteen minutes. Carter snores. I've always been a light sleeper."

Despite my sour mood, I find myself smirking. "He does snore, but only when he's really tired. He denies it, though."

Kate chuckles. "I know. His dad did the same thing."

Kate limps along on her bad ankle without complaint, both of her feet bare. Pink patches of calamine lotion cover the poison oak on her arms and neck. Her skin is sallow, stretched thin from physical strain and not enough nourishment. The gray roots of her hair have grown out a full inch. She looks like hell, but for some reason, I like it.

I can't help but compare her to my own mother, with her breast implants and BOTOX injections and bottle-blond hair. I can only imagine the nasty things my mom would say about Kate.

She glances at me. "Does Carter talk about his dad much?"

"Yeah. He talks about him a lot." I pause, trying to find the right words. "I can tell he misses him. He talks about him even more since the zombie outbreak."

"Yeah. He talked about him yesterday, too."

Was that before or after our fight? I realize I'm not ready to talk about Carter with Kate. It's awkward and skirts too close to my assholishness. I want her to like me, after all.

We hit the third-floor landing and turn around, walking back down.

"I have a plan for today," I tell her, searching for a way to break the silence.

"What's that?"

"I'm going to start going through the cleared kitchens in Creekside. I'm going to gather up all the food and organize it. Once that's done, I'm going to convince the others to help me clear more of the rooms so we can access those supplies, too."

"That's an excellent idea, Jenna." Kate's eyes flash with approval that warms me. "I have to tell you, it's a relief to know that not everyone in Creekside is waiting around expecting to be rescued."

I let out a breath. "I agree."

"I'll join you," Kate says. "Maybe we can get Carter to help us, too. The three of us will be enough to do the clearance."

"That would be great." I glance at her, relieved she's volunteered to rope Carter into this. "Tell me about training on stairs. I want to know more about ultrarunning."

Kate's eyes light up. It's clear she loves the subject, even if running here almost killed her.

"Ultrarunning isn't like regular road running," Kate says. "For one thing, almost all ultras are on trails. That means you aren't running on flat surfaces. It means you spend a lot of time climbing hills. That's where stair training comes in." She pats one hamstring. "You need to build up this muscle." Her hand moves from her hamstring to her right glute. "And this muscle. Climbing stairs activates these muscles."

"What about your calves?" I ask, noticing that I use those as I climb.

"Yes, those too. Stairs help you engage all those muscles."

I listen, fascinated, as she talks about running. I ask her questions, listen to some of her stories about races. I barely notice when I work up a sweat from the exercise.

"Did you run track all four years in high school?" Kate asks.

"Yeah."

"And your mom didn't want you to run?" Kate's brow furrows at this.

For her, I realize this is akin to not wanting your child to breathe. "I think it's because my dad ran track in college when they met. She always said the guys who ran track were too skinny."

"Huh." Kate is too polite to say what she really thinks. "I take it your parents aren't together?"

I shake my head. "Dad ran off with his yoga instructor." Mom dealt with this blow by getting a tummy tuck and making all her daughters get push-up bras. Like I need a push-up bra. "I actually like my stepmom. She's nice. Or was nice. I hope she and my dad are okay."

"I hope so, too," Kate replies, giving my shoulder a soft squeeze.

The gesture is so kind and so unexpected my eyes well up. I swallow and change the subject before I make an idiot of myself.

"Carter told me a lot about his Uncle Rico," I say. "I'm sorry he didn't make it."

Kate nods, eyes dropping. "He was the best friend I've ever had, aside from my husband."

We continue to talk. Kate tells me about Frederico and some of the crazy runs they did together. It's with some surprise that I realize how easily conversation flows between us.

I laugh as Kate relays a story about Frederico having to drop several "deuces" in the woods after a night of bingeing on chili. I'm about to tell her the story about pulling over at a Denny's in the middle of the night on a road trip so one of my friends could do the same thing when the stairwell door bangs open.

Carter stands there, looking at us with flat blue eyes. The mirth whooshes out of me. The shock of his bare, handsome face hits me all over again.

"What are you doing?" he says to his mom, ignoring me.

The dismissal is like having my legs swept out from under me.

"Just doing a morning walk," Kate says mildly. "Besides, you snore."

Carter scowls at her, his eyes never once flicking in my direction. It's like I'm invisible.

I clench my jaw. I messed things up. It's up to me to fix them. Carter is worth it.

"Carter," I say, "can we talk?"

He ignores me. "I'm going outside to work on Skip," he tells his mother. "Just wanted you to know where I was so you wouldn't worry."

"Alone?" Kate's voice sharpens.

"Yep." Carter strides past us, heading down to the first floor.

I leave my pride on the floor and rush past Kate to catch up with Carter. Falling into stride beside him, I say, "Carter, please, can we talk? I—"

He stops, giving me a look so cold and so angry it takes my breath away. I shrivel inside, feeling about two inches tall. When he turns and stalks away, I don't try to stop him.

Kate gives me an apologetic smile. "We'll have to scavenge for food another time." She hurries after Carter, leaving me alone.

13
Scavenging

JENNA

I stare at the empty space only seconds before occupied by Carter. The memory of his hard blue stare hangs in the air.

I try to align the angry guy to the person I've dated for six months. I almost don't recognize him, and not because he shaved off his beard and hacked his hair. He's never looked at me the way he did just now.

I have royally fucked up. How can I fix things if he won't even look at me?

Heart aching, I decide the best thing I can do is keep myself busy. It's time to start stockpiling supplies and organizing them. I'm sure there's a scientific ratio to figure out how much food is needed to feed the seven of us, but I'll worry about that later.

I head to the dorm suite we cleared yesterday. Between that one and the partially burned one, I have two rooms guaranteed to be zombie free. Maybe when everyone sees what I'm doing, it will be easier to enlist help for the clearance of other rooms.

I dive into the nearest cabinet and pull out food. It's a jumbled mix of refried beans, mashed potato flakes, cereal, and boxed cake mixes.

Eric will like the cake mixes. He's good at making

cakes on the barbecue, even if we don't have eggs. He—

I stop, reaching back into the cabinet. My hand emerges with a bag of Carter's favorite granola. Cinnamon apple from Granny's Kitchen. Imagining him smiling at me as I hand him the bag, I hug it to me.

Against my better judgment, I go to the window that overlooks the back of the dorm. Peering through the slits of the cheap metal blinds, I see Carter and Kate with paint brushes and a can of blue paint.

It's a gorgeous robin's egg blue paint that I picked especially for our Ultra Brew logo.

It should be me down there painting with him, not Kate. Hell, we should be working on beer recipes, not preparing to survive the zombie outbreak. Life is shit like that, I guess.

"It's you," Reed says, wandering into the room. He grips a joint between the thumb and index finger of his right hand. He's shaped his afro into three mini mushroom plumes, each going in a different direction on top of his head. It's the first time I realized hair could be multidirectional.

"I thought I heard a mouse in here," he says.

"Really, Reed?" I gesture at the joint. "It's not even ten in the morning."

"Best breakfast a guy could ask for. What are you doing?" He flops onto the sofa, pulling a blanket around his shoulders.

"What does it look like I'm doing? It's not like we can run to the grocery store and get food anytime we want. I'm going through all the kitchens in the building and organizing the supplies."

"Jeez. Someone is testy this morning. But don't worry, I get it."

Thinking he's making some stupid PMS joke, I whirl on him. "You get what?"

He takes a puff off his joint. "You and Carter got in a fight."

I turn my back on Reed, not wanting him to see how upset I am. I move onto the next cabinet, which contains pots and pans. I slam the door and move onto the next cabinet.

"You want a hit?" Reed holds out the joint. "It'll make you feel better."

"No." I fling open the cabinet. This one has a mishmash of stuff, everything from half-open rice bags, to trail mix, to crackers.

"You know what would make me feel better?" I say.

"What?" He blows two smoke rings.

"If you would help me."

He wrinkles his nose. "I'm allergic to work. Besides, I promised to share my joint with Eric. Will you keep an eye out for pot while you're cleaning? We're down to the last few grams."

And then he leaves.

Just leaves.

A scream of frustration builds in my throat. I'm trying to make sure we don't starve to death, and all he can think about is weed. What would he say if I refused to share any of the food I gathered? That would get him off his lazy ass.

I don't have it in me to pick a fight. The last thing I need is an argument with two people in the dorm.

This is not the first time I've pissed off a boy.

There was the football jock who lost his shit when I refused to shave my armpits, but I'd been hoping for that reaction. It was the only way to get out of the prom date my mother had coerced me into.

There was the journalism boy who had me fooled into thinking he was sweet. Then he went through my underwear drawer and posted pictures of my bras and panties on Instagram. That earned him a hole in the radiator of his car.

There was the rich dumb kid my mom bribed me to go out with because his dad was some fancy corporate lawyer. I should have known better. That asshole only wanted to take me to the restaurant where his ex worked to make her jealous. The prick got a pitcher of water dumped on his head. The new pair of track shoes I received for the ordeal had been worth it.

So yeah, I'm no stranger to having guys pissed at me.

But this is the first time I've hurt someone I care about.

It takes me several hours, but I finally have every scrap of food pulled from the kitchen and organized on the floor and table. There are groups of grains, pastas, canned vegetables, canned and dried fruit, desserts, and other snackables like granola bars, crackers, and chips.

I pick up the bag of cinnamon-apple granola, again hugging it to my chest. I peek out the window. Carter and Kate are still working on the van.

Maybe Carter is cooled off by now. Maybe the granola will make an effective peace offering. He must be hungry by now, right? It's lunchtime, after all.

Steeling myself, I grab two energy bars and the bag of granola. I head outside to Skip, determined to make things right with my boyfriend.

14
Paint Job

KATE

"You know, some people would pay extra for texture from a paint brush," I tell Carter as I smear paint onto the side of the van.

Carter snorts. "Yeah, right."

I can't believe I'm painting a van in the middle of a zombie apocalypse. The only thing more unproductive would be getting stoned, but Reed and Eric already have that base covered.

"You know, it's not every day a crazy mom runs two hundred miles to repaint a Dodge Caravan with her kid. You better tell all your friends I get to ride shotgun. Where are you planning to take this thing, anyway?"

Carter doesn't rise to the bait.

I need my kid to get his head out of his ass.

"Carter, look." I set down my brush and stand in front of him. "I know the van is important to you, but there's a lot of other things we need to be thinking about right now."

"Like what?" His mild tone rankles. He refuses to make eye contact.

"Like gathering food supplies. Like clearing the rest of Creekside. Like fortifying the bottom floor of the dorm so no one can break in. Like finding some solar panels so we can get a washing machine working."

He shrugs. "You don't have to stay out here with me."

"You're the one who made a big deal about coming outside. You know it's not safe to be out here alone. We need to stay in pairs."

"Are you taking her side?" He glares up at me.

"Sweetie, this has nothing to do with Jenna. This is about us surviving—"

"You're taking her side."

I ball my fists in frustration. "I'm *not*—"

"Hey, guys." Jenna steps around the building, carrying something in her arms.

I turn toward her and smile, relieved for a break in my near-argument with Carter. Who disappears to the other side of the van as Jenna approaches.

"Hey, Jenna. What are you up to?" I make my voice chipper, hoping to dispel the tension.

"Hey, Kate. I've been going through the kitchen of one of the cleared dorms. I found some food I thought you might like." She sets two energy bars just inside the open door of the van.

"Thanks. Good timing." I rip into the bar, realizing it must be around lunchtime. "I bet Carter is hungry," I add in a low voice, gesturing for her to go talk to him.

Her face brightens. She circles around the van.

I shouldn't eavesdrop. I should just walk away. Go into the bushes to pee or something. Give them some privacy.

Instead, I slink toward the back of the van, head cocked to listen.

"Hey, Carter."

Silence.

"I found your favorite granola in Kevin's dorm," Jenna offers. "I thought you might be hungry."

More silence.

"Carter, please talk to me."

"There's nothing to talk about, Jenna. You've made your feelings clear."

"No, Carter, I—"

"Go away, Jenna."

"Carter—"

"Are you deaf? I said, go away!"

I emerge around the back of the van just in time to see Jenna hurl the bag of granola onto the ground at Carter's feet. Then she stalks back to Creekside.

"Why did you do that?" Carter demands.

I decide to play dumb. "Do what?"

"Tell Jenna I was hungry."

Guess I hadn't been so quiet after all. Playing dumb was a bad idea anyway. "I thought some alone time would give you guys a chance to talk through things."

"There's nothing to talk about."

"I don't pretend to know the details of your fight," I reply. "Whatever she did, Jenna is sorry. Just talk to her. Give her a chance to say whatever it is she's been trying to say to you."

I am rewarded with a look of profound disgust. "Are you still going to try and convince me you're not on her side?"

I decide to keep my mouth shut. He wouldn't believe me if I told him I was on his side, that seeing him hurt makes me hurt.

With a soft sigh, I pick up my brush. As much as I want to join Jenna, protecting Carter will always be my first priority. Even if that means painting a van in the middle of a zombie apocalypse.

The day drags by. I can't help but think that if Frederico knew that I ran two hundred miles to paint a van with Carter, he'd turn over in his grave. Or laugh. He was good at laughing when things were shitty.

"Remember how Dad always used to help me?"

Carter's voice jars me out of my thoughts. I glance over at him as he rounds the side of the van.

"Helped you with what?" I ask, not in the mood to guess.

"With the beer. I know we only made a few batches together, but it was fun. It was sort of our thing."

"Dad loved making beer with you."

"This is my dream, Mom." Carter's gesture takes in the van and the fermenting kegs in the back. "This is what I want to do with my life. Dad knew that."

There's a reason Carter keeps bringing up Kyle. I know there is. I know it has something to do with the funk he's in, but I can't put my finger on it. I can't unravel the mystery that is my son. As he looks at me, I see how lost he is.

I wish the world hadn't taken away his dream, or his father for that matter. I wish some elbow grease and hard work would restore things to the way they were. I can protect my son and do my best to keep him alive, but I can't restore his dream.

"I know this is important to you, sweetie, but the world has changed. We can't hold onto the past if we're going to survive."

I make my voice as gentle as possible, but Carter's face hardens with every word. Shoulders stiff, he turns his back on me and resumes work on the van.

Which leaves me with exactly two choices. I can go inside and find Jenna and help her get some real work done. Or I can stay here with Carter and paint a van we likely will never be able to use.

It's not safe to be outside alone, and so I stay and paint.

And paint.

And paint.

15
Ham

JENNA

It's been three days since Carter and I got into a fight and he started sleeping on the living room floor.

It's been two days since he started painting Skip with Kate instead of me.

It's been exactly one day since my hurt evaporated and turned into anger. Carter wants to be an ass and ignore me? Two can play that game. There will be no more groveling or apologizing from me. If he wants to talk, he can come to me.

I throw myself into my new routine. In the morning, I work out with Kate in the stairwell. The rest of the day, I keep myself busy by plundering kitchens and bedrooms in Creekside. I converted the burned dorm suite into a storage area, which is starting to resemble a small grocery store.

After some cajoling and bribing with a pack of Oreos, Eric, Reed, and Johnny helped me clear half a dozen rooms and drag the bodies downstairs. Other than that, they have yet to lift a finger.

Eric and Reed spend their days playing video games. I swear Eric's potbelly is getting larger every day. Johnny is glued to his ham radio. Lila is busy reading and making her concoctions. The only thing useful any of them has done is agree to wash dishes and take out the trash to keep the ants at bay.

"Oh my God," Johnny says into the ham radio as I deposit my latest collection of food stores on the kitchen floor. "I can't believe you guys have a whole fucking fort. That is so cool, man."

"A fort?" I pause, a case of Kraft macaroni and cheese in my arms, intrigued despite my grumpiness. "Who has a fort?" And are they talking about a blanket fort, or some other type of fort?

"There's an old Russian fort somewhere on the coast," Johnny replies. "This guy, Alvarez, is living there. His handle is Foot Soldier. Here, say hi."

I drop the case of mac 'n cheese and take the ham from Johnny. "Hello?"

A response crackles through the radio. "Hello? This is Foot Soldier. Over."

"Tell him your name," Johnny prompts.

"My name is Jenna. What's this I hear about a fort?" Are there normal people out there who believe in surviving? If so, I want to meet them.

Johnny elbows me. "Say, 'over.'"

"Over," I add, feeling self-conscious.

"I'm in a Russian fort built in the early eighteen hundreds," Foot Soldier replies. "It was preserved and converted into a state park. We have a windmill to mill grain, an orchard, and space to garden. There's a big wall around the fort and a few old houses inside. We need more people to help run this place. I told Wandering Writer you guys should come here. Over."

"Wandering Writer?" I ask.

"It's my handle on the ham." Johnny grabs a map, spreading it out on the table. Grabbing the ham from me, he says, "Foot Soldier, this is Wandering Writer. What's the closest town to your location? Over."

"Timber Cove. Seriously, you guys gotta come here. Over."

While the idea of joining up with a bona fide survival group does sound good, I'm skeptical we could safely travel far.

Johnny traces the coastline of California. He starts at the Oregon border and works his way down. My heart sinks as his finger drops lower and lower on the map.

"Foot Soldier, did you say you're in northern California? Over," Johnny says.

"Yeah. Just look for Timber Cove. South of Mendocino. Over."

Johnny's finger continues along the coast. Down, down, and down.

"Fuck me." Johnny stares down at the map. "Fort Ross might technically be on the north coast of California, but it's a long way from here."

I lean over the map, taking in the tiny dot of Arcata and the long, long way between our tiny town and Johnny's finger.

"That's gotta be a few hundred miles," I say. Not only that, it looks like there's only one major highway near Fort Ross and the only way to reach it is by backtracking through much of the territory Kate traveled to get here. Seeing how bad she was when she arrived doesn't make me think any of us could make it. Kate is tougher than all of us combined.

"No go," Johnny says into the ham. "You're too far away, Foot Soldier. No way for us to get there. Over."

"Damn," Foot Soldier replies. "Too bad. We could have used you guys. Over."

I don't bother telling him he's better off without the dead weight Creekside boys.

Johnny and Foot Soldier continue to talk, exchanging survival stories. I listen as I return to organizing our stores.

Foot Soldier was in the military when all hell broke loose. His platoon was assigned to a roadblock. They were overrun. No one made it out except him. The guy traveled all the way to Fort Ross on foot. That's probably how he came up with his handle.

At least the guy is being proactive. He's not wasting his days away playing video games and smoking joints or painting a van.

The door opens. Carter and Kate enter, laughing over something. Carter's laugh fades as he spots me watching them. He looks away when our eyes meet.

Frustration wells in my chest. Fuck him. Fuck all these idiots.

I brush past Carter and Kate, grabbing my shoes, spear, and jacket.

"Where are you going?" Kate asks.

I don't look at her when I answer. "I'm going out to get some beer."

"Beer?" Kate's brow creases. "Can't you just tap the kegs in Skip?"

I shake my head. "Carter is doing a double fermentation on them. They won't be ready for another few weeks."

"That's a great idea," Reed says, looking up with bloodshot eyes. The guy is so stoned it's not even funny. "We should go to the Depot."

"That's my plan," I reply crisply. So what if none of us has ventured beyond the parking lot since the outbreak? We have to cross the threshold of our little bubble eventually. Might as well be right now. I can't think of a better reason than beer.

"There are solar panels at the Depot," Eric says. "I've been wanting to check them out." He glances at Kate. "You asked about a washing machine. I think those panels might be large enough to power one. If I can get one of them off the roof, maybe I can get a washing machine running."

Reed pops one of Eric's brownies into his mouth. "I am so high right now."

"You guys aren't going anywhere," Carter declares.

"You two"—he points a finger at Reed and Eric—"are stoned."

"I'm only a little stoned," Eric says.

"You"—Carter points a finger at me—"can't go out by yourself. It's not safe."

Anger hits me like a brick. Carter ignores me for three days, then has the nerve to think to can tell me what I can and can't do?

I can't stay here. I have to move, have to do something. The dorm is too small, too confining, too close to Carter. I have to get away from him and his stupidly handsome face.

"Fuck it," I say to Reed and Eric. "Let's go get solar panels and beer. I want to be drunk and I want to wash my clothes."

"Now you're talking." Eric grins, rising to his feet.

"Reed," I say, "you can only come if you promise not to attract the attention of psychotic drug mules."

Reed waves a hand, drifting toward the sofa. "I think Carter is right. I'm too stoned to go on a beer run. I'm taking a nap." He falls onto the cushions, eyes closing before his head hits the pillows.

"I'll go," Johnny says. "I can write about this."

Kate looks at me. When our eyes meet, I feel exposed. She knows exactly why I'm acting out like a toddler. She must think I'm an idiot. She probably thinks I'm not good enough for Carter.

"I'll go with you guys." Carter grabs a spear. He gives me a look, daring me to argue with him. "I'm going," he says to me.

"Do whatever you want." I stalk past him and out the door.

16
The Depot

JENNA

We walk in a tight cluster along the northern edge of the campus. The school is eerily quiet, not filled with the normal hum of human activity like it used to be.

"I'm going to pretend it's summer session out here and everyone has gone home for a few months," Johnny whispers.

"Good idea," I reply. It would be easier to do if there weren't so many dead bodies everywhere.

We head deeper into campus toward the Depot. It's one of a few buffet dining options at the university.

It's the only one that served beer.

We pass more bodies than I can count. Most bear signs of gunshot wounds to the head. The soldiers definitely did a number on Humboldt State University.

"Is that people over there? Or am I just stoned?" Eric points off to our left.

I squint in the direction Eric points. The sun is halfway concealed by the horizon, casting long shadows and dim light. At first, all I see are trees and bushes and looming buildings. Then I see what Eric sees.

Just outside the glass windows of the Depot is a group of three people. It's clear from the way they move that they're human, not zombie.

"People!" I hiss, pointing.

Carter grabs me, pulling me toward the ground. I yank free and give him a dirty look, but stay down.

Eric and Johnny crouch beside us. There isn't anything to hide behind, but hunkering down seems smarter than standing up where we can be seen. Assuming we haven't already been seen.

"Maybe it's other students," I whisper. "Maybe we should say hi to them."

"Are you kidding?" Johnny says. "Have you ever seen a horror movie? We're living out a classic scene right now. This is the part where trusting people call out in greeting, only to find out the other guys are psychos who collect eyeballs."

"Just because three other people survived hell doesn't make them eyeball collecting psychos," I argue. "We should see who they are."

"Too late now," Eric says. "They're gone."

The four of us squint through the growing darkness. I study the spot where I saw the figures. Sure enough, whoever had been there is gone.

"Let's just get to the Depot." I don't even really want beer anymore, but my pride won't let me back out. This was, after all, my idea.

The courtyard of the Depot looks like a killing ground. There are bodies and dried blood everywhere. I gag as we enter the courtyard. Johnny and Eric cover their mouths, trying to block out the smell.

I force myself to take in the carnage. The dead people here are all my age. I could have easily been one of them. Their lives are over. By some stroke of luck—maybe a few strokes of luck—I'm still alive.

"You okay?" Carter puts a hand on my shoulder.

I shake him off. He doesn't get to be nice to me only when it suits him. I sure as hell don't need his concern.

"What . . ." Johnny raises a shaking hand. "What is that?"

I follow the line of his finger. Past the bodies, past the blood, all the way to . . .

"Oh." My eyes lock on the gruesome sight.

A soldier is staked to a tree. Long knives have been driven through the flesh right below his shoulders, holding him in place. Around his neck are red abrasions, making me think he may have been strangled to death before he was strung up.

"Who would do that?" I whisper. Cold sweat beads along my spine.

"Sickos." Carter stands too close to me, his stance protective.

I can't stand it. It makes me hurt all over.

Clenching my fists, I move into the courtyard and away from Carter.

"A writer can't hide from reality," Johnny murmurs, brandishing his chair leg. "Although I have to admit, I've never been on a high stakes beer run before."

I draw my own chair leg. "Will this make it into your book?"

"Depends on what happens when we get inside," Johnny replies. "There's the implication of danger. That means there's a good chance something scary or bad will happen, which makes for good storytelling. There's also the possibility we'll go inside and nothing at all will happen. Which means there's no scene, just a setting with dead bodies where nothing happens."

"I vote for the scene with dead bodies where nothing happens," I say.

"You guys go ahead," Eric says. "Me and Carter will stay out here and keep watch."

"I'm not staying out here," Carter says.

"You have to," Eric replies. "That way I'll have an excuse to stay with you. If you go inside, I'll look like a pussy out here."

"Let's quit arguing and just go," I say. Standing around out here in the growing darkness is creeping me out.

We move through the courtyard, edging around bodies and avoiding pools of coagulated blood as best we can. Johnny curses when he accidentally steps in a small patch and almost trips.

"That's definitely going into my book," he grumbles.

"Do you have a title for your book?" I ask.

"*Voices of the Apocalypse*," Johnny replies. "Subtitle, *First Days*. I already have fifty pages just from the interviews I've done with people over the ham. Not to mention our own story of surviving the military attack."

The front of the Depot is floor-to-ceiling glass. Several windows have been smashed. Glass crunches underfoot as we near the building. When I glance down, I see it's not just window shards underfoot. Cylindrical tubes of brass roll beneath my shoes. Discarded bullet casings. How many students were murdered by the military?

Still in a tight cluster, we pause outside and peer into the gloom. More dead bodies are inside. I count at least half a dozen killed by headshots.

Nothing moves. Just to be sure, I take my chair leg and tap it against the ground a few times.

An answering growl comes from inside the Depot. A second growl follows hard on the heels of the first.

This was all a bad idea. It seemed reasonable back in the dorm when I was angry and upset. I really don't need a beer. Or my pride. Both are overrated.

Carter taps the spear a second time. Once again, two growls answer.

"There's only two of them," he whispers. "Both came from over there." He points to the buffet, where spoiled food sits. It sends up a rancid smell, though it's not nearly as bad as the smell from the rotting bodies.

"The beer kegs are over there." I point to the other side of the Depot.

"Let's get a keg and get the hell out of here," Reed says.

"What about the solar panels?" Eric points to the roof where half a dozen panels sit. The only way up there is with a ladder or through a second-story window.

"We can come back for them another time," I say. Preferably in full daylight. Besides, getting a panel will be an all day excursion by the time we figure out how to get onto the roof, dismantle the panel, and get it back to the dorm.

"Cool. I don't mind wearing the same clothes every day," Eric says. "Hell, it's pretty much every nerd's dream not to have to worry about clothes."

"Let's just get the beer and get out of here," Johnny says.

No one argues. We inch inside, our feet crunching on the debris.

Carter creeps in my direction, drawing closer with every step. He keeps flicking glances my way, too. I don't know what his deal is. I make it a point to edge away from him. He doesn't get to ignore me then play my protector.

The growls increase in intensity from the buffet area.

"Maybe we should check it out and get rid of whoever is over there," Johnny whispers. "Put them out of their misery."

"No," I reply. "In and out with the keg. That's it." I hold my spear in front of me like a bat, eyes flicking to the left and right.

The beer counter is a half-moon of wood with three taps. I peer behind the bar. A crumpled body lies there.

I prod it with my spear to make sure it's dead. It doesn't move. Carter slides in and detaches the first of the kegs. The fact that they're still here is a sign of just how deserted the campus is.

"How are we going to tap into them when we get back to the dorm?" Eric asks.

"We'll have to take one of the tap handles," Carter replies. "Here, I brought my mom's screwdriver." He passes it to me.

I decide not to read anything into his action. I just happened to be standing closest to him when he pulled out the screwdriver.

Within a few minutes, we have a keg and the tap handle in our possession. Carter removes a second keg.

The fading light illuminates his profile. For a moment, I let myself imagine things are good between us. I imagine we're not surrounded by dead bodies in a shot-up college cafeteria. Instead, we're at a trailhead somewhere, selling our beer to racers after they cross the finish line.

For just a few seconds, I let myself be transported to another time, another place. I miss Carter so much I ache.

"Boo!"

The unexpected voice rings out like a gong.

17
Neighbors

JENNA

The shout sends me into a crouch. In my surprise, I drop the tap handle. It hits the ground with a loud *clunk*.

Eric and Johnny drop to all fours and crawl behind the bar with me and Carter. We fill in around the dead body, trying to hide and avoid the corpse at the same time. Carter is mashed up against me, the smooth skin of his shaven cheek wedged against my elbow.

"Who was that?" Eric hisses.

"I was hoping it was one of you guys," I whisper back, even though I know they wouldn't be hiding behind the bar if that was the case.

"If it wasn't us and it wasn't you guys, then who was it?" Johnny's whisper is thin.

"Probably just some jackasses who survived the outbreak," I say in a soft voice. "Maybe it's those people we saw earlier."

"They're messing with us." To my horror, Eric raises his voice loud enough to carry. "You got us, assholes. You scared us. Now come out."

Silence.

We wait. Somewhere outside is the squeal of a bat. Then the growls of the buffet zombies roll through the room.

I decide Eric is right. Someone is messing with us. "Hello?" I call.

Only the snarling zombies answer us.

Unease drips across my shoulders, followed by an urge to get the hell out of the Depot as fast as we can.

Palms sweaty around my spear, I creep around the edge of the bar and peer out into the common room. It's darker than ever and difficult to see. In the gloom, nothing moves. The growls of the buffet zombies still roll across the tile, but there's no visible sign of them.

"It's clear," I call back in a low voice. "Come on."

Reed and Johnny each heft one of the kegs. They're five-gallon kegs, a smaller format preferred by many of the local microbrews. I jam the tap handle through my belt. The four of us scurry across the commons, Carter and I in the lead.

As we near the exit, a figure rises from behind one of the buffets.

"Howdy, neighbors."

To my dismay, I let out a girlish squeal and jump at least twelve feet into the air. Reed drops one of the kegs. It rings against the tile floor with a reverberating *bang*. Carter jumps in front of me.

The figure doubles over laughing. It's a boy, a student in his university sweatshirt. Two other figures join him. It's three boys, all of them in baggy sweatshirts and jeans. All of them laughing at us.

"You should see the look on your faces," says one boy, pointing a finger at us. They practically fall over one another in their hilarity.

"Assholes," I growl. "Let's get the hell out of here."

"Wait, wait," says the first boy. "Just hold up a sec."

He looks me up and down, scanning me in a way that makes me want to scream. Even in an apocalypse, guys are all the same. I cross my arms over my breasts, blocking them from his view, and scowl at him.

If he notices my hostility, he covers it with a grin.

"Look, we were just messing around."

"Yeah, we were just messing with you," says the second boy.

"We're survivors from College Creek," says the third boy. "We were out gathering supplies when we saw you."

"College Creek?" Carter says. "We heard that place was overrun."

That sobers the boys. "It was," says the first one. "A few of us survived after the military took down the zombies."

"How many of there are you?" I ask.

"Sixteen of us back in the dorm."

Sixteen. More than twice our number.

"Do you have a good set up?" Eric asks.

The lead boy shrugs, eyes flicking toward me. "It's okay. What dorm are you guys in?"

"Pepperwood," Johnny says, flashing all of us a *look*. I don't correct him, glad for the lie. "We have two kegs of beer. Do you guys want one?"

"Really?" The second boy takes a few steps in our direction.

"Sure," Johnny says, giving us all that *look* again. I'm not sure what he's trying to tell us but we go along anyway. Maybe relinquishing one of our kegs will dispel the uncomfortable tension in the air.

Johnny takes a few steps forward and deposits his keg in front of the College Creek boys.

"I'm Johnny. My friends are Carter, Eric, and Jenna. Who are you guys?"

"I'm Ryan," says the lead boy. "My friends are Henry and Adam."

"Nice to meet you," Johnny says. "Maybe we'll see you guys around sometime."

"Maybe we'll come visit," Ryan says.

God, I hope not.

"Cool. See you around." Johnny waves a non-committal hand before hustling us all for the exit.

Right before we pass through the shattered windows, I spot the buffet zombies. Carter sees them at the same time. "What the . . ."

Their legs have been hacked off, leaving nothing but bloody stumps protruding from their hips. Their arms have been cut off just below the shoulder. The discarded limbs are scattered between the salad bar and drink station.

Johnny and Eric, now holding the keg between them, crash into us. They curse before catching sight of our faces.

"Holy shit." Eric's voice is thin and high-pitched. "Did you guys do that?" he asks Ryan and the others.

"What, that?" Ryan points to the writhing undead, who are no more than three feet away from his shoes. He shrugs. "Just messing around, that's all. Not like they can feel it."

"They're nasty enough when they're in one piece," Johnny says.

My feet feel like lead. I'm glad Johnny didn't tell these fuckers where we really live. I've dispatched my fair share of zombies, but not like this. Their dismemberment is a mockery and disrespect to the people they once were. Mouth dry, I advance on the struggling things.

"Jenna, no." Carter lays a hand on my arm.

I ignore him, licking my lips. I recognize one of the creatures. Reggie. He lived in a neighboring dorm. We took statistics together. He was a nice guy. He doesn't deserve what happened to him.

I pass the College Creek boys, untouched by their amused disdain. Carter is by my side. For the first time today, I'm grateful for his presence. He's like a shield between me and the College Creek guys.

I stop in front of Reggie's wriggling body, the smell of the rotting food and rotting bodies washing over me.

I slam the sharpened end of my chair leg through his skull. Reggie shudders, then goes still.

I administer the same mercy to the second creature, a girl with a pixie cut who had been cute and petite when she'd been alive. My spear punches through her skull, the impact of the crumpling bone traveling all the way up my arm.

"I like to make sure they're really dead," I say to Ryan and his friends. "Just in case. See you guys around."

When I rejoin Carter and the others, no one says a word. We hurry into the night with our beer keg.

18
Goodnight

JENNA

By the time we get back to the dorm, the last thing I want is a beer.

"Now *that* was straight out of a horror movie script," Johnny announces as soon as we are inside. "We need to steer wide of those guys."

"What guys?" Reed sits up on the couch. His eyes are no longer bloodshot.

"I can't believe you guys left so close to dusk," Lila says. "That was stupid."

"What happened?" Kate asks. "Are you guys okay?"

I deposit the keg handle on the table and leave the others to relate the tale. All I want to do is shower and go to bed. Since there's no hot water, and heating up water on the barbecue is tedious, bed is the only option left for me.

"Jenna?"

My hand freezes on the door handle. I turn as Carter enters the hallway after me.

My heart swells at the sight of him. I want so badly to bury myself in his arms, but I force myself to stand tall. His blue eyes pin me in place as he approaches.

"What?" I ask, voice raspy with fatigue.

He stops a foot away, so close I could reach out and

touch him. I don't.

"I just wanted to say . . ." He pauses to swallow, dropping his eyes. "I just wanted to say you did a good thing at the Depot today. Killing those maimed students."

His words warm me, but it hurts seeing him hold back from me. "It was the right thing to do. Those College Creek guys are sickos."

"Yeah." He stands there, hands shoved in the pockets of his jeans, not quite meeting my eye.

Out in the sitting room, Johnny gives a loud, dramatic blow-by-blow of the encounter with the College Creek students.

"Carter . . ." I struggle to form words.

He doesn't respond, but he doesn't leave, either. His blue eyes are guarded as he looks at me.

There are so many things I want to say. I've worked on at least half a dozen long-winded speeches in my head the last few days. Now that I'm finally face-to-face with him—now that he isn't giving me the cold shoulder, or telling me to go away, or straight up being a jerk—they all fly out of my head.

"Carter, I . . . I wanted to say you look great. With your new look, I mean. I like it."

"Do you think your mom would like it?"

I flinch, but I don't back down from the challenge. "I deserve that." I swallow, searching for more words. "Do you remember the night when we met? At the Creekside dorm party?"

"Of course."

"I never told you this, but I'd had a crush on you for a while. I wanted to meet you. I made it a point to bump into you at that party."

"What do you mean?" he asks with a frown.

"I saw you the first day we all moved into the dorms at the beginning of the year. Do you remember when that girl dropped her mirror and cut open her hand?"

"Mary. Yeah, I remember."

"You took off your T-shirt and wrapped her hand to stop the bleeding."

He shifts, frown deepening. "I had on an undershirt. I wasn't trying to show off or anything."

"You don't get it. It wasn't about you taking off your shirt. It was about you taking off your shirt to help a girl with a cut hand. All I could think was that I wanted a guy who would give me his clothing if I was hurt and bleeding." I chew my bottom lip. "It wasn't about how you looked. It wasn't about getting back at my mom. It was about you. Beard or no beard. Short hair or long. You're still the guy who gave away his shirt to help a bleeding stranger. I-I . . ."

I love you, I want to say, but the words won't come out. They seem all wrong. They're not the sort of thing you say to someone you've hurt.

"You never told me that." Carter's eyes are wide in the darkness.

"I know." I give him a sad smile. "I'm sorry. I should have."

He hesitates, then reaches out and draws me close. I fall into his arms. Burying my nose in the crook of his neck, I inhale deeply. I pull his scent into my lungs, drawing comfort from it.

He kisses the top of my head and releases me. I watch him, desperate for more, but all he says is, "Goodnight, Jenna."

The smile he gives me is the first one I've had since our fight. And even though he turns and walks away, I'm left feeling lighthearted.

19
Reunion

KATE

I wasn't happy when the kids left on their beer run. However, since it was the first thing they had done that resembled a supply run, I didn't try to stop them. As Johnny wraps up details of the College Creek encounter, I vow to go with them next time.

Reed taps the keg and Eric rounds everyone up for *God of War*. I watch the entrance to the hallway where Carter and Jenna disappeared, silently praying they'll make up.

When Carter emerges a few minutes later, eyes brighter than they've been in days, I inwardly cheer. I wait a few more minutes, hoping Jenna will show.

When it becomes apparent she isn't coming, I sigh. Maybe things are going in the right direction, but they haven't completely made up yet.

I retreat to the kitchen to find dinner. I select a can of baked beans and join Johnny at the kitchen table, clearing myself a small spot between his notebooks, radio, and maps.

"I'm glad you all made it back safely," I say to Johnny, cracking open my can. I could warm up the beans, but it doesn't seem worth the effort. Besides, room temperature isn't all that bad.

"I got good material for my piece on the fall of Humboldt University." Johnny extracts a notebook out of the stack, scratching a sideburn with his pen cap. "The run-in with the creeps makes for a good story."

"How long have you been writing?" I ask.

"Ever since junior high when I joined the school newspaper," Johnny says. "I never wanted to go to college. I wanted to travel the world, meet people, and write about them. Mom and Dad freaked out when I told them my plan. They said that if I agreed to go to college and get my degree, they would sponsor a one-year trip around the world when I graduated."

"Sounds like a pretty good deal," I say around a mouthful of beans.

"I thought so." Johnny fills two cups with beer from the keg, passing one to me. "That's when I got my idea to interview people around the world using a high-frequency ham radio. I put an antenna up on the dorm roof at the beginning of the semester when I first moved in. Did you know that if you lock into the right receivers, you can talk to people on the other side of the globe? It was sort of like traveling. Before all this zombie shit happened, I was interviewing two ladies from Manhattan. They sold all their possessions and moved to Thailand to run an elephant sanctuary. I probably know more about elephant breeding habits than most people. Did you know the average elephant is pregnant for twenty-two months? And that baby elephants are blind when they're born?"

I shake my head, guzzling down half my beer. It's warm but still tastes delicious.

"Anyway," Johnny continues, "that book is called *Voices From Around the World*. The subtitle is *Why Are We Here?* The premise is that I ask each person what led them to being where they are today."

"So, what led the two women to sell all their belongings to open an elephant sanctuary?"

"One was a life-long vegan who ran a successful

bakery in Manhattan. She felt like she needed to give back to the world in a big way. Her partner was a corporate lawyer who got sick of all the greed. She wanted to find work that was rewarding for her soul, rather than her pocketbook."

Up until this point, I hadn't realized how interesting Johnny was, or what part the ham radio played in his life.

"You said you're compiling a story about the fall of Humboldt," I say. "What's that one about?"

"It's going into my collection entitled *Voices of the Apocalypse*," Johnny replies. "Subtitle, *First Days*. I've been writing down all that's happened to us, but I also have eight interviews from other people so far. Five in the U.S., two in Canada, and one in Germany."

I still, his words sinking into my chest. "You're interviewing people in other countries?"

He nods.

My mouth goes dry. I had assumed the world—or at least *my* world—was changed forever. In my head, I saw wasted American cities cluttered with the undead.

What I had not considered were other countries.

"You okay, Kate?"

"Have you had contact with any countries besides Canada or Germany?" I ask.

"Sweden and India, but no official interviews so far."

The scope of the outbreak spreads in my mind. I glance up as Reed lets out a whoop in front of the Xbox.

"Have you mentioned this to anyone here?" I ask.

"I don't know. Maybe."

Even with this information, Johnny hasn't stepped into the new world. He's so consumed with his project that he's let important details—like the gathering of food and water—slide.

Johnny rifles through the maps on the table, pulling out one of Europe marked with red dots. "These are the places where I made contact with people."

I sort through the maps, noting red dots in the towns

and countries where Johnny interviewed survivors.

"What are people saying?" I ask. "Is it as bad in other places as it is here?"

"Yeah. As far as I can tell, it started here in the U.S. in Portland. At the port, to be exact. But there were attacks in other ports around the country not long after. Same thing in Europe."

"What about other continents? South America? Africa?"

"I haven't talked to anyone in those parts of the world. But some of my contacts have mentioned outbreaks in those places. I-I think there's a chance it's worldwide."

"Johnny." I search his face. "You more than anyone else here knows we're at the beginning of a new world. Why are you spending your days with your notebooks and ham radio when we need to be stockpiling food?"

He shuffles through the maps, not meeting my eye. "I'm a writer. That's it. I can talk to people and record their stories." His voice drops. "I don't know how to do anything else."

"But you can find out." I point to his radio.

"What?"

I slam my palm against the tabletop in my excitement, which makes him jump. "Johnny, you're collecting survival stories. Don't you see how important that is? You have firsthand information on how other people are surviving the apocalypse."

"Oh." He blinks, scratching at his sideburns. "I hadn't thought of it that way."

"I need you to keep talking to people. Keep interviewing. Start asking people for survival tips. Make a list. Write down every little tip and piece of advice you can glean, even if it doesn't seem important."

Johnny perks up. "A survival guide." I can tell he's deep in thought as his eyes un-focus. "*A Post-Apocalypse Survival Guide.* No, too generic. That sounds like something that could have been written before the shit hit the fan."

It takes me a moment to realize he's formulating another book title. "*Zombie Survival Tips from the Living?*" I suggest.

"Too clunky." He chews his bottom lip. "How about . . . *How to Survive: Tips From Survivors of the Zombie Apocalypse* . . . no, that uses *survive* twice."

"*How to Persevere? How to Carry On? How to Tough It Out?*" I chuckle at that last one. I could write a book on how to tough it out, though I'm sure no one would read it.

Johnny laughs too, a smile creasing his pensive face. "*How to Survive and Thrive?*"

"*How to Thrive?*"

"*How to Thrive in the Apocalypse.*" Johnny seizes a new notebook and scribbles out the title. "Yes! That's it. I love the word *thrive*. It's more than just *surviving*. Surviving can mean hiding out in the latrine and drinking your own piss to stay alive. I don't want to write about that. I want to help people do more than just survive. I want to write about *thriving*."

"We want to thrive," I agree. After a beat, I add, "I have your first tip on how to thrive."

"What is it?" Johnny leans forward, pen poised over the pale blue lines of his notebook.

"How to thrive, rule number one," I say. "Even if the world has ended, don't steal from drug dealers."

This inspires a peal of laughter so loud the commotion around the Xbox lulls.

"What are you guys laughing about?" Reed asks.

"Kate and I are just making a list of ways to thrive in the apocalypse," Johnny replies.

"Cool," Eric says before his attention shifts back to *God of War.*

Johnny hunches over his notebook, writing as fast as he can. "Number two: avoid everyone in a uniform."

"I disagree," I say. "Not all soldiers murder college kids. I met a young soldier on the way here. He helped me bury my friend's daughter. His name was Alvarez. Guy had a good heart."

I take another long pull off the beer, remembering that nightmare of a day. I'd probably still be digging Aleisha's grave if Alvarez hadn't been there to help. Hand-dug graves always look like neat rectangles in the movies. In reality, you're lucky to get a lopsided hole wide enough to hold a corpse in the fetal position.

Johnny stops scribbling and looks up at me. "Wait, what did you say the name of that guy was?"

"What guy?

"The guy who helped you bury your friend."

"Alvarez."

"Alvarez." Johnny grabs the ham. "I've been talking to a guy named Foot Soldier. He's living in an old Russian fort on the coast."

"Fort Ross?" I ask.

"Yeah. You know it?"

"Yeah. I've been there. Carter had a field trip there when he was a kid. I was one of the chaperones."

Johnny's eyes light up. "Foot Soldier says it is a big ass fort with a twenty-foot wall all the way around it."

"Sounds like Fort Ross. That wouldn't be a bad place to weather the apocalypse. Too bad it's so far away from here."

"The point is, this guy's real name isn't Foot Soldier. That's just his handle. His real name is Alvarez. What if it's the same guy?"

"You mean, what if this Alvarez is the same Alvarez I met?"

"Yeah." Johnny adjusts the dial on the ham, then leans forward to speak into it. "Foot Soldier, this is Wandering Writer. Are you there? Over."

Seems unlikely, but I don't have it in me to burst Johnny's excitement. The young man I met in Laytonville was as green as they come. He was also on foot. The chance that he made it all the way to Fort Ross is slim to none.

The ham crackles in Johnny's hand. "This is Foot Soldier. How's it going in your neck of the woods? Over."

Johnny oozes excitement. "Hey, Foot Soldier, I have a friend here. Her name is Kate. We think you guys might know each other. Did you by any chance help a woman bury someone on your way to Fort Ross? Over."

"Holy shit," comes the response. "Yeah, I did. Are those crazy runners with you?"

20
Map

KATE

My jaw falls open. I snatch the ham away from Johnny.

"Alvarez, is that really you?" Tears of emotion fill my eyes. "This is Kate."

"Say 'over,'" Johnny whispers.

"Over," I say.

"Holy fucking shit," comes the response. Even through the static, I hear the emotion in Alvarez's voice. "Damn, woman. I've thought about you and Frederico every day since I left you. Meeting you guys saved my life. Every time things got hard, I told myself, *Alvarez, if those two old fools can run two hundred miles on foot, so can you.* I can't believe you guys made it! Over."

"Frederico didn't make it." My throat constricts. I blink to keep tears from spilling. "Over."

"Shit. I'm sorry to hear that. He was a tough old bastard. I could tell that much. Over."

I nod, then realize he can't see me. "I know," I croak. "He was a good friend. How did you get to Fort Ross? Over."

"Long story. The short version is that I met up with some people along the way. A few of them were going to the fort and let me tag along. Are you safe? Over."

"As safe as can be expected. Over."

"I wish you could come here. We need good people to get this place up and running. Over."

I sigh, my eyes traveling over the maps. Fort Ross is probably a solid two hundred miles from here. "Too far," I say. "But I'm glad you're safe and alive."

"How's your arm? Over."

I glance down at the atrocity on my arm that is the stitches from Alvarez. "It's healing."

Johnny takes the ham from me. "Foot Soldier, this is Wandering Writer," he says. "Are you the one who gave Kate those stitches?"

"Yeah, that was me."

"Dude, those stitches make her look like the bride of Frankenstein. Did you sew those with a blindfold?"

Alvarez bursts out laughing. Johnny grins at me to show he's joking. I roll my eyes, glancing down at the jagged black thread marring my arm. The stitches should be ready to come out soon. And Johnny isn't far off from his Frankenstein comparison.

"I'm putting together a thrive list," Johnny continues, speaking into the ham.

I tune him out as he rattles off the idea for his book. My eyes stray to all the maps Johnny has compiled.

Another cheer goes up from around the Xbox.

Alvarez has a group of survivors. He and Johnny are talking about farming, raising cattle, and fishing.

My survivors are playing video games.

They all need a drop kick into the present.

And I think I finally have a way to do it. I gather up Johnny's maps.

The walls of the sitting room are covered with a mish-mash of posters and flyers, most of which pertain to music, bands, and ironic slogans. I pull out the thumbtacks, replacing the posters with maps from around the world.

"Mom, what are you doing?" Carter, taking a break

from *God of War*, glances at me from his seat on the floor.

"Johnny has been talking to people around the world," I reply. "Apocalypse survivors. All the red dots indicate towns where he's spoken to people."

One second, all eyes are glued to *God of War*. The next second, a hush falls on the Xbox enthusiasts. Johnny, having switched off the ham, is also silent. Every head stares at the maps on the walls.

I move to the side, letting them take in the breadth of the global epidemic.

"Dude," Eric breathes, breaking the silence.

"There are dots in other countries," Carter says dumbly. He looks like someone delivered a wicked left hook to his brain. Emotion ripples across his face.

It makes a part of me break inside. Instead of the twenty-year-old young man before me, I see the little four-year-old who fell off his bike. More than anything, I wish I had a Band-Aid to cover his wound like I did when he was four.

"The outbreak isn't isolated to the American northwest." I raise my voice, pitching it loud enough to fill the room. They need to hear me. They need to see the maps. "It's worldwide."

Johnny rises, crossing to point to a city in England. "Robert the butcher. Single dad, widowed. Three kids. He was butchering a pig when riots started outside his shop. When a man with a missing throat ran in and attacked him, Robert fought him off. It wasn't until his cleaver went into the man's head did it dawn on him that he was dealing with a zombie. He closed the shop and rushed to get his kids from school." Johnny's voice drops. "He was able to get the two smallest. The older one, who was at a different school, never made it home. Robert hopes she's still alive. He and his two youngest kids are back in the butcher shop. He boarded up all the windows. He and his kids are aging and drying the meats. They have enough to survive for a few months."

Johnny moves to another red dot, this one a port town in Texas. "Pamela Winchester. A manager of Target who moonlights as an amateur marksman. She's got a thing for guns. When people started eating each other inside the store, she went straight home to her guns. She's teamed up with a group of other amateur marksmen. They're holed up in an apartment complex on tight rations. Pamela isn't sure what they're going to do when they run out of food, but she's ready to start shooting anything that doesn't look alive."

God of War is completely forgotten. All eyes are riveted on Johnny.

I study the group of young men and women before me. There's Lila, who looks like she wants to hide in a closet and never come out. Reed and Eric grip the Xbox controllers like they're lifelines. Even Johnny, with all the information he's gathered, looks like he prefers denial to reality. My son looks like he's been run over with a freight train. I wish Jenna was here to embrace the moment with me.

I push on, determined to make them see. "You can't spend your days in front of the Xbox anymore. The food will run out. The water will run out. Something else could happen and we might need to leave. No one is going to come rescue us. We either take care of ourselves, or we die."

"What are we supposed to do?" Eric asks.

This is my chance. Eric has given me an opening. I don't intend to waste it.

"Tomorrow, we go to Trading Post." That's the outdoor shop in downtown Arcata. "We stock up on survival gear. We make sure we each have a bug-out bag in case things go to shit and we have to make a run for it. After that, we scavenge. Every day. We clear every room in this building and gather supplies. We get solar panels and hook up the washing machine. We fortify the downstairs lounge. We figure out how to plant a garden.

We make Creekside our home. A real home. And we always, always have a contingency plan in place."

There it is. My sixty-second soapbox speech. I scan their faces, trying to gauge the impact of my words.

Carter lets out a long, slow exhale. "I'm in, Mom."

"Me, too," Johnny says.

"I'll help, but I'm not going outside," Lila says.

"I've been working out how to set up the solar panel," Eric says. "Count me in."

"So long as I can get high at the end of the day, I'm in, too," Reed says.

Eric smacks him. "Dude."

"What?" Reed says.

Chuckles ripple through the room. For the first time since arriving here, I feel a sense of hope.

21
Surrounded

KATE

As I look at my tired face in the mirror, something occurs to me: I'm healthy. I'm almost recovered from my two-hundred-mile run. I have a few achy twinges here and there and the poison oak is still hanging out, but overall my body feels good. The swelling in my ankle is almost gone. I can lace on a shoe without discomfort. Even better, I'm not showing any signs of a waterborne illness. I'd been forced to drink unfiltered water on my way here, a risky move at best.

I may have hair badly in need of a cut and color, and I could benefit from an extra ten pounds, but in light of how bad things could be, I find it hard to care about my physical appearance.

I exit the bathroom and head into the living room. Everyone has gathered there, eager for the expedition to Trading Post. The exception is Lila. She still refuses to leave Creekside.

"This is going to be epic," Reed is saying as I enter the room. "It's my childhood fantasy to walk into a store and take whatever I want without paying for it."

"Your childhood fantasy is stealing?" I ask.

He shrugs, unapologetic. "I grew up in the Oakland 'hood. Stealing is practically in my DNA. Except that my dad would have whooped my ass if he ever caught me."

That gets a few soft chuckles.

"You should come," Jenna says to Lila. "What if more of those drug mules show up, or those College Creek guys?"

"You have a bigger chance of running into them out there than I do in here," Lila replies.

"I'll stay back," Eric says casually, flipping through his collection of video games.

"I don't need a babysitter," Lila says.

Eric rolls his eyes. "Who says this is about you? I want the Xbox to myself for a few hours."

The others groan, but I see the way Eric looks at Lila. They might argue and bicker, but under the surface, I suspect Eric likes Lila. He has a lame way of showing it, usually goading her into an argument.

"No way," Jenna says. "You guys have to pull your weight if you stay behind."

"What do you want us to do?" Lila asks cautiously.

"Go through the cleared dorm rooms and find all the toilet paper, Kleenex, and paper towels," Jenna says. "Find all the cleaning supplies and first aid supplies. Make an inventory and find a logical place to store it in room two-oh-four. That's our supply room."

Lila's mouth is set in a thin, scared line, but Eric shrugs and says, "Okay, we can do that."

"You gather the stuff," Lila says. "I'll organize it and write up the inventory."

Should I be worried that Lila is so uncomfortable leaving the apartment? It's a problem to be chewed on another time.

Twenty minutes later, Carter, Jenna, Reed, Johnny, and I are all astride bikes. Three of them came from the cleared dorm rooms; the other two were liberated from the rack outside the dorm. Reed was surprisingly savvy when it came to opening the U-Lock bike locks. A simple ballpoint pen was all it had taken to jimmy them open.

"It's amazing what you can learn on YouTube," he told me with a proud grin.

The five of us now pedal our way down Granite Avenue. I'd prefer to be on foot. It's quieter and, to be honest, I'm more comfortable on foot than on a bike. But the others aren't in the necessary shape to make a journey of several miles on foot, so I agreed to the bikes. At least they'd been smart enough to know we couldn't use a car.

The silence of the road is broken only by the squawk of birds and the buzz of flies congregated on the dead bodies. I scan the blank-faced buildings. My shoulder blades itch like I'm being watched, but there's no telling if that's my paranoia or my instinct talking.

The smell is worse than ever. We have handkerchiefs over our mouths and noses, but flimsy pieces of fabric aren't enough to combat the stink of the rotting dead, which are fully encrusted with black flies and carrion birds.

We're going to have to figure out a way to deal with the bodies sooner or later. Living around the smell and rot is not a good thing. I make a mental note to keep an eye out for a bulldozer or some kind of CAT while we're in town.

"We should try to find some essential oil or perfume for the handkerchiefs," Jenna says. "It would help combat the stink a little."

"How about some patchouli?" Reed asks. "I know a few shops where we can find that."

Everyone snickers. There's an ongoing joke in Arcata about the hippies who use patchouli oil instead of deodorant. I had been nervous that Jenna was one of them when I first met her. And though she doesn't shave her armpits—something I've come to overlook since getting to know her—she does use standard deodorant.

She and Carter pedal beside one another in easy silence. I'm not sure what transpired between the two of them last night, but things are different now. The stiff resentment is gone, and they've even smiled at each other a few times. That, coupled with the fact I finally have this group of kids looking forward instead of at the Xbox console has me in a good mood.

We slow as we reach the end of the street and make the turn onto the road that hugs the outer perimeter of the main campus. This part of the college isn't in much better shape than our area. Bodies are everywhere, along with abandoned cars and military Jeeps. A wrought iron fence stands between the road and the large sports field on the front end of campus. Dozens of undead mill around on the field. A few turn at the sound of our passage, but most are too far away to hear us.

The world around me flips back and forth. Part of me sees the campus Carter called home the last two years: the white stucco buildings, the vast green lawn where students congregated to play soccer and football, the salty tang of the ocean air that's always in my nostrils, and the redwood trees rising up alongside the buildings.

The rest of me sees the wreckage of the present. The burned buildings. The bodies. The death.

Only the smell of the ocean is unchanged, but even that mingles with the stench of rotting corpses.

We reach the edge of the campus. Humboldt State University sits apart from the rest of Arcata. Between us and the town is a wide freeway that sits below the street level, making it possible to look down on the abandoned road where there are more cars, bodies, and zombies.

An overpass spans the freeway, connecting the college to the town of Arcata. From where we stand, the town doesn't look all that different. If you ignore the burned-out buildings. And the bodies. Even from here, I see bodies in the streets.

We pause at the edge of campus, all of us in a silent semicircle. There's no telling what we'll find in the streets of Arcata.

"Keep your weapons ready." I heft my screwdriver to emphasize the point. "Make as little noise as possible. If something happens and we're separated, get back to Creekside."

We exit the campus, weave through the cars clogging the overpass, and cross into downtown Arcata.

"Slow down," I call as the sound of moaning reaches my ears. "I hear them."

Everyone slows, the bikes falling into line behind me. I pull to a stop at the corner of a strip mall and look into the street beyond.

Two dozen zombies mill around in the street. The closest is a good ten yards from where we stand, giving us a decent amount of clearance.

"We can get by them," I whisper-shout. "Just pedal fast."

We zip across the street, pedaling hard for the next turn. The zombies rotate at the sound of our passage, their bodies moving in strange synchronicity. I lead the kids in a hard left turn, angling deeper into the town.

Old houses spring up on either side of us, colorful bungalows leftover from the logging era. They're a mixture of storefronts and small shops.

I bite my lip as we turn onto another street, this one with more zombies in the middle of the road. I wish we were on foot. It would be easier to sneak through the town undetected. The soft whir of the bike pedals sound like gongs going off in these dead-quiet neighborhoods.

I mentally trace the map of Arcata in my head. I know the streets well, having run through them many times over the past two years when I visited Carter. We can turn and backtrack to another street that leads to the central square where Trading Post is located, or we can push through this street.

I count ten zombies in front of us. Less before us than behind.

"We pedal through them," I murmur, brandishing my

screwdriver. "Kill any that get too close. Stay together."

I pick up speed, gripping the handlebar with one hand and the screwdriver in the other. Around and behind me are Carter and his friends, every one of them wielding their wooden spears.

The first zombie half runs, half shuffles in my direction. His legs are partially decomposed, and he can't move too fast. Flies and maggots swarm his left thigh, leading me to believe that's where he was bitten.

I aim my bike in his direction, jamming my screwdriver into his eye socket as I do.

The bike keeps going, but the screwdriver gets stuck in the socket. I tip sideways, dragged down by the dead weight of the impaled body. My leg shoots out, catching me, and I manage to yank the screwdriver free without falling off.

Johnny isn't so lucky. As his spear punches through the face of an oncoming zombie, the creature falls on him. The bike makes a loud rattle as it tips over, pinning Johnny's leg to the ground.

I leap off my bike and race toward him. The zombie he stabbed is dead, but the body is draped across the bike with Johnny underneath. I reach for the body as three more zombies close in.

Jenna wheels her bike around, planting herself between us and the oncoming zombies. Carter wheels up beside her, the two of them striking out with their spears.

Reed rolls up behind us and faces off against a zombie of his own. I fling aside the dead body, freeing Johnny. He scrambles up, jumping back onto the bike.

"Go!" I hiss.

Jenna and Carter finish off their zombies and push hard against the bike pedals, breaking free of the melee. I race back to my bike, which is tipped over in a clump of bushes. Just as I grab it, a figure looms up from the other side of the greenery.

He was homeless when he was alive, his skin sun-darkened and half his teeth missing. He growls at me, bunching his legs to spring.

I don't give him a chance. Straddling my bike, I lunge across the bushes and bury my screwdriver in his forehead. I yank my weapon free, not waiting to see the body hit the ground before slamming down on the pedals.

I race to catch up with the others, who keep glancing back in my direction to be sure I've made it. We race in a clump down the street. There are a few more zombies. We pick up speed and swerve around them.

Reaching the next intersection, we slow long enough to scan every direction. We need to go left, toward the plaza, but that way is clogged with cars, zombies, and dead bodies. By the amount of shell casings shining on the ground, I'd say a shootout happened here.

The ways forward and to the right aren't much better.

"Which way?" Reed hisses.

"Straight," I say.

We pedal another few blocks, breaking up as we swerve around zombies.

The moaning has increased in the streets around us. Somewhere nearby, several high-pitched keens rend the air. I look over my shoulder and see a large pack of the undead rounding the corner.

We're making too much noise, drawing too much attention.

"There's an alleyway half a mile up the street," I call, pitching my voice as loud as I dare. "On your left. Turn down that way."

With any luck, the zombies will have a hard time figuring out how to follow us into the narrow opening.

I zip around one of the undead only to find myself in a near head-on collision with another. I grit my teeth and rise up on the bike pedals, giving myself leverage over the oncoming creature. I stab it through the eye. As it drops from the blow, I yank my screwdriver free.

Two creatures converge on Jenna, each of them a silver-haired woman in a flowing skirt. Jenna spins to take out the nearest of them, her spear missing the old lady's head and instead punching through her sternum. The impaled zombie claws her way toward Jenna, bloodied hands reaching.

Carter drops his bike and sprints to her side, his face a mask of fear and determination. He grabs the impaled zombie by the hair and hauls her backward. He swings his spear like a bat, clubbing the old lady so hard her skull cracks.

Jenna spins around to face the last of the old ladies. She's lost her spear, but her expression is fierce. She leaps free of the bike and shoves both hands against the zombie. As the creature topples backward, she pounces. One booted foot comes down on the old lady's face, smashing through bone. Bits of blood and bone fragments spray in every direction.

"There's too many of them," Johnny wheezes, dispatching an undead with half a dozen facial piercings.

He's right. Zombies flood the street from both directions, their eerie keening cutting the air. There's no way to break through them without getting killed.

"Into that house." I charge up the steps of a pink bungalow.

I raise my screwdriver, ready to shatter the window if need be, but the door swings open under my hand.

"Inside!" I hold it open as the others rush past me.

A zombie scrambles up the steps, hard on the heels of Reed. I slam the door in its face.

22
On Foot

KATE

Carter and Johnny wedge a sofa against the door. Outside come several thumps as the undead barrel into it.

We lean over our knees, breathing hard. My hand is covered up to the elbow in blood. More of it spatters my clothing.

"Everyone okay?" I ask between gulps for air. "Anyone bit?"

They shake their heads, casting wide-eyed looks of fear in the direction of the door.

"We go on foot from here," I say. "We won't make as much noise and we'll be more nimble."

"We'll also be slower," Johnny points out.

"Slower is okay if we aren't running for our lives," I reply. "I made my way on foot through Arcata without attracting any attention."

A glance out the window shows me more and more of the undead pouring into the street. We can't linger. If we don't move now, we risk getting trapped inside the bungalow.

"Out the back." I spin, ushering Carter and the others toward the rear of the house.

We pass through rooms with shag carpet and flowered wallpaper in hues of green, orange, and metallic gold. Gaudy light fixtures of black wrought iron with bulging glass bowls of olive green hang from the walls and ceiling. The house looks like it was transported from the set of *That 70s Show*.

The air smells like decades of nicotine. I sniff, trying to discern the smell of death over the cigarette residue. I detect none, though there is a smear of blood across the wall. Other than that, the place looks like it's been undisturbed for forty years.

We enter the kitchen at the back of the house. I snatch a serrated knife out of the butcher block, knowing my screwdriver might not be enough to get us through this. I'm a fan of having plan Bs. Speaking of which, we all need some backup.

"Hold up," I whisper. I pull out the longest knives, passing them around to the others. They take them from me with tense expressions, each of them sliding the knives into the belts they wear.

Jenna ends up with a giant cleaver. She grimaces, but slides it into her belt without complaint. She looks like a *Buffy the Vampire Slayer* caricature.

I lead the way out the aluminum porch door. The backyard is quiet and empty. The moans and keening of the undead pepper the air. They bang on the front door and rattle against the windows.

We need to get off this street and around the hoard. At this point, the best way to do that is by moving through the backyards.

This yard is surrounded with a cheap bamboo fence, the type you get at Walmart. I peek through the slats to make sure we aren't going to blunder into a barbecue gone bad. When I see nothing but a rusted old car and a cracked fountain, I push against the bamboo.

It gives way beneath the pressure. I trample over it. The others follow me, Carter bringing up the rear.

"We're going to go through the backyards and circle around the zombies," I whisper. "Stay alert. There's no telling what we might encounter."

They nod at me in grim-faced understanding. I can see they're scared.

Scared is good. I'm fucking terrified, though I do my best to hide it.

The next fence is made of wood, but it's old and rotting and lists to one side. Once we determine there are no undead on the other side of it, Carter yanks two boards free to create an opening we can pass through. I notice him staying close to Jenna, his stance alert and protective. Maybe after this near-death experience, they'll get over themselves and make up completely.

We pass through the next two yards without incident. The moaning and keening from the street haven't let up. The sound of shattering glass tells me when they've broken through the front window of the house we escaped into.

This knowledge hits me with a shockwave of urgency. There are four houses between us and them, but what if they bash their way into the backyard? Did we close the back door or just the screen? Shit, I can't remember.

I hurry to the next fence which, as luck would have it, is the first sturdy fence we've encountered. Sturdy *and* tall. Carter hauls himself up to peer over the side.

No sooner has he popped his head over the side than a dog lets loose a string of frantic barks. The animal throws itself against the fence as Carter leaps backward. It barks and claws at the planks.

The barking is like a beacon to the blind zombies. Out on the street and back in the house, their keening goes off like a jumble of alarm clocks.

"Back fence," I hiss.

Carter checks over the top of this one, then drops down and nods.

The dog is still going nuts, barking and growling and throwing himself at the fence. Where is his owner? There must be an owner if the dog has survived, right?

Carter grabs Jenna around the waist and heaves her up. She grabs the top of the fence, hauling herself up and over.

"Your turn." I jump in surprise when Johnny grabs me and hoists me up. He's not a strapping kid by any sense of the imagination, but he lifts me like I weigh nothing more than an oversized stuffed animal. Bits of blood and gore are spattered in his sideburns.

I drop down beside Jenna on the other side. She crouches and scans the yard. It's overgrown with weeds and faded lawn ornaments. To the left is a deer with a broken antler. Hiding in the grass near my feet is a garden gnome that looks like it tangled with a weed whacker and lost.

The boys follow us over the fence. Carter is the last one to drop into the weed-choked yard with us. As he does, I hear the sound of splintering wood, frantic barks, and the crescendo of moaning zombies.

"They've broken through the fence into the yard with the dog," Carter whispers.

Poor animal. I might not have a warm fuzzy spot for dogs who attack my son, but I wouldn't wish the zombies on it. Hearing its pain also brings back memories of Stout, the sweet dog who ran with Frederico and me before some assholes thought it would be fun to shoot her.

I take our group toward the gate that leads onto the next street. I pause, straining my ears and peering through the gap in the fence boards. I can't be certain, but it sounds like all the zombie commotion is behind us, not on the neighboring street.

The barking of the dog rises in pitch. It yelps then barks some more.

I suck in a breath and ease open the gate. It creaks on rusted hinges, but the sound is lost in the keening of the zombies in the dog's yard. The poor animal gives two more pitiful cries before going silent. I try not to think of its fate.

We creep onto a street lined with more colorful bungalows. There are only a few zombies in sight, all of them bumping against houses and cars as they try to figure out how to get to the keening pack one street over.

It's with a sense of relief that I set out on foot. If it's one thing I know how to do, it's how to maneuver on my own two feet.

I resolve to do something about the fitness levels of the kids if—*when*—we make it back to Creekside. They won't survive in this world if they insist on being couch potatoes.

We hurry to the end of the block, pausing as a zombie lumbers into our path. Jenna takes an experimental swing with her cleaver, pursing her lips in satisfaction when the blade sinks deep into the skull and the undead drops to the ground.

Carter stands nearby, hovering as he watches the operation. Jenna, putting one boot on the shoulder of the monster and yanking the cleaver free, doesn't notice.

"I could get used to this thing," she whispers to me.

At the end of the block, we drop behind a hedgerow that hasn't been trimmed in months. The runners grow wild in all directions, creating a decent barrier for us to hide behind. The blind zombies can't see us regardless, but it's still comforting to have something between us and them.

I peer through the foliage, gauging the threat from the street we just escaped. A mob of zombies is congregating, so large it balloons out into the intersecting street.

"We have to get around the horde," I tell the others. "Stay light on your feet and we should be fine."

We make it another block without incident, only having to dispatch another few zombies. The horde behind us still makes a ruckus, drawing the attention of every undead within earshot.

We pass two zombies who claw at a fence, trying to reach the sound of their keening brethren. Neither notices our passing.

"Much better on foot," Jenna whispers to me as we hurry along.

"No more bikes," I reply. She nods in agreement.

The next intersection is passable, but instead of turning left and heading toward downtown, I hurry up another block.

"Kate," Reed says, "that street was clear. Trading Post is that way." He gestures to the street I bypassed.

The poor kid is panting, sweat dripping down his temples and saturating his shirt. Some of that must be fear induced, but I decide Reed needs to smoke less pot and start running. They all need to start running.

"We don't know how far the mob stretches," I reply. "I want to make sure we have at least another block between us."

He swallows, nodding in understanding, chest heaving as he sucks in air. "I can't believe you ran two hundred miles to get here. I can barely run two blocks."

I squeeze his shoulder in sympathy, but don't slow down.

The next connecting street is also clear, except for a few stray undead. I lead our group down it. At the following cross street, we see a thick knot of zombies. Luckily, they're gathered around a cluster of cars that blocks the road and all their attention is away from us.

Most of the keening has died down, but the moaning hasn't subsided. The crowd shoves at one another and the cars, all of them trying to move in the same direction. Several zombies are on the ground, trampled by their brethren.

Our group makes little noise as we continue through the streets of Arcata, eliminating zombies as needed. It takes us another thirty minutes to maneuver into the center of town.

The Arcata plaza is a quaint grass area divided like a compass with cement walkways. In the center is a circular area with a statue of a United States president. I can't remember which one.

The plaza throngs with zombies. Two wrecked Hummers are there, one tipped on its side, the other smashed through a storefront. The zombies are a mixture of college kids, locals, and tourists, with a handful of homeless mixed in.

"There's Trading Post." Carter raises a finger, pointing across the plaza to a blue Victorian storefront. Between us and the shop are several hundred zombies.

"We could try and go around the back," Jenna says, crouching beside us. "Maybe it's clear behind the shop."

I nod. It's our only option.

We fall back, working our way around the plaza. We're forced to drop back several more blocks when the subsequent ones have more zombies than we're comfortable taking on. Many are in military uniform. I even spot a few rifles strewn among the undead.

I consider trying to snag a few of them but dismiss the idea. We have a mission today, and it's not gun retrieval. Besides that, the few guns I do see are not easy to retrieve, thanks to the undead wandering around the streets.

There are more real dead in this part of town, too, people killed during the chaos that exploded here. The bodies I see are riddled with gunshot wounds. How many were killed because they were zombies, and how many were unfortunate enough to be in the wrong place at the wrong time?

It takes us nearly an hour to work our way around the plaza to the backside of Trading Post. And though it's slow going, we don't attract any attention.

"Damn," Carter swears as the alleyway behind Trading Post comes into view.

It's crammed with zombies.

23
Distraction

KATE

We fall back, taking shelter against the building between the plaza and the alleyway behind the shop.

"This was a bad idea," Reed says. "We should just go back."

"No way," Jenna says. "We worked our asses off to get here. No way are we turning around now."

"What are we supposed to do? Wade into *that*"— Reed gestures to the milling undead—"and hope for the best?"

"We just need a distraction to draw them away," Carter says.

Johnny grunts in disgust. "Well, we're all out of dogs."

"All we need is a car radio," I say. "We—"

"What good will that do?" Reed demands. "It's not like there are any radio stations that work."

I want to suggest that Reed take himself back to Creekside if he isn't going to be helpful, but remind myself that he's scared.

"Frederico and I used a trick on the way here," I explain. "We find a nearby car with the keys still in the ignition. Preferably one with a CD or old-fashioned tape player. We crank the music and let it draw the zombies."

"I'll do it," Carter says. "I'll find a car."

"We'll go together," I begin, but Carter shakes his head.

"You know better than anyone what supplies we need in there," he replies. "It'll be getting dark in another two hours. We don't want to get stuck out here. You guys go and get started. I'll create the distraction and make my way back to you."

"I'm going with you," Jenna says. Carter opens his mouth, the argument plain on his face, but Jenna cuts him off with a fierce shake of her head. "Don't even try to talk me out of this, Carter Stephenson. You need someone to watch your back. That someone is me."

"The two of you need someone to watch both your dumb asses," Reed says. "I'm not going in there." He gestures to the alleyway.

Johnny looks at me. "I guess that means you and I are on our own, Kate."

"Only until we create the distraction and get back to you," Carter says.

I nod, even though a knot has formed in my stomach. I don't like the idea of splitting up the group. Still, Carter's plan makes sense. It would be better to have Reed with us for the extra hand in searching for supplies, but he's so shaken I'm not sure how much good he'll be. At least if he's with Carter and Jenna, they'll have one more person to look out for them. He's proven proficient at killing zombies.

"We need a rendezvous point in case something happens and you can't reach the store," I say.

"If we can't get to the store, that will mean you're trapped inside," Reed says. "A rendezvous won't do any good at that point."

"Will you stop being a complete ass for thirty seconds?" Jenna demands. "Just shut up." She turns to me with a forced smile. "Kate, if for some reason we can't make it to the shop, we'll meet you at the overpass that leads back to the university."

I nod. That's a logical place. "We'll wait for one another until sunset. After that, get back to Creekside."

They all nod in agreement. I hesitate, wanting to gather Carter into a hug and cover him with kisses. But he's twenty, not two. He doesn't need me going to pieces on him.

"Be safe," I whisper.

"You, too, Mom." Gripping his spear in one hand and his kitchen knife in the other, he, Jenna, and Reed set out. I make a mental note to find them all decent hunting knives in Trading Post.

"It's hard for you to let him go," Johnny observes.

Leave it to the writer to notice what I'm trying to hide. "I traveled two hundred miles on foot through hell to find him. So yes, it's hard to watch him walk away from me into danger."

"He'll always be your baby." Johnny gives a small sigh. "This is a moving moment. I'm going to write about it when we get back. I still want to interview you about your journey here, you know."

I fold my arms across my chest. "To be honest, I don't want to talk about it."

"Too fresh." Johnny nods. "I understand. Someday, then. Promise me someday you'll tell me about your journey."

I think of the night Frederico sacrificed himself to save me. Of the day our dog was shot by a bunch of crazed assholes. Of the hunger, thirst, and fear that plagued me every step of the way. The memories claw at me. I haven't even shared much with Carter. "If I ever decide to talk about it, I'll let you know."

"Deal." Johnny flashes me a wide smile, settling against the wall of the building while we wait.

And wait.

And wait.

I fidget, watching the sun sink in the sky. If we don't

get into the store soon, we'll be forced to turn back. Or worse, find a place to sleep for the night. It's not worth risking our lives traipsing back to the university in the dark.

Johnny straightens, tilting his head to one side. "Do you hear that?"

I strain my ears, listening. A few seconds later, I feel it more than hear it. A deep, pulsing rhythm that makes the ground beneath my feet vibrate.

The sound grows, rippling outward over the buildings. *Just beat it, beat it!* Michael Jackson unfurls in a wave of glorious sound. Carter, Jenna, and Reed got us our distraction.

Johnny and I peek around the building where we're hiding. The zombies in the alleyway stir at the sound, walking in uneven lines and bumping into each other. Their agitation increases by the second as they search for a way out. White eyes roll as they hiss and moan, scratching at the walls as the music drives them.

"They can't figure out how to leave the alley," Johnny says.

"Let's check the plaza," I say.

We cross the length of the building toward the plaza. Before we reach the other side, a stream of zombies staggers by. We fall back, pressing ourselves against the wall.

Johnny grabs my arm, gripping it with both hands. From the look on his face, I don't think he even notices he's clinging to me.

"Fall back," I hiss, prodding Johnny back the way we came. It doesn't take more than a finger in the ribs before he shakes himself out of his stupor.

We hustle back toward the alleyway. As we do, another stream of zombies staggers into view. They extend their arms, probing the open air in front of them as they find their way out of the alley. In the long shadows of the late afternoon, their silhouettes look like the zombies on the poster of a B-rated movie.

We scurry back, ducking into the alcove of a doorway. We're trapped. Zombies are on either side of us, some on the move from the plaza, some on the move from the alley. My mouth is dry, and I have a terrified college student gripping my arm so fiercely it feels like he's going to break it off.

I press us back against the alcove and stand stock-still. Johnny copies me, going rigid. I test the knob of the door behind us, but it's locked.

"They're trying the find the music," I whisper. "We have to stay here until they pass."

The look he gives me is one of complete incredulity. I don't know if he thinks I'm crazy for proposing we stand here and do nothing, or crazy for suggesting the zombies might actually pass by en masse without realizing we're here.

My skin crawls, fear raising the hair along my shoulder blades. I take deep breaths, forcing air into my chest and belly.

Two zombies blunder in our direction. My breath catches. Johnny's grip turns white-knuckled on my arm. I didn't think it was possible for him to squeeze me any harder.

My free hand strays to my screwdriver, resting on the handle. The zombies draw closer. They bump against the wall, take several steps sideways, and then continue forward. They draw so close I could reach and stab the nearest through the ear.

I don't move. There are too many zombies on either side of the alcove that shelters us. The smallest sound could draw their attention. I look at Johnny, hoping to convey my intent with my eyes, but he isn't looking at me. One hand has loosened from my wrist, straying to his knife.

I poke him in the neck to get his attention. He startles before turning to look at me. I give an emphatic shake of my head. He licks his lips, but stays his hand.

The zombies lumber past us, joining the stream on the other side of the street. They are swept into the crowd and away from view.

Johnny sags beside me. "How did you know they would pass by us?"

I recall that awful flight from Mr. Rosario's zombies with our bell collars. When Frederico and I crouched in the darkness of the tunnel, the zombies blundered by us without noticing.

Just thinking about it brings back the potent fear of those miles. My throat tightens at the memory of my lost friend. I would give anything to have Frederico here now.

"I'll tell you later," I reply.

Johnny's eyes search my face. I'm thankful he doesn't ask questions.

A break in the zombie pack opens near the entrance to the alley. I gesture to it with my chin. Johnny follows my gaze and nods. We run on light feet, rushing for the opening. We stop short when a single undead lumbers into sight. The twenty-something man wearing a torn Starbucks barista shirt never turns in our direction before disappearing from sight.

"Come on." I grab Johnny's shirt and haul him the rest of the way to the mouth of the alleyway. I pause long enough to make sure the coast is clear.

A near-empty street yawns before us, clear of all but a few zombies. Carter's music has done the trick.

Be safe, baby, I think, before dragging Johnny the rest of the way to Trading Post.

24
Beat It

JENNA

Humboldt County isn't known for wealth. Unlike the town where I grew up, there aren't fancy SUVs and electric cars at every turn. A newish car—meaning anything with a paint job that isn't scratched or faded—is a reason to be noticed.

Finding an older car with a CD player or a tape deck isn't hard. The hard part is finding one with keys still in the ignition and not surrounded by zombies. It also needs to be far enough away to draw the zombies from the plaza, but near enough to be heard when we blast the music.

"That one." I point down the street at a battered brown four-door. It sits in the middle of the street five blocks from the plaza. Only two zombies mill near it.

"I'll take the one on the left," Carter says. "Reed, you get the one on the right."

Color has returned to Reed's face after our earlier near-misses. He still looks like he might pee his pants, but when he brandishes his spear and kitchen knife, there's determination behind his eyes.

"I'll take care of the window." I heft a small rock out of a front yard.

We advance down the street. Carter and Reed branch off, each of them moving toward their targets.

Carter's eyes follow me. My throat is tight with worry. I swallow and force myself to give him a small smile. He smiles back. If I wasn't so tense, I'd probably appreciate his smile even more than I already do.

I pull off my sweat jacket, wrapping it around the rock. There's a chance the door is unlocked, but I don't want to waste time checking. The car sits askew in the middle of the road, as though the owners jumped out and fled on foot. Not so different from what we did when we were forced to abandon our bikes. Around the car are a few bodies, all of them felled by headshots.

I smash my rock through the glass, shattering the window. The glass makes soft cracking sounds and tinkles onto the seat inside. I open the door, glass crunching as I rest a knee on the cracked leather.

I glance up long enough to see Carter ram his spear up through the neck and brain of his zombie. A sick squishing sound follows as he pulls the spear free. Our eyes meet through the windshield of the car.

Everything inside me loosens at the sight of him standing safe on the other side of the car. I return my attention to the dashboard.

An old tape deck sits before me. Dangling out of it is a wire that leads to an honest-to-God Disc Man, one of those old-fashioned portable CD players. This is the way my parents used to listen to music back when they were teenagers.

There are no keys in the ignition. Damn. I check the cup holder, glove compartment, and visor. Nothing.

By this time, Reed has also dispatched his zombie. "What are you waiting for?" His eyes flick up and down the street, shoulders hunched. He looks like he's on the run.

"No keys." I hurry to the nearest body on the ground near the car. A man in a button-up shirt and blue jeans lies on his stomach. I almost flip him over with my boot, but the number of flies and maggots crawling over his body change my mind. I twist my hand, angling it into his jeans pocket.

Carter, understanding my plan, doesn't waste time waiting for me to complete my search. He hurries to the next body, a woman in jeans. "Found them," he says, raising a set of keys in triumph.

"Awesome, babe." I hold out my hands for him to toss the keys to me before I realize I've called him babe.

His expression morphs into a guarded one. I keep a smile on my face, trying to act casual, but my jaw feels stiff. He tosses the keys to me without comment.

Later, I tell myself. *Worry about boyfriend stuff later.*

When I fire up the engine of the car, I crank the radio to full blast. Michael Jackson's *Beat It* thumps out of the speakers. The car may be old, but at some point, someone upgraded the sound system. The bass vibrates against my skin.

A few zombies stagger around a nearby corner, drawn by the sound. We have to get the hell out of here.

Using Kate's trick from earlier, we duck through a fence into a backyard. It's dog and zombie free. We hop the fence a second time and exit one street up.

Now we just have to avoid the horde of zombies we've drawn from the plaza and get back to Kate and Johnny.

This all seemed like a good idea thirty minutes ago when we hatched the plan. But as I catch sight of the zombies twitching to life up and down the street, I wonder what we've gotten ourselves into. When the keening starts up, I wonder if we should hide in one of the houses for a while.

But Kate and Johnny are still out there. We have to get back to them.

The trick is going to be maneuvering around the zombies we've drawn. Time to pull out one of Kate's tried and true methods: I break into a run.

Carter and Reed share my sense of urgency. They

huff along on either side of me, pumping their arms as we run through the streets. We kill a few zombies that get too close, choosing to avoid and outrun the rest. Michael Jackson's voice continues to thump in the distance, growing fainter the farther we go.

We make it several blocks without incident before I pause to look over my shoulder. A stream of zombies clogs the intersection behind us, all of them heading toward the car.

I slow, struggling to catch my breath. Carter and Reed wheeze like asthma patients.

"How does Kate do it?" Reed puffs between gasps for breath. "I feel like I'm going to faint."

"Training," Carter replies, also huffing. "She trains her body."

"We're past the bulk of them," I say. "Let's circle back to the plaza."

We move at a brisk walk, none of us willing to run now that the immediate threat is out of the way.

We pause one block away from the plaza, surveying the scene. Nearly all the zombies are gone, drawn to the music. The few still present bump into storefronts or abandoned vehicles, hissing and moaning as they try to figure out how to get to the noise.

Something moves in the park. At first, I think it's more zombies, except the two figures don't move like zombies. Their movements are curt and efficient, their heads on an axis as they scan their surroundings.

It's two men in their thirties, clean-shaven with dark hair. They wear sturdy boots, jeans, and leather jackets.

Fear curdles in my gut. Zombies are scary, but after our run-in with the College Creek kids, people scare me more. I'm not eager to be seen by these guys.

Carter backs up, his hand grabbing mine. I only have a second to wonder if the act is a conscious one before I see Reed's face break into a grin. Before I can say anything, he rushes past us—straight toward the two men.

25
At Gunpoint

JENNA

"Reed! What are you doing?"

"I know those guys." He hurries into the open. He waves his arms, catching the attention of the two guys.

Shit. I exchange a look with Carter, who looks as worried as I feel. This time, when Carter takes my hand, I know it's on purpose. He squeezes my fingers, glancing into my eyes as we hurry after Reed.

"Carlos. Jesus." Reed grins at the men. "Am I glad to see—"

The smaller of the two men raises a gun and shoves the barrel up against Reed's nose.

Carter pushes me behind him, herding us both back. I freeze as the taller man pulls a gun and aims it at us.

"Stop right there," he drawls.

"What the fuck, Carlos?" Reed says, pushing the gun barrel out of his face. "Why are you being an asshole?"

"Inside." Carlos gestures with the gun at a gem and mineral shop. "We need a word with you, Reed."

"Can you put the guns away?" Reed demands. He points to Carter and me. "These are my friends. You're scaring them."

"Get your asses inside," Carlos barks.

The bigger guy, Jesus, gestures to us with the gun.

"He said, get your asses inside."

Reed grumbles, but waves for us to go into the store. How does he know these guys? What sort of shit has he gotten us into this time? I make a mental note never to let Reed leave Creekside again. Ever. I'm sick of having firearms pointed at us.

Carter keeps one hand in mine, pulling me close to him as we enter the shop. I don't pull away.

"Over there." Carlos points to a spot on the floor between a rack of crystal necklaces and a giant purple geode.

"Dude, can you put the guns away?" Reed asks, following their orders and taking a seat on the floor.

Both men wait until Carter and I take seats beside Reed. I scan the shelves, making note of which rocks would make decent weapons. There are more than a few fist-sized ones that could be used against these men.

"Seriously," Reed says. "Why are you guys being like this?" He tries to make his tone casual, but I don't miss the quaver of fear.

Carlos and Jesus just stare, guns still leveled at us. Seconds tick by. It takes all my willpower not to squirm.

A slow grin spreads over Carlos's face. His shoulders shake with mirth. A long moment passes before I realize he's laughing at us.

"We're just fucking with you, bro," Carlos says.

Jesus lets out a loud guffaw. "You should see your face!"

"You fuckers!" Reed leaps to his feet, slugging both men in the arms with strikes that are half affectionate, half angry.

The two older men round on Reed and slug him back. They're all grinning by this time and, thank God, the guns have been put away. The flurry of slugging turns into a group hug with lots of backslapping.

"We just wanted to fuck with you," Carlos says.

"You know I'm loyal to Granjero. Have you guys

been in Arcata the whole time?" Reed asks.

"We were up here making a drop when the shit hit the fan," Carlos replies. "We tried to get out but our car was mobbed. We lost Timmo and Rick. Me and Jesus barely got away." The dark-haired man shakes his head. "That's how it is for Mr. Rosario's men, too. We're all stuck here."

It all clicks together in my brain. These guys are from a rival drug faction. They're stranded here, along with Mr. Rosario's guys.

"Was that you guys that set off the music?" Jesus asks.

Reed nods. "We're on a supply run. We needed to draw the zombies away from the plaza."

I'm grateful he doesn't mention Kate or Johnny or Trading Post.

"Was that you guys who set off the zoms a few streets over, too? Where the dog was?"

Reed hesitates, then nods. "Yeah."

"You guys are waking up the whole fucking town," Carlos says. "That dog belonged to one of Mr. Rosario's crew."

Jesus chuckles. "We should probably thank you for that. We were scoping out their hidey-hole from across the street. Three of them didn't make it out. The fucking dog neither. The survivors are mad as hell over the dog. You better watch yourself if you go back out there." He jerks a thumb to indicate the plaza.

"We didn't know," Reed says. "Like I said, we're on a supply run. We got mobbed."

"We can't let Rosario's bastards roam free. They'll take over our territory if we let them. We—" Carlos is interrupted by the sound of a gunshot.

It came from the plaza. I look past the shelves of rocks in the window, trying to see into the street and the park beyond.

"Go check it out," Carlos orders.

Jesus, mouth tight, nods and slips out the door.

26
Trading Post

KATE

Trading Post is a porn shop for the outdoor athlete.

I revel in the merchandise, all of it clean smelling and still crisp in its packaging. Running shoes. Handheld water bottles. Headlamps. Running packs. Waist packs. Compression sleeves. A bunch of other outdoor gear, but I only have eyes for the running equipment.

There is the issue of the five zombies bumping around in the racks. The stockroom muffled our entry through the back, which means they haven't noticed us and we aren't in any immediate danger. They are, however, separating us from the supplies we need.

"Behind the counter," I say to Johnny.

He doesn't have to be told twice. We hustle on tiptoe to the cash register and take up position behind it, weapons raised.

"I'm going to draw them to us," I whisper.

"Is this like the Attack and Stack thing you told Carter about?"

"This is just keeping something big between us and them." I tap the counter, making just enough noise to draw the undead.

Heads swivel, tracking the direction of the sound. Two of them are store employees dressed in brown

Trading Post polo shirts. The other three are customers, the outdoorsy type as evidenced by the name brand clothing they wear. North Face. Patagonia. Osprey.

The group rushes toward us. Two crash into racks, but the remaining three have a clear path. They collide with the counter so hard I hear ribs crack.

Johnny jumps back at the onslaught. I grab the nearest undead by her polo shirt and drag her toward me. She can't be any older than Carter, probably a college student at Humboldt when all this went down.

Her teeth gnash. The other two zombies lunge toward me, but I move fast, yanking myself out of reach while keeping an iron grip on the polo shirt of the girl. My screwdriver goes into her eye and I release her body, leaving it slumped on the counter.

Johnny recovers himself, joining me at the counter-top. He swings his spear at the head of the zombie in the brown polo. Instead of cracking open his skull, he hits the beast in the shoulder and pisses it off.

I lunge and strike, my screwdriver punching through the thing's nose as it goes for Johnny. Dark, reddish-black blood sprays everywhere. I finish off the third zombie as the last two reach us.

This time, Johnny gets the hang of it. When the outdoors zombie lashes out, he snags the thing by the wrist, drags it forward, and jams his kitchen knife into the skull. Blood spatters across the countertop.

"Nice work." I finish off the last zombie with a screwdriver through the ear.

The interior of the store is drenched in blissful silence. No more zombies. Surprisingly, the large front windows are intact, not shot out like some of the other windows on the plaza. Even the interior is untouched. Perhaps all the zombies in the plaza kept others from scavenging here.

Whatever the case, Trading Post is gloriously intact. It's just us in this building chock-full of gorgeous running gear. I'd roll in it, except that would be weird, even for me.

"You know," Johnny says, "I had a friend growing up with a crazy mom. She was from Mexico and had a temper. If my friend missed a homework assignment or got caught ditching school, she'd lay into him in Spanish. Sometimes she laid into him just as a preventative measure if she thought he was thinking about doing something he shouldn't. Or if she was having a bad day. She was always yelling in Spanish and I always thought she was scary." Johnny's eyes rove over the dead zombies draped over the countertop. "That lady was like a hyperactive kitten compared to you. *You're* scary, Kate."

"Johnny, I think I'm going to take that as a compliment. Come on. Let's go look at shoes."

I can practically hear the angelic choir playing in my head as we reach the back wall where all the shoes are. There might as well be beams of holy light shining down.

"Oh my God," I breathe. "This is a beautiful sight."

Johnny frowns, looking around. "What, the neat racks?"

"No. The shoes."

"The *shoes*?"

"Yeah. They might not be designer Italian pumps, but they could save our lives."

I have a list of shoe sizes I compiled before we left Creekside. I pull it out, automatically adding one shoe size to each. Feet swell when used for extended periods of time. A larger shoe will help prevent blistering.

Not knowing each person's individual footwear requirements, I scan for brands with a wider toe box. More room for toes also means fewer blisters. If someone has a narrow foot, we can tighten the laces.

I also consider the amount of cushion in the sole. Running shoes range from soles that are like thick marshmallows, all the way to soles that are only a few millimeters thick for those who like a stronger connection between their foot and the ground. The latter is definitely out; a person needs tough feet to survive thin-soled shoes. I'm not willing to risk stress fractures.

There are also different treads to take into account. Those with the biggest lugs are meant for mountain runs with lots of vertical. The flatter ones are for road running.

I find shoes with medium tread, thicker cushions, and wide toe boxes.

"Here." I rip the list and hand half to Johnny. "Let's go. These are the models we want." I show him the men's and women's shoes I've picked.

The back stockroom is dark. I retrieve headlamps for us, which luckily come with pre-charged batteries. The stockroom is neat with not so much as a splash of blood anywhere. The scent of decaying bodies is nearly lost to the smell of new shoes.

Once we have the shoes, I move onto other gear. It isn't long before we have a huge pile of supplies mounded on the floor in front of the shoe racks. Headlamps. Hunting knives. Waist packs. Socks. Gloves. Hats. Compression gear. Waterproof jackets. Water purification tablets. Dried food. Lighters. A few small tents. I even add several boxes of energy bars and gels for good measure. Running fuel is as essential as dried food.

"Check this out." I hold up a microfiber sleeping bag that compresses into a small bag the size of two fists. "These things are a hundred and fifty bucks each. We're taking seven." I toss them into the pile.

"What about a portable stove or pot?" Johnny asks.

"Already threw one into the pile. Here, look at this. I saved the best for last." I lead Johnny to the backpack section, where all the running packs are.

"You're enjoying this," Johnny observes.

"It's the apocalypse," I reply. "A woman has to get her kicks when she can."

"Yeah, but I bet you were like this before the apocalypse."

"Like what?" I raise a brow, even though I know exactly what he means.

"This is your kid in a candy store moment."

"Maybe a little," I admit. "Don't take me to Nordstrom. I'd be bored. Take me to a store with running gear and I can geek out for hours. Look at this." I hold up a blue running pack. "You can carry twenty liters worth of gear in this thing. And the design still makes it possible to run if necessary."

"I just visualized twenty cartons of milk crammed into that thing. And then I imagined trying to wear it and run from zombies," Johnny says.

"This is one of the bigger packs on the market. It has a two-liter water bladder in the back plus more room for water bottles in the front. It's mostly used for fast packing."

"What's a fast packing?"

"A cross between ultrarunning and hiking. Slower than a race but faster than a hike. Fast packers carry all their own food and gear. Some of them go into the wilderness for days or weeks at a time. They can go for hundreds of miles with packs like this."

Johnny makes a face. "Do they ever change their underwear?"

"Most runners don't wear underwear unless it's built into the clothing. Too much chafing."

Johnny makes a gagging sound. "TMI, Kate. I could have gone to my grave without knowing that."

"Don't joke about going to your grave." I pile seven packs into his arms. "No one is going to their grave on my watch."

"I'm oddly comforted by that statement. It's all the more meaningful because you're covered in blood and have a contact high from all the shit we have."

"This shit could be the difference between living and dying. With this stuff, we can travel fast and light." Looking at the pile of gear makes me think of Carter,

Jenna, and Reed. "The others should have been here by now."

"They set up a distraction to lure a huge pack of zombies away from the plaza," Johnny replies. "They probably had to cut a wide path to get back to us."

He has a point, but I can't help the uneasiness that steals over me. Granted, I experienced the same feeling when Carter was sixteen and missed his curfew by ten minutes. He wasn't dead and dying in a ditch back then; I shouldn't assume the worst now.

Johnny and I take everything out of its packaging and set about the tedious task of condensing all the gear into five packs we can carry back to Creekside. By the time we're finished, the sun is lower in the sky than I'd like. We've been here at least an hour and still no sign of Carter.

Johnny sees my expression. "We should wait another fifteen minutes or so. If they don't show up, we should make our way to the rendezvous."

I don't like it. I pace, fidgeting with a rack of T-shirts. I peel off my sweaty, bloody shirt and replace it with a clean one. For good measure, I pull a second over the first. No telling when I'll get my hands on moisture-wicking fabric again. I consider making a joke about the best bug-out bags the world has ever seen, but I don't have it in me to joke.

Where are Carter, Jenna, and Reed?

"They just want us to carry all the shit," Johnny says, gesturing to the five enormous backpacks we've crammed full of stuff.

I try to laugh, but it comes out weak and strangled.

"We need to go." I pick up the first of the packs and swing it onto my back, grunting under the weight. I put another one in front, feeling like a pregnant lady with the bulge over my stomach.

Johnny does the same with two of the packs. We're in the process of trying to figure out how to carry the fifth and final backpack when I hear shouting.

I hurry to the big glass windows, peering into the plaza. On the far side of the street are two men in blue jeans and leather jackets. My breath catches in my throat. With them are Carter, Jenna, and Reed.

"Oh, fuck," Johnny breathes. "Fuck and fucking shit."

As we watch, Carter, Jenna, and Reed are ushered by gunpoint into a gem and mineral shop.

"Do you know who those guys are?" I ask.

Johnny shifts, giving me a wary look. "What if it's more of those drug dealer guys?"

"Fuck." I ball my fists. "They don't look like Mr. Rosario's flunkies. Her people dress like hobos. Could they be guys who work for that other guy Reed mentioned?"

"Granjero? Yeah, that's what I was thinking."

"Fucking shit." Now what? "I'm going to strangle Reed."

Johnny shakes his head. "Don't be too hard on Reed. He's from the Oakland ghetto. His dad was a truck driver and his mom a cocaine addict who took off when Reed and his siblings were kids. Reed couldn't afford college."

"It's called a student loan," I say icily.

"It's called who-wants-to-be-in-debt-for-the-next-thirty-years?" Johnny shoots back. "Look, Reed is a good guy. He did what he had to do to make a better life for himself."

"If he cared so much about his life, he shouldn't smoke so much."

"No one's perfect, Kate."

I stew on this. I want to be furious. Reed's extra-curricular activity has earned Carter and Jenna the wrong end of a gun. But Johnny isn't wrong about how hard it is—was—to pay for college.

I take a deep breath, trying to focus my thoughts. "What do you think those guys want from them?"

"If I had to hazard a guess, I'd say they either want their money or their product back."

"The world is over. Why do they care about their money or drugs?"

"Can you think of a better reason to use drugs?" Johnny shrugs. "I don't smoke a lot, but there are days when I think Eric and Reed have it figured out. Being stoned makes all this easier." He points at the pile of dead bodies draped on the cash counter.

When all this is over, Johnny and I can have a philosophical discussion on the pros and cons of drugs in an apocalyptic world. Right now, we have to figure out a way to get Carter and the others out of there.

"We need to draw them out." I scan the store for inspiration. "Lure the bad guys out into the open." For the first time, I rethink my decision to leave our guns stashed under the living room couch. We could really use them at a time like this.

Too bad there aren't any in Trading Post. It might be an outdoors store, but it doesn't sell firearms.

"You think we can get the drop on them?" Johnny looks at me hopefully.

I shake my head. "I got lucky with Mr. Rosario's men. I could just as easily have gotten shot or killed myself. We need to get closer and see what our options are." There has got to be a way to get to Carter.

"Recon." Johnny nods, dumping his packs to the floor. "I didn't really want to carry these all the way back to Creekside without help anyway."

In any other instance, it would be painful to leave behind all the running gear. Now, I barely noticed when my packs drop to the ground. My world is full of the gem and mineral storefront and thoughts of my son.

A gunshot sounds. I jump, dropping into a crouch and scuttling across the floor to take cover behind a rack of pants with Johnny.

A peek through the new-smelling clothing reveals one of the thugs slinking out of the gem and mineral shop, gun raised.

27
Trapped

JENNA

We wait in tense silence as Jesus disappears out the front door of the shop. Carlos keeps his gun aimed at the window. The guy is like an animal poised to spring.

Seconds pass. They stretch into minutes. Carlos grows visibly more concerned. Sweat beads around his temples. He swears to himself in Spanish, shifting his weight back and forth between his two feet.

I lick my lips and pick up a large rock from a shelf. Not that a rock is going to do me much good in a gun fight, but I feel better having something in my hand. I catch Carter's gaze and cast a pointed look at the rocks. He nods, also picking up a rock.

We both jump when two gunshots sound from outside. Three more answer it, these much closer than the first.

"Fuck." Carlos gestures at us with his gun. "All of you need to get back." He herds us to the back of the shop, stopping in front of a small supply closet. "Inside," he orders. "You'll be safe here."

"But—" Reed begins.

"Rosario's men are armed and pissed about their dog," Carlos replies. "Without a weapon, you'll be dead meat. Just sit tight and let us take care of them."

It's hard to believe this is the same guy who held us at gunpoint. My throat tightens as I realize he truly cares about Reed.

We pile into the tiny storeroom, which is lined with boxes of rocks, shopping bags, and register tape. Carlos closes the door, leaving us drenched in complete black.

The sound of shattering glass and gunfire booms from inside the store.

"Motherfuckers!" Carlos screams.

More gunshots. Something outside the storeroom door crashes to the ground, making the door rattle in its frame.

"We have to get out of here," Carter says. "It's not safe."

I couldn't agree more. Sitting around in a closet while men shoot each other just outside is not my idea of a good time.

"Let's see if there's a back way out," I say.

"We should sit tight and wait for Jesus and Carlos," Reed says.

"Be my guest," Carter replies. "Jenna and I are getting out of here."

I flounder for the doorknob and give it a shove. The knob turns, but the door won't budge.

I throw my shoulder against it. The door is old and made of solid wood. There's a dull thud as my shoulder connects. The door doesn't move.

"Shit." I grit my teeth in frustration.

"Let me try." Carter takes over, slamming his shoulder several times into the door. After several minutes, he succeeds only in getting the door to move a half inch. Gunfire continues, though it sounds like it's moved out of the shop.

"What the fuck is on the other side?" I kick the door in frustration.

"I think a piece of furniture fell over in front of it," Carter says.

"Those guys do know they don't have to kill each other, right?" I ask. "I mean, turf isn't all that important if there aren't any people left alive to sell to."

"Turf is always important to those guys," Reed replies.

Of course, it is. I kick the door again, for good measure. And because I'm mad and scared and I can't think of what else to do in this pitch-black room.

Even though the world has ended, these idiots have decided to perpetuate their stupid turf wars. What is it with all these people who insist on dwelling in a world that no longer exists? There's probably a psychology word to describe the phenomenon. The fact that more of these drug people are in town makes me glad we're taking steps to gather supplies and fortify Creekside.

The gunfire outside has grown more distant. For the moment, the fighting has apparently migrated away from the rock shop.

"I'm going to try and climb the shelves and see if there's a way out through the ceiling," Carter says.

"We just need to wait," Reed says. "Carlos and Jesus will be back for us."

"They could get shot out there," I say. "They're having a street fight with Mr. Rosario's men right now."

"Move closer to the door," Carter says. "The shelves seem sturdy, but I don't want to land on you if I fall."

"Be careful." I reach through the darkness, groping for him, not caring that I don't know where we stand as a couple. We've landed somewhere between fighting and not fighting. My hand lands halfway between his nose and cheek. "Shit, sorry, I—"

His strong hand wraps around mine. My breath catches when he tugs me forward into an embrace.

"I was an asshole," he whispers in my ear. "I'm sorry, babe."

Emotion wells in my throat. "Me, too." I tighten my arms around him, reveling in the sensation of the tension between us melting away.

He kisses my forehead. "We'll talk more later," he murmurs.

"Okay." I kiss the side of his neck.

When I slip out of his arms, I feel good knowing I'll be in them again soon. Just as soon as we get the hell out of this place.

The shelf rattles under Carter's weight but doesn't tip over. He knocks over unseen boxes as he climbs, all of them making a racket when they hit the floor.

"Dude, watch out," Reed complains.

"Sorry." *Thunk.* "Ow. Shit," he grumbles.

"Find the ceiling?" I ask.

"Yeah."

Any hope that he'd encounter a cheap fiberglass ceiling is dashed as his knuckles rap on something hard.

"I don't think we're getting through that," Reed says. "It sounds like solid wood.

This town was founded during the redwood-logging era. All the old buildings around here are made of solid redwood.

"Either of you have an axe?" I try to make my words light, but they come out dull.

"I think Paul Bunyan has one we can borrow," Carter says, voice equally glum. He fumbles around for another few minutes, knocking on the ceiling. Everything is solid. "Damn it. I don't feel anything resembling an attic door, either."

Another loud crash sounds inside the store, followed by gunfire. This time, the shots are at close range. My ears echo with the blasts.

"Motherfuckers!" comes the voice of Carlos. "Jesus, get that fucker!"

28
Ignite

KATE

I watch the scene unfolding before me in increments of ever-increasing horror. Inside the gem and mineral shop are two dark-haired men. They are ducked beneath the large front window, which has been obliterated by gunfire.

Behind a car outside the shop are three people I peg as belonging to Mr. Rosario. Their hobo clothing, coupled with the fact that they're packing firepower, is a dead giveaway. They pop from behind the car and shoot at the gem and mineral shop. The men inside return fire. All the while the two groups yell obscenities at one another.

"What the hell?" Johnny says. The two of us crouch behind the statue of the president in the plaza. "Rival drug gangs?"

"I think so." Honestly, I don't care who the fuck they are. They have Carter, Jenna, and Reed.

"What are we going to do?" Johnny asks.

"Our people are in the shop. We're going around to see if there's a back way in." With any luck, we can free them, get the hell out of here, and let these drug goons kill each other off.

"Okay." Johnny licks his lips. "We could really use

some guns of our own right now."

He isn't wrong. As it is, we have our new knives from the shop and the kitchen knives we took earlier. Johnny has his spear and I have my screwdriver. We're not exactly armed for a gunfight.

Thanks to Michael Jackson, who still blares in the distance, the plaza has remained mostly empty of the undead. The few still milling around don't notice us; their attention is on the gunfire.

Good. Let the idiots with the guns deal with the undead.

It doesn't take long for Johnny and me to make our way to the parking lot behind the row of shops. We dispatch three zombies on the way. We're getting so used to this, it doesn't even slow us down.

A row of doors faces the parking lot, all of them leading into the various storefronts on the other side.

"Which one goes into the gem shop?" Johnny asks.

"That one, I think." I point to a metal security door. Above it hangs a wooden painting of a purple amethyst.

I try the handle. It's locked. *Shit.* I yank and pull, but the door doesn't budge.

"We're not getting through that," Johnny says. "Those security doors are strong."

I glare at the row of doors. Of course, the gem shop is the only one with the metal security door.

"Maybe we can get in through one of the adjoining shops," Johnny suggests.

"Good idea."

We try the shop to the immediate left. Locked. We hurry to one on the right.

A hiss of relief escapes my lips as the door swings open. Finally. A stroke of luck. "I was beginning to wonder if—"

A growl cuts me off. I turn in time to see a zombie rushing at me out of the dark. It's a woman in jeans and a blazer. Her hair is in a neat bun. If not for her ripped sleeve and the blood soaking her right side, I could almost mistake her for one of the living.

I raise my knife, but Johnny is faster. He leaps in front of me. The zombie woman plows right into his spear. It crumples the front of her face. Black blood and pasty brain parts spill out.

Johnny and I remain in the doorway, waiting and listening. Nothing else moves inside the shop.

"Thanks," I whisper. He nods, lips compressed in a tight line.

We creep into what turns out to be a futon shop. It isn't until I take in the various brightly colored fabrics and grain of the wood frames that I realize the lights are on.

"This building has electricity," I say.

"Must be solar power," Johnny replies. "A lot of businesses have them. The city gives out big tax credits to anyone who installs them."

With the sun setting outside, I appreciate the electricity to see by, although I worry about being spotted by the gun-toting psychos outside. All the more reason to get out of here as quickly as possible.

I explore the wall shared with the gem and mineral shop. It's a slim shot, but maybe there's a connecting door between the two.

No such luck.

"We're going to have to go through the wall," I tell Johnny.

"How are we going to do that?"

"It's just sheet rock." I pick up a small end table, hefting it into the air. "We just bash our way through."

To illustrate my point, I slam the table into the wall. Under normal circumstances, I'd worry about all the noise. Between Michael Jackson and the gunfire outside, our noise is muffled.

Johnny picks up a large paperweight and joins me. We hammer and smash at the sheetrock. Hope flares in my chest as the white plaster crumbles away beneath the onslaught. Another few minutes, and we'll have a hole large enough to fit through.

My table connects with something hard. Really hard. The impact sends a shockwave up both arms, causing me to stumble back.

What the hell? Whatever I hit is most definitely not sheetrock.

Johnny comes to the same conclusion. He lowers the paperweight and reaches through the hole we made. His knuckles wrap on something solid.

"Damn it," he mutters. "These buildings are made of old redwood planks. No way we're busting through it without an axe." He hurls the paperweight to the ground.

I could go back to Trading Post. I could find an axe there. Except that would take too much time. Who knows what could happen in the twenty or thirty minutes it would take to retrieve an axe? Carter could be dead by then. Carter, Jenna, and Reed.

I grit my teeth. *Fuck.* I slam my end table against the wall a few more times in a fit of frustration.

The sheetrock crumbles against my attack. A spark arcs out in my direction.

I yelp in surprise and jump back. A tiny arc of flame licks out from the wall.

"Woah," Johnny says. "Electrical fire. You must have hit one of the live wires—"

The tiny flame abruptly goes from a dancing finger of light to a burst of fire. It races up the exposed length of redwood. A gust of black smoke rolls over me. Coughing and waving the smoke away from my eyes, I fall back.

When half the wall suddenly bursts into flame, I shout in surprise. In retrospect, I should have considered the fact that the redwood is old and dry.

"Um, Kate?" Johnny says. "I think we need to get out of here."

29
Chair

KATE

Too much smoke. It pours into the room, down my lungs, and across my eyes. Coughing and choking, I reach for Johnny. I find his arm and latch on.

Panic claws through my chest. Carter. How am I going to get to him?

Johnny drags me away from the flames. Our way back to the parking lot is blocked by a wall of flame. I pull my shirt up over my nose, struggling to breathe.

"We have to get out of here," Johnny chokes.

He's right. I can't help Carter if I die of smoke inhalation.

We rush to the front of the store. Johnny throws himself at the swinging glass door, but it doesn't budge.

"Damn it!" he shrieks, yanking on the handle.

I fumble at the door, searching for the deadbolt. There's no latch, just a keyhole. The only way to turn the deadbolt is to use a key.

Instinct takes over. No way are Johnny and I going to burn to death in a fucking futon shop.

I seize the object closest to me. A chair. A simple metal chair with four legs.

I hurl it at the window.

The glass blows outward, no doubt helped along by

the pressure building inside the shop. I grab Johnny and haul him toward the opening. We use our elbows to knock aside lingering pieces of glass, then climb free of the shop.

The street is in chaos. One of Mr. Rosario's men writhes on the ground beneath a swarm of zombies. The other two are still behind the car. One fires at the rock shop while the other fires at the zombies eating his friend.

One of the dark-haired men who took Carter stands on the sidewalk, backing away from the burning building. Several zombies loom out of the gloom and latch onto him.

I don't bother to watch as he's pulled down.

The remaining guy, still inside the shop, rises into a half crouch. "Carlos!" he bellows.

This is my opening. I snatch the metal chair off the sidewalk. Screaming, I charge at the man. I half expect a bullet to punch through me, but I don't care. I have to get the kids out of that shop. They are not going to burn to death on my watch.

The man's mouth sags open. I can't tell if he's staring at me in shock, or at the zombies that drag his friend to the ground.

I smash the chair across his face. He lets out a shout. His gun thumps to the ground.

"Don't you ever, *ever*, lay a finger on my kids!" I scream at him. Rage and fear beat in my chest. "Touch them again and I'll kill you. Do you understand? I'll fucking kill you!"

"Lady, wait—!" the man begins.

I swing a second time, hitting him so hard blood sprays out of his nose.

Eyes bulging as he grips his bleeding nose in one hand, the man scrambles up and runs away. He streaks past his fallen friend, past the drug dealers behind the car, and disappears.

I sweep my eyes through the front of the shop. It's in complete disarray. Display cabinets are knocked over. Rocks and gems are strewn all over the floor.

There is no sign of Carter, Jenna, or Reed.

"Carter!" I scream. "Carter, where are you?"

30
Fire

JENNA

More gunfire and shouting.

Carter and I find each other in the dark. We huddle on the floor in one another's arms.

"I was a jerk," I whisper, pressing my forehead against his neck and not caring that Reed can hear everything I say. "I—"

"I'm the jerk." His arms tighten around me. "You tried to talk to me but I shut you down. I'm sorry. I was in denial. It's just . . . it was like the world ended when my dad died, you know? I wasn't ready for it to end a second time."

"Carter." I whisper his name, feeling like complete shit for not seeing his turmoil. I'd noticed him talking a lot about his dad after we witnessed the military slaughter, but I hadn't put the pieces together. "I'm so sorry, babe. I didn't understand what you were going through."

"Neither did I."

Something large hits the shop floor with an echoing thud. More cursing and gunfire.

"My real hair color is blond," I blurt.

"What?"

"My hair isn't brown. It's blond. Junior year a stupid

football jock asked me to prom. My mom found out and threatened to take away my cell phone if I didn't go with him. The guy was from a rich family and mom wanted a piece of it." I give a soft, bitter laugh. "I said yes to the date, dyed my hair brown, and grew out my armpit hair. It didn't take long for the jock to change his mind."

"God, babe. Every story I hear about your family is more fucked up than the last." He rocks me in his arms in the dark amid gunfire and shouting. God, I hope we don't die here.

"Looking like a real-life Barbie doll made me a magnet for jerky guys," I continue. "I wanted them to like me for who I was on the inside, not what I looked like on the outside." Does he understand what I'm trying to say? Does he understand why I flinch away from compliments? "When I moved away from my mom, I promised myself I would never date until I found a guy I liked on the inside," I whisper. "Then I acted like an asshole when I got in front of my family and did to you what so many guys have done to me. Sorry I fucked everything up."

He kisses my temples. "Remember when we ran out of that frat party?" he asks.

"I remember."

"I pushed people out of the way to get to you. I didn't care what happened to them. I didn't try to help them. All I could think about was getting you to safety." His breath rattles in his chest. "I didn't want to believe I was living in a world where I had to choose between protecting you and hurting other people."

A bullet punches through the wall above us, sending dust and grit raining down. Reed shouts. I scream. Carter holds onto me, gripping my arms like lifelines. I imagine the drug guys having an old-fashioned Wild West shootout right here in the shop.

"How about we shave your pits when we get out of here?" Carter says in a shaky voice.

I bark a laugh, understanding that he's attempting to crack a joke. "I would love that. I never liked having hairy pits, but they became a security measure to keep assholes away."

"Oh my God," Reed says. "Can you two stop with the couples therapy session? I feel like I'm on the set of Maury Povich. I—wait, do you guys smell that?"

I take a long sniff. "Is that . . . ?"

"It's smoke!" I hear Reed jump to his feet. "Fuck, something is on fire!"

Carter and I scramble up. The smell of smoke is distinct now.

Carter attacks the door with all his might. Reed joins him, the two of them struggling to get it open.

"Help us!" I shriek. "Somebody help!"

The gunshots and yelling have stopped. Replacing it is the crackling sound of flames. Smoke makes its way into the tiny storage room. I can't see it, but I smell it and feel it sliding into my lungs. We start to cough.

"Help!" Carter shouts, banging on the door. "We're stuck in here."

Of all the things I worried about today when we left Creekside, burning to death in the closet of a rock shop was not on the list. Getting eaten by a zombie, yes. Getting chased by bad guys with guns, yes. But not this.

The smoke is getting worse. Reed and Carter keep up their constant barrage against the door. They've managed to move it an inch or so, but all that does is let in more smoke.

"Carter?" From somewhere in the shop comes a voice. "Carter?"

It's Kate. Thank fucking God.

"We're in here," I scream. "Kate, help us!"

"The supply closet," Carter shouts, grabbing the knob and banging the door repeatedly against whatever piece of furniture is blocking our escape. "Mom, over here!"

"Hold on, guys." Johnny's voice carries over the din.

Outside the door is a loud scraping sound.

"Fuck this," Kate growls. "Move over, Johnny." There's a huge crash followed by the sound of shattering glass.

Reed throws himself against the door. He tumbles out into the smoke. Carter and I hurry after him, emerging in the dark shop.

A large curio cabinet lays in shattered remnants in front of the closet. Rocks and gems lay among broken glass and splintered wood. It had been knocked in front of the door during the conflict.

Kate grabs Carter in a fierce hug. "Are you okay?"

"We're okay," he says. "Thanks for the rescue."

Reed throws his arms around Kate, hugging her around the waist like a little kid. "Oh my God," he gasps. "I love you, Kate. You have to be my mom, too. I need someone to look out for me the way you look out for Carter."

"What about me?" Johnny demands, annoyed. "I helped rescue you guys, too."

"You wanna be my dad?" Reed asks with a sarcastic frown, never loosening his grip on Kate.

"We can talk later," Kate says, giving Reed a squeeze on the shoulder before extricating herself. "We have to get out of here. The fire is going to draw the zombies and some of those maniacs with guns are still out there."

She leads the way out of the shop. It's not yet full dark outside, but dusk is in full swing.

The blaze burns hot and thick in the futon shop next door. Zombies might not be attracted to light due to their blindness, but the roar of the flames as it consumes the old buildings makes enough noise to draw them.

Reed stops dead, mouth sagging open at the sight of the drug dealer on the sidewalk. Five zombies crouch over him, sinking their teeth into various body parts. My chest seizes at the sight.

"Carlos," Reed whispers.

"He can't hurt you now," Kate says. "Come on."

"But—" Reed begins.

There's no time to explain that Carlos tried to keep us safe from Mr. Rosario's men. I grab Reed's arm, urging him to keep moving.

"But what about Jesus?" Reed asks.

"We have to go," Carter tells him, taking Reed's other arm.

The undead advance from all directions, hands outstretched as they moan and hiss and fumble their way forward. They pour in from every street corner, coming straight for us.

31
Run

A fundamental change in the wiring of the brain happens when a person becomes a mother. I don't know if it's ever been officially documented by scientists, but I know for a fact that I never viewed the world as a scary place until I had Carter.

The moment I held my son in my arms for the first time, the world emerged around me in new colors. Everywhere I looked was a new threat I'd never seen before.

The corner of the coffee table became a vehicle of death for my toddling twelve-month-old. The sun became a peddler of skin cancer. Television became a potential brain scrambler. A tree was nothing more than a broken arm waiting to happen. Cold weather was a portent of pneumonia and other deadly illnesses.

The list of paranoia-inducing panic was long, unending, and ever evolving.

And while I might not have to worry about coffee tables or trees anymore, I still worry about my son's wellbeing. Finding ourselves in the middle of a fire with zombies converging all around and gun-toting psychos out there in the dark is a mother's worst nightmare.

I grit my teeth. No way is Carter going to die tonight.

Not Carter, not Jenna, not Reed, and not Johnny. Whatever it takes, I'm going to get them through this.

"Follow me. We're going back to Trading Post. Make as little noise as possible." I plunge forward, racing as fast as I can toward the opposite side of the plaza. I have my screwdriver in one hand and my Trading Post knife in the other. We dodge and weave around the zombies, killing those that stand in our way.

We reach the far side of the plaza. Two zombies bump against the glass doors of Trading Post. I bury my knife in the skull of the first. Johnny is by my side, taking out the other with his knife.

We rush inside the shop. Our packs are there, waiting where we left them.

"Everyone grab a pack," I order. "We go out the back."

No one argues, and no one comments about the weight of the packs. I lead them through the storeroom to the back door of the shop that opens onto the alleyway. I spot a few zombies. More than a few, actually.

Under normal circumstances, I would not advocate charging through a tight cluster of zombies blocking our only way out. Tonight, there's no choice. The alley is our best option. It's a shitty option, but less shitty than going out the front door or hunkering down and waiting to burn to death if the fire spreads.

"We have to punch through that cluster," I say. "Once we're on the other side, we run like hell. Stay together. Look out for each other. And kill any of those undead fuckers who get in our way. Got it?"

No one says anything, but they all nod. I adjust the grip on my weapons. We glance at one another, each of us taking a moment to ready ourselves for the push.

Reed says, "I have a serious mom crush right now." The answering laughter is shaky at best, but I appreciate his attempt at levity.

We move into the alleyway, which by this time is

drenched in shadow. The sky is a pale gray lanced with fingers of yellow. Somewhere on the plaza is a loud *boom* as something explodes.

The zombies rotate in unison, all of them drawn to the sound. I pounce, sinking a knife into the skull of the closest of them. I spin, stabbing the next nearest through the skull.

The kids fall in around me, slashing and stabbing in silence. When Johnny slips in a puddle of blood, Carter grabs his arm and keeps him upright. When Jenna's knife gets stuck in the forehead of a zombie, Reed yanks it out for her.

We break out of the alleyway and into the street beyond. I suck in a breath at the sight of a dark horde coming straight at us. They move at a lumbering gait, growling and snarling as they fumble their way forward. As of yet, they haven't sensed us.

I point, making eye contact with the group to make sure they understand. When they nod, I sprint for the nearest intersection. The heavy pack pulls at my shoulder blades. I grit my teeth, knowing it's just going to get heavier the longer I wear it.

We dodge through the next several streets, avoiding the larger groups and slashing our way through smaller ones. Labored breathing is all around me.

Johnny grips his side, stumbling from a cramp. Carter's face is red. Reed sucks in breaths like an old man. Even Jenna, who's in the best shape of them all, is drenched in sweat.

We haven't even run half a mile.

As I pause, giving them all a moment to catch their breaths, a giant fireball explodes into the air, momentarily bathing the world in orange light and black shadows. The noise that accompanies the fireball is immense, as if someone punched a mountain-sized drum.

My heart beats faster, fear driving me.

"Fire can spread fast," I tell them. "All the noise is

going to stir up the zombies and draw them. We need to keep moving."

"I think I'm gonna puke," Reed wheezes.

I give his shoulder a pat. "When it's ready to come out, just tell me and I'll stop. Until then, we keep going." It will be good practice for Reed to keep running with an upset stomach.

"Can't we go into one of the houses?" Johnny asks, staring with longing at a nearby bungalow.

I shake my head. "We keep moving. We don't want to get penned in or trapped if the fire spreads. Come on."

Carter nods, miserable but resolute. He's crewed enough ultras with me to know the name of the game. Jenna's face is set, determination etched in her jaw. I take heart in her resolve. Our group needs as much of that as possible.

A group of zombies rounds the corner, coming in our direction. Another boom goes up from the plaza, eliciting keens and groans from them.

"Hug the houses," I murmur, shoving the kids off the road and in the direction of the homes. "Give the zombies a wide berth."

I keep them moving, stepping quickly through the front yards. Thanks to the fire, the zombies don't hear us.

We near the corner, but there are more and more zombies pouring around it. Keening travels through their midst, a signal to draw more of their brethren.

"Back," I hiss, realizing our exit has been cut off. There are too many of them now and no way to squeeze by without risk. "Turn around!"

We hurry back in the direction we came. We're forced down a street that takes us farther away from campus. It pushes us south, toward the edge of town.

I set a decent pace. It's not a sprint, but it's not a stroll either. I stay just far enough ahead of the kids to keep them moving fast.

Rain begins to fall. It's a cold, saturating drizzle, the

kind this part of California is known for. It soaks right to the bone, chilling our clothing and skin.

"This blows," Reed says.

"Maybe it will put out the fire," Carter says.

"Thank you, Mr. Optimistic," Johnny grumbles.

I ignore the commentary and keep pushing forward.

The stitch between my shoulder blades increases, but I ignore it. Johnny runs bent at the waist, hands behind his back as he tries to support the pack's weight.

"Straighten up," I tell him. "I know the pack is heavy but running like that could injure your back."

"My shoulders," he moans.

"I know. You have to ignore it. The supplies are too valuable to leave behind."

That could change at any moment, but for now, I want us to do our best to hang onto the supplies. We paid a high price to get them, and they might save our lives at some point.

"If an old lady can do it, we can do it." Reed's voice is strained, his face is pale.

"That's the spirit," I tell him.

Three zombies loom up before us, arms stretching forward as they moan. We fan out. Carter and Jenna take the one of the left. Reed and Johnny take the one on the right, while I kill the one in the middle.

I push the kids as hard as I dare. We run hardest through the clear streets and creep through the ones with zombies. Too many times we're forced farther south to avoid the larger packs. The kids slow and stumble, but I don't cut them any slack. Sympathy won't keep them alive.

"Push through the pain," I tell them. "Your job is to stay alive. If that means you have to hurt, so be it."

They raise tired, scared eyes to me. Their chests rise and fall as they gulp in air. The packs are like giant crabs on their backs. The rain slicks across their skin and clothing.

As usual, Reed has to have the last word. "When we get back to Creekside—oh, God—" He bends over his knees and heaves. A stream of vomit hits the pavement, splattering all over his shoes.

Good thing I have a new pair for him.

"Keep moving," I tell Reed as soon as he's finished, barely giving him time to spit the residual vomit out of his mouth.

"Lady, you're crazy."

"This crazy lady is going to keep you alive."

We move deeper into the night, skirting the edge of town and moving farther away from the fire.

We reach the cinderblock wall that separates the town from the freeway. I scan in both directions but don't see any zombies. By this time, the drizzle has turned into a downpour.

"Three minute break," I tell them.

Reed and Johnny collapse, sagging back against the wall. Jenna leans over her knees, sucking in gulps of air. Carter rests against the wall. He pants with the rest of them, but gives me a wry smile and shakes his head.

I'm happy to see him and Jenna holding hands. They stand near one another, intimacy thick between them. I don't know what happened in the gem shop, but I think they made up. That's another good thing to come from this disastrous outing.

"Time's up," I tell them. "We have to keep moving."

Johnny and Reed, looking miserable, climb back to their feet. For once, Reed has no witty comeback, although I do hear him grumble about chunks of vomit still in his mouth.

"I can't do it," Johnny gasps as I take them down yet another street, zigzagging our way back to the university. "I can't go any farther."

"Bullshit," I tell him. "You might be tired, but your legs are just fine. Keep moving."

His mouth sags open. "I—"

"Move," I bark. If I let up now, they could all die.

Johnny moves, half running, half staggering.

It takes us over an hour to get back to Creekside. We couldn't have covered more than three miles, but to these kids, I may as well have dragged them on their first ultra.

They limp and stagger by the time we get back to the dorm. Lightning streaks across the sky. Eric rushes down the stairs to meet us, shouldering the packs from Reed and Jenna. I watch the kids climb the stairs, their bodies bent with fatigue but very much alive.

At least the university is on the other side of the freeway. It doesn't hurt to have a large asphalt barrier between us and the flames. It's no guarantee of safety, but it gives us a measure of security.

"What the fuck happened out there?" Eric asked. "Half the town is on fire."

"We'll fill you in upstairs."

We deposit the packs in one of the deserted dorm rooms. I want to spread out the gear and organize the packs, which will be easier in a space I don't have to share with six other people.

Back in our dorm suite, Carter, Reed, Jenna, and Johnny sprawl on the sitting room floor. They look like they've been run over by a truck. Lila, sitting in the middle of them, has her cannabis salve out.

"Dude, Lila, they don't need lotion," Eric says. "They need a joint."

"Dude, Eric," she says, "the skin is the largest organ on the body. Applying salve will get the needed relief to their muscles faster."

The usual rancor is missing from their exchange. In fact, the two of them smile at each other like they're sharing a private joke. Maybe they bonded while worrying about the five of us and watching Arcata explode in flame.

As I look at the four exhausted young men and women at my feet, resolve hardens within me. This new world requires fitness.

And I'm not talking about normal, thirty-minutes-of-cardio-three-days-a-week fitness. I'm talking about ultramarathon fitness. One way or another, I'm going to get these kids in shape.

32
Meeting

JENNA

I rouse from a deep sleep in Carter's arms. His long limbs are snug around me, holding me close. I want to stay here forever, safe and warm and with Carter.

It's still raining outside, the water pattering against the glass. Yet another reason to stay in bed with Carter. It can rain for days at a time in this part of the state. I can't think of a better place to wait out the storm.

But someone keeps tapping on the door.

"Jenna!" Lila's voice calls through the hollow wood. "Are you guys decent?"

I am most certainly not decent. When we returned home last night, Lila took one look at me and Carter and resigned herself to the living room with Kate.

"Give us a sec," I call back.

Carter stirs, eyelids fluttering open. His face splits into a big grin when he sees me. I kiss him, drawing it out and savoring his warmth.

"It's been more than a second," Lila says. "Don't make me come in there."

Sighing, I flip off the covers and attempt to pick my clothes up off the floor. Carter grabs me around the waist and drags me back. I shriek as he playfully bites my shoulder.

I shove at him, struggling free. "They're going to hear us." I gesture in the vague direction of the living room as I sweep up my clothes. Realizing they're still covered in the grime, blood, and sweat from yesterday, I release them with a grunt.

I spot a fresh haul of clothing Lila must have brought in yesterday: three paper bags filled with clean garments. I pluck off jeans and a shirt and shimmy into them, not caring that both are too big.

"You better get up unless you want Lila to see you naked," I tell Carter.

He quirks an eyebrow. I see the joke forming on his lips.

I plant my hands on my hips and raise my eyebrow, daring. He melts into a chuckle. Closing the distance between us, he gives me one last kiss before climbing into his clothes. Which are filthy from yesterday's trip into town. If Carter cares, he doesn't let it show.

"Finally," Lila announces as we emerge into the hall. "Everyone is waiting for you guys."

As we enter the sitting room, we find she was not exaggerating. Kate, Johnny, Eric, and Reed are all there. The air in the room is somber. I pause, surveying everyone.

"What's up?" I ask.

"I've called a Creekside meeting." Kate rises from her seat on the arm of the sofa, planting herself in front of the flat screen. Whatever is going on, she means business.

"A meeting about what?" Carter asks.

"About the fact that all of us almost died last night."

Oh. That. Do we really have to talk about it? Other than Carter and I making up, I'd like to bury all memories of last night.

Johnny raises his hand. "Should I take minutes?" His joking smile wilts under Kate's flat stare.

"First," Kate says, "I want to know who those guys were who locked you up."

Carter and I turn to Reed. He wrinkles his nose and scratches at his head.

"They didn't lock us up on purpose," Reed says. "They put us in the closet to keep us safe, but the curio fell over and we got locked inside . . ." His voice trails off under the weight of Kate's scowl. He swallows and begins again. "They were, uh, guys I worked with back in Oakland. Granjero's guys sort of have a serious turf war with Mr. Rosario's group. Guys from both groups got stranded here at the start of the outbreak."

"I was afraid of this," Kate says. "There are two warring drug factions out there, and even though we're in a zombie apocalypse, they still fight over territory?"

Jenna, Carter, and Reed all nod.

"Shit," she growls. "Not good." She paces up and down in front of the flat screen.

"At least the fire didn't jump the freeway," Reed says. "And the rain put out most of the fire."

"Reed," Kate says, "this is not a glass half full situation. Men from Granjero or Mr. Rosario could show up here. They already did once."

He shrinks under her glare, subconsciously running his hands through his afro.

"We need to secure this building," Kate says. "But we also need to be ready to evacuate if a bunch of them show up here with guns, or if something equally dangerous happens. Last night shows us just how much we need to be able to rely on our own two feet."

I see where this conversation is going. Kate is walking us into her conclusion.

"We need to be in shape," I say.

Kate nods. "Correct."

Horrified eyes turn in her direction.

"I can't run," Lila declares.

"I almost died running last night," Reed says.

"Running isn't an option for normal people," Eric says.

"That attitude is the reason we nearly didn't make it out of Arcata," Kate replies, voice level and eyes unyielding. "When was the last time any of you did anything resembling strenuous exercise?"

"Carter and Jenna were being pretty strenuous last night," Johnny says.

I roll my eyes. Carter says, "You're just jealous, dude."

"Damn right I'm jealous. You've got one of the two pretty girls around here all to yourself." His eyes dart to Kate. "No offense."

Kate shakes her head, refusing to be drawn into the banter. "It's a new world out there." She thrusts her index finger in the direction of the small kitchen window. "Physical fitness counts. You all need to get into shape. I'm going to help you."

Silence. Eyes bug.

Then everyone starts talking at once.

"You can't make us into ultrarunners," Lila says.

"Did you see this guy run?" Johnny waves his hand at Reed. "He almost tripped over his own pants."

"And what about you?" Reed shoots back, tugging on his baggy jeans that barely cover his boxer shorts. "Like you weren't huffing and puffing with the rest of us."

"I'm a writer," Johnny says. "I can write about running, but I can't do it."

"You're all wrong." To my surprise, Carter steps into the center of the room. "I've never run a race, but I spent a lot of time at ultras growing up. I saw all types of people on the trails. Fat people. Skinny people. Young people. Even grandparents. It's all a matter of training. Anyone can run if they decide to."

"Thank you, Carter." Kate steps up to stand beside him. "You took the words out of my mouth." She turns her eyes on the rest of us. "I'm going to train all of you. Feet are the safest form of transportation. All of you are going to learn how to use them."

"I'm in." I step forward to join Carter and Kate in front of the flat screen. Kate's words make perfect sense, but that's not the real reason I'm stepping up. Kate could propose that we all learn to be ninjas and I'd still step up.

I want Carter and Kate for my family. My family is gone from my life. Even if I hated them half the time, their loss hurts. I'm determined not to lose my new family. Kate and Carter might not know it, and they might not feel the same about me, but I'm determined to be part of their unit. If that means training and working out, that's what I'll do.

"What the hell." Johnny tosses his notebook across the tabletop. "I'm in. On one condition." He points a finger at Kate. "I want your story."

Kate's mouth tightens, resistance in every angle of her face.

"How about when you're ready?" Carter intercedes. "You don't have to give the interview tomorrow, or even six months from now."

"One year," Johnny agrees. "I want it sometime in the next year.

Kate hesitates, then nods. "Okay. If you apply yourself to training, I promise to share my story with you."

"I'm in, Mama," Reed announces. "But you have to adopt me. I need a mom not addicted to crack."

No one laughs. We know he's dead serious. About Kate and his own mother.

"Fine, Reed," Kate says. "I'll adopt you."

"I mean it," he says. "You have to love me like you love Carter."

"Dude," Carter says, frowning.

"Fine, whatever," Reed says. "But I want to be adopted. I want a badass mom."

"Consider yourself adopted," Kate says. "Eric?"

"Okay," he says. "I guess if the rest of you are doing it."

"I'm not doing it," Lila says. "How do you expect us to train, anyway? Where are we supposed to run with zombies everywhere out there?"

Kate smiles. "I'm glad you asked, Lila. Come with me."

33
Course

KATE

"What the fuck is that?"

I'm not sure who speaks, but the obstacle course elicits the same reaction from all the kids.

We stand on the first-floor lounge, where five dead zombies have been arranged down the center of the room. The sofas and tables have all been pushed to one side.

"You brought them *inside*?" Lila demands. "That is so disgusting."

"Welcome to Humboldt University's first ultra-marathon training camp," I say.

Six sets of eyes bug at me in horror. Everyone starts talking at once.

"We can't train for an ultramarathon in a lounge," Eric argues. "That's just stupid."

"What if those things carry disease?" Lila asks. "Oh my God, I think I see maggots."

"Can I get stoned before my workout? That's the only way I'm going to be able to deal with the smell," Reed says.

"Hear her out." Jenna raises her voice. "Just shut up and hear her out!"

"Thank you, Jenna. Training for an ultra isn't

necessarily about having lots of places to run," I tell the kids. "I once knew a guy who worked on a cruise ship. He trained for ultras on the treadmill. He'd do four hours of uphill power walking interspersed with interval sprints. It's all a matter of perspective." I gesture at the dead bodies. "You could run in circles, but I figured you'd get bored. And to be honest, it's good to work different muscle groups. Jumping over and dodging around zombies is valuable practice for what you'll encounter out there. And it's good to remember exactly *what* is out there." I point to the world outside the dorm building. "Come on. I'll show you the next station."

"Station?" Lila says. "What are you talking about?"

"I set up three endurance training stations," I reply. "You'll rotate through them. Today, you'll do each station for twenty minutes. We add five minutes every third day until you get to a four-hour workout. That's a good endurance base."

"Four *hours*?" Reed exclaims. "Just because you're my mama doesn't mean you can abuse me."

"This is what it takes," I reply. "You need to be strong. All of you. I'm going to make you strong."

The grumbling continues. I take them back into the stairwell, which I've cleared of all debris and set up with cups and a water pitcher.

"Stair repeats," I tell them. "You don't have to run them. Just go up and down as fast as you can."

Reed groans. "I'm going to die. Just kill me now, Mama."

We head upstairs to the third floor, where I've set up the last station.

"What are these?" Johnny hefts one of three backpacks I've staged just inside the door. Each weighs seven to ten pounds.

"Weight training," I reply. "We might have to move with supplies on our backs like we did last night. Supplies can be the difference between living and dying. Jog up and down the hall with the backpacks. When you get tired, speed walk. When you're too tired for that, just walk. The most important thing is to be on your feet and moving."

"You're sadistic. I'm not doing any of this." Lila storms away, the stairwell door slamming shut behind her.

"Anyone else?" I ask those that remain.

They hesitate, looking at one another, each waiting for someone else to speak.

Jenna and Carter are the only ones who don't look like they've been hit with a fifty-pound sack of rice. If anything, Jenna looks eager; that's the track girl inside of her. Carter looks resigned, probably because he's witnessed crazy training routines his entire life. He knows what's in store for him.

Eric, Reed, and Johnny look like they want to melt into the floor. But none of them leave. The fact they're still here listening makes me proud of them. The mental aspect of ultrarunning is seventy-five percent of the game.

"When do we start?" Jenna asks.

"Right now," I reply. "Put on your shoes and some workout clothes. I expect everyone back here in fifteen minutes."

*

I assign Carter and Jenna to the first-floor zombie obstacle course. Reed and Eric are sent to the weight station. I pair up with Johnny and tackle the stairs.

I pick up the old-fashioned kitchen timer I found in a drawer and turn it to twenty minutes. Johnny takes off at a run, tearing up the stairs. I start at a fast power hike.

Five minutes into the exercise, I pass Johnny. Sweat drips down his nose and temples.

"This sucks," he wheezes.

"I used to do hill repeats with my running buddy," I

tell him as I plow past. "There was a hill near my house one mile straight up. The views were great. We would go up and down that hill four or five times. It was great for building climbing muscles."

This time, he only grunts in response. I take this as a good sign. I need to wear him out. I need to wear them all out. Push them to the point of exhaustion, let them rest, then do it all again. It's the only way to make them stronger.

When the kitchen timer dings to signal the first twenty minutes is over, Johnny looks like he's been in a sauna for two hours. His face is red and his clothes are drenched in sweat. Even his sideburns glisten with perspiration.

"Two more intervals, then you're done for today," I tell him cheerfully.

"I think maybe I should have tried to work out once or twice a week instead of, you know, screwing around on the ham in all my free time," Johnny says.

"Exercise is now a survival tactic," I reply. "You can put that in your book. Come on."

We enter the first floor as Jenna and Carter are finishing their workout. Jenna's cheeks are flushed, but her eyes are bright.

"I should have kept up with running after I graduated," she says. "I'm out of shape."

"I think I have a new idea for a beer name," Carter says. "Just because we can't have a mobile beer business doesn't mean we can't make beer, babe."

"What's the name?" Jenna asks.

"Obstacle."

Jenna's eyes light up. "I have some label ideas. I'll sketch them out when we're finished."

"They're too chipper for their own good," Johnny grumbles, but he resolutely accompanies me into the zombie obstacle course I've created.

"Fast as you can," I tell Johnny. "Back and forth as

many times as you can. Ready?" I hold up the kitchen timer.

"No, but yeah," he says.

We're off, charging around the room side by side. All told, it's three or four hundred yards long.

"Tell me again why you thought bringing bodies in here was a good idea?" Johnny asks when we reach the far wall, turn around, and start back the other way.

"Life isn't a smooth all-weather track," I reply. "Last night, when we were running through Arcata, there were obstacles everywhere. Bodies underfoot. Zombies coming after us. Cars to dodge around. You have to train yourself to be aware of your surroundings, particularly of your next few steps. You always need to watch the terrain in front of you. This gives your brain time to make adjustments for any obstacle you might encounter. You're basically getting a two-for-one on this part of the course. Endurance and environmental awareness."

"You couldn't have used a coffee table or something instead?" he gasps. "There's perfectly good furniture everywhere."

"I wanted to give you guys a realistic simulation of what you would encounter outside."

The stink *is* bad. I may have been a little too enthusiastic when I dragged the bodies in here. I'll replace them with furniture tomorrow, but for now, I hope they serve as reminders of the danger that awaits outside.

We reach the end of the lounge, turn around, and start back the other way. Johnny sucks in great gulps of air, still tired from the short stairwell workout.

We run a few more laps, Johnny falling behind with each one. I slow my steps to stay in sync with him.

"How are the shoes?" I ask him.

"Huh?"

"The shoes. You helped me pick them out last night. How do they feel?"

He scowls, which tells me how much of a toll this

workout is taking on him. "Like shoes."

"Pay attention to your feet. If you start to feel any abnormal pain, let me know. There was a time I ran a one-hundred-kilometer race with my laces too tight. I ended up with a giant bruise on the top of one foot. It hurt like a son-of-a-bitch. During the run, I thought I had a stress fracture. I didn't want to be pulled from the race so I kept running. If I'd just taken off my shoe and inspected my foot, I would have figured out what was going on. It would have made the last twenty miles much easier. My point is, pay attention to the little things. Don't let them become big things."

Johnny grunts. We continue back and forth until the timer dings, then head upstairs for the last part of the course.

This time, we pass Reed and Eric as they drag themselves down to the first floor. Reed has pulled his hair into a tight ponytail that stands over his head like a nuclear cloud. Eric looks at me and says, "I hear weed can provide pain relief to endurance athletes."

"Not on my watch," I reply. "You guys need to learn to function through pain. If you insist on smoking, save it until the workout is over."

"You just told us we have to function through pain," Eric says, staring at me like I'm crazy. "Who says stuff like that?"

"That's the whole point of this type of training. Didn't you all hurt like hell on our run back to Creekside last night?" I wait for their nods. "What if we have to run twice as far next time? Or farther? You're going to hurt. You have to learn how to mentally and physically keep going when your body hurts."

"Carter," Eric yells up the stairwell, "you didn't tell us your mom is a certified masochist."

I shrug, dragging Johnny with me up the stairs to the third floor. When I hand him the weighted backpack, he groans and shrugs into it.

"Think of it this way," I tell him. "When I decide to share my story with you, you'll have firsthand knowledge to add to the writing."

"I'm reconsidering our deal," he replies sourly. "Maybe I don't want to write your story as much as I thought I did."

I clap him on the shoulder. "You'll be thankful you put in the work the next time we go into town."

I break into a jog, trotting down the corridor. The backpack bounces against my spine and lower back as I run. It's a regular college backpack, not one of the running packs we snagged from Trading Post last night. I'm saving those to make bug-out bags for everyone.

I hear zombies bump against the closed doors of the dorm rooms. They scratch and moan against the wood, agitated by our presence. As I continue up and down the long hallway, I make a mental note to get everyone up here and clear the floor as soon as possible.

Johnny doesn't even try to keep up with me. Misery paints his face.

"There are some ultras that require runners to carry a certain amount of gear for safety precautions," I say, attempting to distract him from his physical discomfort. "Solar blankets, crampons for shoes, even extra food and water and emergency kits. Stuff like that. Just think of this as a chance to get strong enough to carry everything essential for survival on your back."

"How . . . can . . . you . . . talk . . . so . . . much?" Johnny bursts out, taking in big gulps of air between each word.

"Practice," I reply.

When the timer dings, Johnny throws the pack to the ground and collapses beside it.

"I am one out of shape fucker." He sags against the wall.

"For now," I say. "Just keep up the work. It will get easier." Then I'll crank up the workouts to make them uncomfortable again, but I don't say this last part aloud.

Out in the stairwell, Carter and the others gather to drink from the pitcher and cups I set up. Lila passes around her container of CBD salve. Everyone is sweaty and tired.

Eric in particular looks pissed. "That was fucked up."

"She's trying to help us," Jenna cuts in.

"I know!" Eric shouts. "But it totally sucked."

I down a cup of water and return to the stairs.

"Where are you going?" Carter asks.

"I have another few hours of exercise."

"Show off," Johnny says.

I ignore the comment. These kids have to see where each of them needs to be. What they have to train their bodies to do in order to become stronger.

When I reach the second-story landing, I hear Reed say, "Fuck this. I don't want to die."

His feet tap on the stairs as he hurries to catch up with me. I wait for him.

"How long do you plan to go?" he asks me.

"Three hours, maybe four."

"I'm doing it with you. Fuck this interval training shit. I want to be stronger right now. If Mr. Rosario's goons show up, I want to be able to run far and fast."

Pride swells in my chest. I grin at the young man beside me, at the sliver of a future ultrarunner peeking out from behind dark eyes and nuclear cloud afro. "Let's go."

*

Reed and I become a live action show. Everyone, even Lila, brings out folding chairs and takes up residence on various landings to watch us.

Johnny has his ham radio, relating a blow-by-blow of our workout routine to Alvarez on the other end. Eric, not surprisingly, has a fresh joint in his hand and puffs away, slumped in his chair with his eyes closed. Reed and I are about forty minutes into our workout when Carter and Jenna show up with fresh popcorn.

"Who knew you could make popcorn on the barbecue?" Jenna says, grinning at me as we head upstairs to the weight segment.

"Mom, we brought you some trail mix," Carter says, handing me a bag as we pass him.

"Thanks, sweetie." I hold the bag out to Reed. "It's important to stay fueled. Eat some."

He does, and we head to the third floor to grab the weighted bags. We finish the set, then start all over again.

I'm starting to feel good, to slide into the state of a runner's high. I'm leaping over zombies, pumping my arms, and enjoying the feeling of my body's exertion.

That's when Reed doubles over and pukes all over the floor.

The sound brings everyone running.

"Dude, Reed is now puking all over the feet of a zombie corpse," Johnny reports into the ham.

"That's twice now," Jenna observes.

"Mom always pukes during her ultras," Carter adds.

"Not always," I reply. "Just sometimes." I pat Reed between the shoulder blades. "It happens as your body diverts energy to fueling your limbs. There's nothing left to digest the food."

Reed heaves again, bits of trail mix and a brownish mix of whatever he had for breakfast also coming up. I'd say the smell was bad, but it isn't even a blip in the all-encompassing stench of the zombie bodies.

Jenna produces a towel from one of the rooms, handing it to Reed so he can wipe his mouth and face. Carter hands him a bottle of water.

"You okay?" I ask Reed.

He nods, holding himself steady with one hand against the wall.

"Good. Let's finish the set."

"You're making him do more?" Lila asks, mouth hanging open.

"If zombies were chasing you, would you stop because you threw up?" I reply. "There were points last night when stopping wasn't an option."

Reed, face pinched from discomfort, shakes his head. "I'm good. Let's go, Mama."

34
Sleep Deprivation

KATE

I slip into the suite where Jenna has organized all our food. Lila found a survival book in someone's bedroom and calculated we have enough food for six weeks. That's a good haul, and this is just the stuff Jenna pulled in from only a dozen or so rooms in Creekside.

We've since cleared all the dorms on the second and third floors and have begun to organize and inventory the additional supplies. Creekside is officially a safe zone.

Ultramarathon training camp has been going well. Except for Lila, all the other kids have committed to getting in shape. After two weeks, they're up to one-hundred-twenty-minute workouts.

It's time to introduce a new phase in their training: sleep deprivation.

I dig through the supplies and extract a bottle of vodka I found a few days ago tucked underneath a bathroom sink in one of the neighboring dorm rooms. Rain patters against the window as I hold up the bottle to examine it in the dull light. Ketel One.

"Time for a new training technique," I announce as I return to our apartment. Everyone ignores me, wrapped up in the excitement of *Call of Duty*. It's an evening ritual. So long as they're exercising and participating in the necessary chores during the day, I don't mind if they have downtime in the evening.

I set the bottle of Kettle One on the kitchen table, letting it bang against the particle-board surface.

Heads turn. Simulated gunfire cracks out of the flat screen, but I have everyone's attention.

"Sleep deprivation is part of ultrarunning," I say. "You won't finish a hundred-miler if you pull over to sleep the night away. You need to be prepared to be awake and moving for twenty to thirty hours, sometimes more. Sleep deprivation hits us all in different ways. It makes us hallucinate. It makes us exhausted. Worst of all, it makes us want to quit. To throw in the towel. To take the easy way out. That's not an option for you. We need to be prepared and trained for sleep deprivation."

Reed is the first to crack. "You're not going to make us climb the stairs all night, are you?"

There's a collective sigh of relief when I shake my head, forcing me to smother a grin. Their heads had gone straight to the stairwell.

"Nope. We need to practice staying awake for twenty-four-hour intervals. What time did everyone wake up today?"

Looks are exchanged. We don't worry too much about time these days, but there is still a functioning battery-powered clock on the kitchen wall.

"I think we were all up by nine," Jenna says.

"Right." I nod. "Nine in the morning. We are going to stay awake until nine a.m. tomorrow. I'll sweeten the deal with this." I tap the lid of the Kettle One bottle. "We can start with shots."

They shift in a collective mass toward the kitchen table. Johnny is the first to sweep up the bottle, embracing it like it's a beloved stuffed animal and he's a little kid.

"Where did you find that?" Carter asks.

"In one of the cleared bedrooms," I reply. "I wanted

it for a rainy day." I gesture at the kitchen window, where rain makes a smeary pattern across the glass. A punch of lightning follows my words.

"It's definitely raining," Eric says, wrestling the bottle away from Johnny. "Kate, you are the coolest old person I've ever met. Minus the crazy workouts you make us do."

I grin, rounding up some glasses from the kitchen. Everyone gathers on the sofa and floor of the sitting room, *Call of Duty* forgotten.

Eric does the honors, pouring a small shot for everyone. A few months ago, I wouldn't have considered serving alcohol to minors. These days, I figure they've all proven themselves adults. At least a little. Even Carter grins as the clear liquid sluices into his glass.

"Bottoms up," Reed calls, holding up his glass. We raise our glasses in a toast, then throw back our heads and down the liquid.

Lila sputters and coughs, laughing in embarrassment when Jenna calls her a lightweight. Reed flops onto the floor, moaning in mock ecstasy.

"Oh my God," he says. "All we need now are some of Eric's brownies and we'd have a legit party."

"No brownies," I say, giving Eric a stern look when he starts to rise. "This is a training exercise. Brownies will have us all passed out on the floor."

"Vodka can leave us all passed out, too," Eric argues.

"Vodka can turn this into a pleasant training exercise," I reply. "Or we can all just sit around and stare at one another."

"Strip poker!" Reed cries, jumping to his feet. "I'll get the cards."

"Only if you promise to keep your underwear on," Jenna calls to Reed's disappearing backside. "There's only one man around here I want to see in his birthday suit." She and Carter smirk at each other. It's nice to see them happy together, even if the last thing I want to hear is the two of them talk about birthday suits.

Reed shouts protests from the hallway, where he digs in a closet. "I look fucking hot in my birthday suit. You don't know what you're missing!"

"I'm pretty sure we'd all be underwhelmed," Lila replies.

This brings a round of laughter. Lila cracks a smile, something she doesn't do much these days.

"Any more out of you, and I'm going to eat your cannabis salve," Reed announces, strutting back into the room.

"Dude, I'm pretty sure I have dibs on the salve," Eric puts in. "How else are we going to get any decent brownies? We're almost out of buds."

"My salve is not for brownies," Lila retorts.

"We could mix the buds in the vodka," Eric suggests.

"No!" we all shout.

More laughter. The cards come out. The Kettle One makes its rounds. Thunder crashes outside like a punctuation.

Satisfied, I settle in for a long night. Away from the strip poker game.

35
Library

JENNA

"Was I hallucinating, or did I hear Carter say that you shit yourself at a few ultras?" I slump down at the kitchen table late the next afternoon, reaching for a bottle of water to combat the hangover headache hammering at my temples.

Everyone else sits at the table in an equal state of discomfort, water bottles clutched in hands. Kate passes out Tylenol. She alone looks un-phased by the long night of drinking and strip poker.

"Mom thought it would be a good idea to have Indian curry before one of her races." Carter throws the Tylenol into his mouth and chugs down half a bottle of water.

"I'm pretty sure we should save the Tylenol for real illnesses," Johnny says. His sideburns stick out at a severe horizontal angle from his face, giving him the appearance of having stuck his finger in a light socket.

"Your first round of sleep deprivation training is a legit reason for Tylenol," Kate replies, patting his shoulder.

"How come you aren't hung over?" Eric asks Kate.

"I stopped drinking while everyone still had their clothes on."

"Sucks for you," Lila says. "I can't imagine seeing these losers naked without my drunk glasses."

"While you all recover, I need to go to the library," Kate says. "We have a few hours before sunset. Alvarez asked me to find books on farming and canning. His people are having trouble getting their seeds to germinate."

"I'll go with you," Carter says.

"Me, too," I add. Some fresh air might help dispel the headache.

"You sure?" Kate asks. "The library isn't far."

"Very sure," Carter replies, throwing me a look of thanks. "Maybe we can find stuff on hydroponics while we're there. If we can move solar panels to Creekside, maybe we can turn the first floor into a garden. There's too much rain in Arcata to grow a decent vegetable garden outside."

He isn't wrong. It rains nine months out of the year in Arcata.

Kate's brows lift in approval. "That's a good idea. We can't rely on scavenged food forever."

Johnny perks up. "A field trip? Count me in. I just finished writing about our trip to Trading Post. It's practically a novel by itself. Villains, monsters, kidnapping, suspense—I'm telling you, the story has it all."

I roll my eyes. "I'm glad our near-death experience gave you something to write about."

"Think of it this way," Johnny replies. "You are officially immortalized."

Carter snorts. "Yeah, in your notebook."

"Don't knock the notebook," Johnny replies, unruffled.

Carter, Kate, Johnny, and I exit Creekside, leaving the others behind to nurse their hangovers.

"How's your *Thrive* book coming along?" Kate asks Johnny.

"Still working on it," he replies. "I'm a multitasker. The other night I talked to some people in Canada. They've been living in the family tree house for weeks. One of the guys spent an hour telling me all the different ways you can poop and pee when living in a tree house."

Before the outbreak, this topic of conversation would have grossed me out. Now, as we make our way onto a campus littered with decomposing bodies, I find myself curious. "There's more than one or two ways to go to the bathroom in a tree house?"

"He described exactly fourteen different ways to defecate off the side of the platform."

"Good thing you wrote it all down," Carter replies drily. "It could come in handy if we get stuck in Creekside for some reason."

Kate stops, raising a hand to signal silence. We all stop talking, clustering behind her. I study our surroundings, a feeling of unease stealing over me. We'd been chatting like stupid college kids instead of paying attention. Stupid, stupid.

"What is it?" Carter whispers.

Kate shakes her head. "Just a feeling. Come on. No more conversation until we get back to Creekside."

No one argues. We move deeper into campus. There are some undead wandering around, usually in clumps of three or four. We dispatch any within our direct path and leave the rest.

When we pass the Depot, I shudder at the sight of the soldier impaled to the tree. A vulture sits on his head, pecking at the dead man's eyes. It's a gruesome sight. I wish we'd taken the body down the last time we were here. I consider doing it now, but Kate hustles us by the Depot before I can make up my mind. The dead soldier is left behind with his carrion companion.

We reach the library. The building is a two-story mass of gray cement with big pillars in the front. The glass windows and automated front doors are all shattered. We stop in front of the building, scanning the immediate interior. Six corpses litter the front entryway.

"There's a good chance we'll run into zombies inside," Kate says. "We need to stay together and watch one another's backs. No splitting up. Agreed?"

I don't relish the idea of wandering around the stacks alone. "Agreed."

"Agreed," Carter and Johnny say.

We draw our weapons. My spear is in my right hand, the knife Kate got me at Trading Post in my left.

Inside the wide entryway, past the check-out desk, is a wide staircase that leads to the second floor.

"Let's see if the vending machines are still intact," Carter says.

"I wouldn't mind some food myself, especially if we're going to be here a while," I say. "Searching through all the books to find the stuff we need on hydroponic gardening and preserving food could take forever without the electronic catalogue."

"They're by the bathrooms," Johnny says. "This way."

We all look to Kate. It occurs to me we're waiting for her approval. Somewhere along the way, she's become our collective mom.

"Vending machines," she agrees.

The first-floor vending machine has already been raided, the Plexiglas smashed. Several bodies lay nearby in a pool of dried blood.

"No go," Johnny says. "Let's try upstairs."

We climb the stairs in a tight knot, all of us scanning with our weapons out. I hear a few moans, telling me there are zombies upstairs. Luckily, it doesn't sound like too many.

We creep up the last few steps and pause, listening.

"Doesn't sound like more than a few," Carter whispers. "We should go see where they are."

The rest of us nod in agreement.

At first, all we see are rows of tall bookshelves and

study cubicles. The moan sounds again, drawing our attention to the left side of the room. Creeping forward, we find three zombies, each of them in a different row.

"We should get rid of them," Kate says. "Clear out this floor."

Sticking together, we move into each of the aisles. Kate takes the lead on the killing, using her screwdriver to dispatch the undead while the rest of us cover her. It doesn't take long to eliminate them.

"Vending machine," Johnny says when we finish. "I'd kill for a bag of Cheetos."

"Glad the zombies didn't ruin your appetite," Carter replies.

"Admit it," Johnny says. "You'd kill for a bag a Cheetos, too."

Carter lets out a long, mock sigh. "Yeah, okay. You got me. I'd kill for Cheetos."

"You'll both have to fight me for them," Kate says.

We head toward the back of the building where the restrooms are. As we draw closer, a stench reaches my nose. It's not the general scent of rot and decay I'm used to. It smells like . . .

"It smells like piss and shit," Kate says.

"Took the words out of my mouth," I murmur.

"Maybe the bathrooms are backed up," Carter suggests.

We emerge from a long aisle of books and stop short. In front of us are two dead girls.

"Um, guys?" I lower my voice to a soft whisper. "These girls weren't killed long ago. And I think they were people when they died, not zombies."

If someone had told me six months ago that I'd become adept at discerning the age of a corpse, I'd have written them off as weird. Now I've seen so many dead that my mind quickly registers the details of these: The blood is reddish brown, not the blackish-red that flows from a zombie. The fact that there's still a reddish hue to it means it hasn't been exposed to oxygen for weeks and weeks. There are no discernable bite wounds on either of the bodies. The bodies themselves are already encrusted with maggots, but the rot and decay isn't that far along.

"Someone hurt them." Kate crouches beside the dead girls, eyes blazing as she inspects them.

At first, I don't see what she sees. Then I see the blood on the inside of their thighs. The torn panties matted in the thick pool of blood. The deep tears in their abdomens.

This violence wasn't from zombies.

The source of the shit and piss aroma becomes apparent. Someone defecated on the bodies of the girls. No way to know if that was done before or after they were killed.

Carter toes at something in the blood. A key fob. "They were from College Creek dorm. Those are the only dorms on campus with fobs instead of regular keys."

We look at each other. I know we're all thinking of the guys we met in the Depot from College Creek.

"I didn't like those guys," Carter says. "I knew they were bad news."

It's impossible to imagine hurting another human being the way these girls have been hurt. But for some reason, it's not a stretch to imagine those guys inflicting this kind of pain.

Kate rises. "We need to go to College Creek."

"Is that a good idea?" Johnny asks. He takes several steps back when she glares. "I mean, it's probably good story fodder, but is it safe? If those guys are the ones who did this—"

"If those guys are the ones who hurt these girls, we need to know," Kate says. "There could be others who need our help. We have to check it out and put a stop to it."

It's the right thing to do. I know it on a deep, humanitarian level. But all I want to do is look for books.

I want to read about farming, and hydroponics, and preserving food. I don't want to head into the part of campus hit hardest by the plague to look for boys I'd just as soon never see again.

"It's getting late," Carter says. "Look, Mom, I get it. If people need help, we should help. But we shouldn't get stuck on the other side of campus after dark."

Kate hesitates. I see the fire burning behind her eyes, the anger over the dead girls. It's as scary as it is inspiring.

"Tomorrow," she says, voice clipped. "Let's find the books we need and get out of here."

36
Late Night Chat

KATE

I can't shake the image of the dead girls from my head. Their desecrated corpses. The blood of their deaths and their rapes.

We've known we're not alone in Arcata. We've seen evidence of that firsthand. Hell, Carter has been held at gunpoint twice.

But even that pales when I think of the girls. What if there are other girls like them out there? I can't sit by and do nothing.

I toss and turn, unable to sleep. I wish I could scrub today from my brain.

I fumble for the flashlight and rise. An hour or two in the stairwell will help me sleep. I shine the light around, searching for my shoes.

The beam glances off the kitchen table, illuminating the black rectangle of Johnny's ham radio. I cross the room and plop in front of it, resting my forehead in my hands. I wonder if I could talk to someone. It would be so nice to talk to another adult. I can't dump my fears on Carter or any of the other kids, but a stranger is another story.

I flip on the radio, turning the dial experimentally. "Hello, anyone there?" I ask.

Static answers me. I try a few more times but reach no one.

I notice a scrap of paper taped to the top of the ham. There are numbers on the scrap, and next to the numbers, names.

Foot Soldier. Alvarez's name leaps out at me, a barely legible pencil smudge in the dark.

Not really expecting to get a response, I turn the dial to the corresponding channel. "Hello? Foot Soldier, are you there? It's Kate."

As expected, I get nothing. I let out an exasperated huff. It's the middle of the night. Normal people are asleep right now.

I need my stairwell.

As I retrieve my shoes from underneath the table, I hear a crunch of static.

"Kate? It's Foot Soldier. Over."

I snatch up the ham receiver. "Hello? Alvarez?"

"Hey, Kate. What are you doing up? Over."

Now that I have him on the other end, I feel self-conscious for reaching out. "I can't sleep. Today I saw something and . . . and it wasn't pretty."

I know I'm supposed to use official language like *over* and *roger*, but I don't have the energy. On top of that, I don't really know the etiquette like Johnny does.

"I feel you," comes Alvarez's reply. "There's a lot of messed up shit out there. What was it?"

A knot of tension builds in my chest. "Are you sure you wanna hear? It's awful."

A long pause. "On my way to Fort Ross, I took shelter in a campground during a storm. I found an abandoned tent and crawled inside to wait out the rain. When I left the next morning, I realized the tent wasn't there because the owners had left in a rush." Emotion tinges his voice. "The owners had hung themselves. A couple. They shot their three kids then hung themselves."

I press the heel of my hand into my forehead. God,

things are so fucked up.

"I understand, Kate," Alvarez says. "I really do."

Slowly, haltingly, I relate the horror of today. What started out as a simple mission to find some research books turned into a nightmare.

"We found the books," I finish. A dry, bitter laugh climbs out of my throat. Tears press against the back of my eyes. "Jenna is going to read up on gardening and put together some bullet points for you."

"That's nice of her," Alvarez says. "Kate, I'm sorry you had to see that. It's fucked up."

"I don't think *fucked up* begins to cover it."

"Yeah, I know. There are no words. Not really." A long pause. "You know that whoever hurt those girls is out there, right?"

"I know. Damn it, I know. I feel like we should have surveillance cameras and private security, you know? But we can't get any of that shit."

"Do you have a plan?"

"Sort of. It involves going to the place where I think the bad guys are holed up."

"Uh, okay. And then what?"

And then what? I haven't let myself think that far along. "I just keep thinking there might be more girls like the ones we found. What if they have them chained to a bed or locked in a closet or something?"

"I think," Alvarez says, "that you need to take a few steps back, Kate. There are people out there who raped and murdered those girls. Stop for a minute and swallow that. What are you going to do if you come up against them? Do you have a gun?"

My stomach turns. I feel like an idiot. I convinced myself there are more girls out there that need rescuing. Maybe I'm the one who needs rescuing. From myself.

"We have two guns." I don't explain how we came to be in possession of them.

"If you decide to track them down, you do it because

you need to clean house. Don't get caught up worrying about victims that may or may not exist."

He's right. I feel myself hardening as I realize what tomorrow might have in store. Because I *am* going to College Creek tomorrow.

"Kate? You still there?"

"I'm here. Thanks for listening."

"Anytime. Will you radio me tomorrow? I want to know you guys are okay. I sleep better at night knowing there are good people still out there."

I nod before I remember he can't see me. "Yeah, I'll radio. I'm going to try to sleep now." My eyes feel heavy. The talk really did help. "Good night, Foot Soldier."

"Goodnight, Kate."

37
College Creek

JENNA

I feel my body evolving.

The first few days of Kate's workout left me so sore it was difficult to get out of bed. And if I felt sore and achy, I can only imagine how bad everyone else felt, especially the guys like Eric and Reed who made the act of being a couch potato into an art form.

Kate promised us it would get easier. She was right. We're only two weeks into our workout routine, but already I feel stronger. In the beginning, twenty minutes of running with the weighted packs made me want to roll on the floor and pass out. Now, after forty minutes, I feel like I can easily do more.

I'm grateful for the newfound strength. It might very well come in handy today. In less than an hour, we're headed to College Creek. I dread the outing.

The timer dings. Carter and I head down to the first floor for our last interval. Thank God Kate got rid of the bodies after the first day and replaced them with various pieces of furniture. The vending machine is a bit hard to get over, but I'll take it over a rotting body any day.

"I've been thinking more about security," Carter says as we begin our exercises. We can converse during our workouts now, something that hadn't been possible in the beginning.

"How so?" I ask.

"I think we should see if we can find the keys for some of the other dorm rooms so we can lock them."

I don't relish the thought of going through the dead bodies to find keys. "Why?" I ask. "To lock up our supplies?"

"Exactly. We need to start taking more precautions."

How far my boyfriend has come. From denying the apocalypse to chief security planner for our group.

"If you want to go through bodies and look for keys, I'll help you," I say. "But you have to find me a pair of rubber gloves. And a surgical mask."

"Deal, babe."

"We're leaving soon," Kate calls, poking her head in through the stairwell door. "The whole gang has decided to come. Except for Lila, of course."

A short time later, we're in clean clothes pulled from a neighboring dorm—one of these days, Eric is going to get the solar panel installed for the washing machine—with weapons on our belts. I lace up a pair of sturdy hiking boots. Kate, I notice, puts on her running shoes. When she isn't barefoot in the dorm, she wears her running shoes.

I want my ankles protected even if it means I'll run slower. College Creek borders the big playing field on the southern side of campus where several hundred zombies are corralled. They're trapped inside the wrought iron fence that surrounds the field. I'm not sure why the military didn't wipe them out like they did other large bodies of infected.

I don't even want to go to College Creek. It's not the wisest way we could spend our day, although I have to credit Kate for wanting to make sure no one out there needs help.

Where Kate goes, Carter goes. Where Carter and Kate go, I go.

Today, there's no banter as we make our way through campus. A light rain falls.

I scan the Depot warily as we pass by, looking for signs of Ryan or the other College Creek kids. I do the same at the library. Both buildings stare back at us in blank-faced silence.

The next time we come this way, I vow to get the dead soldier off the tree. For some reason, looking at his body is more disturbing than all the other bodies.

"Hold up." Carter raises a hand to halt us. "Listen. Do you hear that?"

Adrenaline pumps through my body, making my breathing rapid and harsh. I hold my breath and strain my ears.

"Zombies," Kate says.

Sure enough, a murmur of moans peppers the air.

"Where are they coming from?" Johnny asks.

"South?" Carter asks.

We inch together to form a tight cluster. The longer I listen, the more moans I hear. There are a lot of zombies out there.

"South," I agree after a few minutes. "Could it be the ones in the field?"

"Seems most likely," Kate says. "We move slow and cautious. If we spot trouble, we turn back around."

Now *that's* a plan.

We slip through campus, creeping along between the buildings and drawing ever closer to College Creek. I take out my weapons, the skin along the back of my neck itching with nerves.

"Am I the only one who feels like this part of campus is different?" Eric asks.

"No," I agree, "it's different." And it's not just the bodies we see everywhere. The backdrop of all the moaning makes it impossible to forget we risk our lives with every step we take.

"There." Carter points to a three-story building that

comes into sight as we round a corner. "College Creek."

College Creek apartments are the newest dorms on campus. They were the nice, more expensive dorms. Kids who wanted a room to themselves generally lived in College Creek, where each suite boasted three single rooms.

Carter, on student loans, chose the older, more affordable housing. I took one look at the pretty stucco buildings and knew I didn't want to live in them. They reminded me too much of my high school in Southern California. I came to Humboldt to get away from those memories. Even though my cosmetic surgeon father offered to pay for more expensive lodging, I picked Creekside. And since I met Carter there, I know it was the right decision.

I'm doubly grateful when my eyes take in the charred half of College Creek. Fire took the rooms on the right-hand side of the long building. The part still standing is stained with soot. I see a few partially burned bodies on the ground.

I shiver, inching closer to Carter.

"This way." To my shock, Kate draws a handgun. She'd hidden it in the waistband of her pants and covered it with her shirt. It's one of the guns she took from Mr. Rosario's people.

"Mom, what's that for?" Carter asks.

"Just in case." Kate pauses, her gaze sweeping over us. "You guys can stay here if you want. I'll check it out and let you know if it's clear."

"No way," Carter says. The rest of us echo his protest.

She gives us a tight nod before heading toward College Creek. "Have your weapons out," she tells us. "Be ready for anything."

College Creek is rectangular. In the center of the building is a big courtyard with seating areas and tables. Where once we would have seen kids hanging out or doing homework, we now see bodies. Lots of them.

Bullet casings glint in the dull light and crunch underfoot. Vultures study us with their beady eyes. When they determine we aren't here to take their food, they go back to their feasting.

The moaning is louder here in the courtyard. Legs tense, ready to run if necessary, I scan the surrounding area. Where are all the zombies?

"They're on the other side of the fence. Look." Carter raises a hand, pointing with his knife.

I follow the line of his hand. Across the courtyard are two breezeways that lead onto the playing field.

That's where the zombies are. The wrought iron gates erected in front of the breezeways effectively cut the zombies off from the rest of the campus.

"That looks like a disaster waiting to happen," Johnny hisses, staring at the zombies milling on the other side of the fence. "Horror story disaster. It's like the smoking gun on the mantle."

"What smoking gun?" Reed asks.

"It's a figure of speech," Johnny says.

"He means they could smash through that fence if they mob it," I explain. "And then we'd be screwed because the whole campus would be overrun." I feel even less safe than I did a few minutes ago, and I haven't felt safe since we made the decision to come here.

"We stay away from the fence and don't incite them," Kate replies. "Come on."

"You haven't seen enough?" Johnny asks.

"Far from it." Kate gestures with her chin.

I look across the courtyard to where she indicates.

"Fuck me," Carter murmurs.

I bump up against him as he grinds to a halt. There, nailed to a door with knives, is another dead soldier. His body is pierced with two long knives through the shoulder blades, just like the one at the Depot. His throat is slit, a dried river of blood running down the front of his fatigues.

38
Death

KATE

The gore doesn't stop at the dead soldier. Scattered around him are half a dozen bodies of college kids. Like the girls we found in the library, these are newly dead. The rain has streaked the blood, turning it into red swirling patterns that fan out around the bodies. Their clothes are wet and wrinkled from exposure to the constant rain.

Blood pounds in my ears as I take in the death. *I'm too late.* The words flash through my mind. Some part of me knows these are the kids I wanted to save. They were slaughtered by whoever it was that murdered the girls in the library.

"Uh, Mom? I think we should go home now."

I turn to look at Carter and the others. Bringing them here was a mistake. I should have come alone.

"Those College Creek kids you met in the Depot," I say. "Do you guys remember what they look like?"

"I do," Jenna says. Carter nods.

"Do you see any of them here?" I gesture to the bodies.

They inch forward, Eric and Johnny with them. Several of the dead lay facedown. Using my foot, I turn them over so we can get a good look at them.

There's a fat boy, a skinny boy, and another kid covered with acne. The rest of the dead are all girls. I count eight altogether.

My eyes sweep to the dead soldier nailed to the door. He's older, with gray stubble and the beginnings of wrinkles around his eyes and mouth. A veteran of probably more than one war, and yet someone got the drop on him.

"I don't see Ryan or the others," Carter says.

"You think they did this?" Jenna whispers.

"They mutilated those zombies in the Depot," Eric says.

While I agree that mutilating zombies takes a special person, I don't think that necessarily means they're the ones who killed all these kids. For one thing, these kids look like they were killed with two shots, one in the head and one in the chest. Average college kids aren't such good shots.

"We should go." Jenna glances in the direction of the fence, at the thin rods of iron that separate us from a field of zombies.

I itch to go into the building, to hunt down whoever murdered these kids. But even I have to admit that would be a colossally stupid idea. I knew things could be bad, but I hadn't expected to find so many dead. Something tells me this wasn't the work of one or two college kids. There's someone else hurting people. Could it be men of Granjero or Mr. Rosario? Just the thought makes my blood pressure boil.

"Let's go back," I murmur. I have one gun and five living kids with me. If there are armed people inside, we don't need to be going in there.

"Wait." Jenna takes a few steps away from us. "I want to take him down." She gestures to the soldier nailed to the door. "It's messed up."

"No," Carter says. "There's nothing we can do for him."

"I agree with Carter," Johnny says. "Evidence suggests we should get the fuck out of here."

Jenna's eyes blaze. I don't know what it is, but something about the hanging body has her more worked up than the bodies on the ground. I can see by the stubborn set of her jaw that she isn't going to budge on this.

"Let's make it fast." I gesture to her, striding toward the door.

I've taken only two steps when a shot rings out. The ground in front of me sends up a puff of cement from the impact of the bullet.

"Stop right there, motherfuckers." The voice echoes through the open courtyard.

I freeze, palm sweaty around the handle of the gun. A chorus of moans rises from beyond the fence line.

"What are you doing here?" the voice calls.

"Can you keep your voice down?" I whisper-shout. "You're upsetting the natives." I scan the building, searching for the owner of the voice.

"Answer the question!"

A cluster of zombies bumps up against the fence. Jenna and Carter clutch each other, while Johnny, Reed, and Eric gather behind them. They all cast nervous looks in the direction of the fence.

"We found two dead girls in the library," I say, voice shaking with rage and fear. Is this the asshole who murdered those girls? Cold sweat drenches my back. My hands tremble from the force of the adrenaline hammering through my body. "They lived in College Creek. Do you know anything about that?"

Silence stretches. My breathing is loud in my ears, rasping in and out through my nose.

I spot movement on a second-story balcony only fifty yards from where we stand. A man is crouched behind a barbecue, some sort of machine gun balanced across the top of it. All I can see of him is a forehead, eyes, and brownish-gray crew cut.

When he finally speaks, his question surprises me. "What were the girls wearing?"

"I couldn't tell you," I reply. "There was too much blood. We came here to see if there was anyone else in trouble." I gesture to the bodies with my screwdriver hand. "I think we're too late."

Another long pause. Then the soft scrape of the machine gun as it's lifted from the barbecue. A man in military fatigues stands, revealing himself on the balcony. He's too far away for me to see the details of his face, but from this distance, I'd gauge him to be in his late forties or early fifties.

"We were both too late," he replies. "The fuckers who did this got away."

The fury in his voice settles me. It is not the fury of a man who murders young men and women. It's a fury that resonates inside me, echoes my own thoughts and feelings.

"Tell me who did this," I grind out. I'll kill them with my bare hands if I have to. Anything to keep Carter and the kids safe.

My eyes meet those of the soldier across the distance. He gives a small shake of his head. "I don't know where they went," he says, "but I intend to hunt them down. Every last one of them."

"I can help."

He barks a laugh. "Get out of here. Stay out of sight and watch your backs."

"Tell me who did this."

"Soldiers. Stay away from anyone in military uniform. If you meet them, it'll be too late for you."

39
Gift

Something fundamental changes in us after College Creek. Every one of us throws ourselves into fortifying Creekside. We dismantle bookshelves and nail planks over every window on the first floor. Carter and Eric pull together enough scraps to build a real door for the front entry, complete with a security bar to hold it in place. No more flimsy swinging glass doors for us.

The Xbox hasn't been turned on once. Eric, Reed, and Johnny make a trip to the Depot to retrieve several solar panels. We finally have a working washing machine. We still have to fill it with water from the creek, but that's a small price to pay for clean clothes.

Carter and I do indeed venture out into the pile of bodies to search for keys to other dorm rooms. Shockingly, we manage to find three for Creekside. All our food and supplies are now behind locked doors.

Lila and Eric have teamed up on the hydroponics project. She's buried herself in the library books while Eric hooks grow lights up to the solar panels. A trip to a neighboring dorm produced the grow lights. Reed had known a few guys who grew pot in their closets.

I think there's something going on between Eric and Lila. Even when they're not working on the hydroponics project, they spend a lot of time together. They still argue and bicker over just about everything, but it has a good-natured edge to it.

All this progress and preparation hasn't done anything to lift the pall that hangs over our group. Gone is the friendly banter. It feels like we're waiting for the other shoe to drop.

At least things between Carter and I have returned to normal. I feel like I can handle anything the world throws at me if we're together.

"Will you help me get water for the washing machine?" I ask him. I'm dying to get out of our somber dorm room, even if it's only for a trip to the creek and back. Besides that, I have a surprise for him.

"Sure, babe," he says. "Let's go."

Outside, the air is clean and fresh from a recent rainfall. Out here, under the trees, I can almost imagine we don't live in a world of death and monsters. All this should make me feel more relaxed, but I can't shake the feeling of a looming threat.

When we reach the creek, I reach into the back pocket of my pants and pull out a folded piece of paper. "Here, I drew this for you."

Carter unfolds it, eyes taking in the graphite lines that outline the shape of a beer label. The word "obstacle" is drawn in angular script. A runner leaps over what looks like a track hurdle. Upon closer inspection, the hurdle reveals itself to be made from bones and body parts.

"It's perfect," he breathes.

"We can still have Ultra Brew," I tell him. "Maybe it won't be what we planned, but it's still ours." I step closer to him. "I feel complete when I'm with you, Carter. With or without our brewery. I'm sorry I ever made you feel differently."

"Babe." He draws me against his chest. "We're past that now. It was just a misunderstanding."

"I know. But I'm still sorry I hurt you."

He cups my face in his hands and kisses me. "It's behind us." He looks down, studying my face. "I want to try something. Will you close your eyes?"

"Okay." I lower my lids, even though standing in the forest with my eyes closed is far from my comfort zone.

We stand there in silence, me with my eyes closed and Carter with his thumbs caressing my cheeks.

"You're beautiful," he whispers.

My eyes snap open.

His thumbs never stop moving over my cheeks. "Those words are meant to be a compliment, babe. That's it. You're beautiful. I've decided I'm going to say it whenever I feel like it. You're going to have to learn to deal with it."

I lower my gaze. "It's just my stupid childhood baggage."

"I know. I'm going to help you get past it, starting today. You're beautiful, Jenna, inside and out. I love you."

"I love you, too."

The emotion of the moment is almost too much to bear. It's like a giant boulder sitting on my chest. I have to say something to dislodge it before I end up in tears. "You're just feeling mushy because I shaved my armpits."

He chuckles, once again folding me against his chest. "You got me. Once you got rid of the armpit hair, you went from hot to steaming hot."

"You're pretty hot yourself, Carter Stephenson."

He raises a teasing eyebrow. "Even without the beard?"

"You are, hands down, the hottest boyfriend I've ever had. Although, I think I like you beardless most of all. I don't have to worry about a zombie grabbing your face."

"I guess that's a good thing, isn't it?"

"It's definitely a good thing. I like you with your face."

We stand together beside the creek, just holding each

other. When we finally fill the water tote and head back to Creekside, I realize I'm even more in love with Carter than ever before.

"I promised to help your mom take apart some desks," I tell him. Now that we've managed to find enough furniture to board up all the windows on the first floor of Creekside, Kate has moved onto a new project. "She wants to try building a garden bed for Eric and Lila."

"I'll help you guys," Carter says.

"Don't you have plans to—?"

Seven people step around the side of the building to intercept us. Four of them are dressed in military fatigues; the other three are college boys. I recognize them as the College Creek kids we ran into at the Depot on our beer run. Ryan, Adam, and Henry were their names.

"There you are," says Ryan, leveling a gun at us with a smirk. "You guys don't live in Pepperwood."

"No, we don't," Carter says, voice flat.

"I'm hurt you didn't trust us," Ryan says. "We are, after all, schoolmates."

"If that really means anything to you, lower your gun," I reply.

Ryan's smile curls as he studies me. The look makes my skin crawl.

He doesn't lower his gun.

40
Tithe

KATE

I sit in a living room on the third floor, a hammer in one hand and a screwdriver in the other. In front of me are two desks. I need to figure out a way to take them apart and reassemble them into a growing bed for Lila and Eric's hydroponics nursery.

"I could really use a saw," I mutter, staring down at the desks. I already tried using the screwdriver to separate the back from the shelves. All I managed to do was bend the screwdriver.

A scream, followed by a shout and a gunshot, brings my head whipping up.

I mentally trace the sound. It doesn't take a genius to deduce it came from downstairs. I'm on top of our living room.

I fly down to the second floor. Every instinct screams at me to rip open the stairwell door and rush to our apartment.

I don't. Instead, I press my ear against the door, listening. One voice carries, loud and commanding, but I can't make out the words.

I crack the door. The hallway is empty; the door to our apartment stands wide open.

I inch my way down the hall, hefting the knife I

239

always carry.

"Now, assholes," booms a voice. "Fill our boxes or we take this pretty little honey right now in front of all of you."

"No!" Lila's voice is shrill with panic. "Let me go!"

A chill seeps through my body. This is not good.

I think of the guns stashed under the sofa. If we survive the next few minutes, I make a silent vow to wear one at all times.

I scuttle down the hallway and peek around the open doorway. I expect to see Mr. Rosario's homeless vagabonds. Instead, I see four soldiers and three college boys, all of them with guns raised. Not a single one looks older than twenty-one or twenty-two. The college boys look even younger.

Carter, Jenna, Johnny, Reed, and Eric are in the kitchen, yanking open cupboards and pulling out precious food. They load the food into several large plastic totes on the kitchen table. Lila is pinned to the floor by one of the soldiers, a gun to the back of her neck.

"That's right," says the boy pinning Lila. "Load 'em up. Make sure you throw in those bottles of booze. We don't care if they're mostly empty. Do we, boys?"

Chuckles bubble up from the rest of the armed boys. Several of them let their eyes wander freely over Jenna as she stands on her toes to pull food off a top shelf.

"Hey, Ryan," Jenna says, "is this how you repay us for giving you a keg of beer?"

Ryan. I remember that name. This is one of the College Creek boys they met at the Depot.

One of the college kids—presumably Ryan—leers at Jenna. "You're lucky we were feeling neighborly that night," he replies. "We could have taken both kegs and then some." What he means by *and then some* is clear by the way he looks Jenna up and down. It makes me want to scratch the kid's eyeballs out.

"You lied to us," Ryan continues. "You said you lived

in Pepperwood. Imagine our surprise when we went there for a visit. All we found is a bunch of undead fuckers."

"You weren't easy to find," says the boy pinning Lila to the ground. "It wasn't until one of you idiots thought it was a good idea to smoke pot on the roof that we found you." His grin is feral. "Thank God for idiots."

I am going to kill Eric. Or Reed. Maybe both of them for good measure. Which dumb fuck thought it was a good idea to get high on the roof?

It doesn't take a genius to figure out what's going on. We're being robbed at gunpoint. And if we don't give these guys what they want, they'll take Lila instead.

Could these be the people who raped those girls and murdered the College Creek kids? The old soldier had told us to be on the lookout for other soldiers. He hadn't said anything about a combined group of students and soldiers.

"Maybe I'll take your friend here, just so you don't forget who's in charge," continues the young soldier. He pulls Lila up by the hips and grinds himself against her. "You'd like that, wouldn't you?"

Lila whimpers. I want to be sick.

"Let her go." Eric balls his fists and glares at the soldier boy with Lila. "We're getting you your supplies. You don't have to hurt her."

"Who's in charge here, motherfucker?" the soldier demands.

"I only meant—"

Ryan strides forward, shoving the barrel of his gun in Eric's nose. "You're not being useful. We have no need of people who aren't useful."

I sense the situation careening out of control. Taking a deep breath, I stride into the room and assume my best mom voice.

"I think everyone can put their guns down. Right fucking now," I say. Terror pounds through me, but I march right into the midst of the commotion and plant myself in the middle of the room.

Hands on my hips, I glare down at the kid pinning Lila. His baby face is covered with acne. His nametag reads *Johnson*.

"We'll fill your boxes." I gesture to the large crates sitting on the kitchen table. Carter, Jenna, Reed, Eric, and Johnny scurry to fill them. "You're scaring my friend. Please let her up. There's no need to terrorize her. None of us is going to fight you."

"Damn right you're not going to fight us." The boy sneers at me. "Brandy is our favorite. It'll earn you extra points if you remember that."

"Will you please let my friend up? You can see we're complying."

The boy's eyes narrow. For a moment, I fear he's going to hurt Lila just to prove a point.

"Sir, it would be a gesture of goodwill to let up the girl." Another soldier steps forward. The badge on his uniform reads *Roberts*. His handsome dark face reveals nothing as he faces off with Johnson. "They are complying with our demands."

"Whose side are you on?" Ryan asks.

Roberts tilts his head at Ryan. "Our side. We want tithers, remember? These guys won't be tithers if we hurt them."

Tithers. I have a sinking feeling I know what that means.

"Whatever," Johnson says. "This bitch is annoying me anyway. She'll change her tune once she gets to know me." He leans forward, raking his tongue along the back of her neck. When Lila chokes on a sob, he laughs. Only then does he rise and remove the gun from the back of her head.

As soon as she's freed, Lila scrambles to a far corner and huddles in a tight ball. Johnson watches her, a leer on his face. Ryan looks disgusted. Roberts' eyes flick to mine for a split second. I sense he's trying to tell me something, but I don't know what.

I hold out my hand, speaking loudly to draw Johnson's attention away from Lila. "My name is Kate. And you are?"

The kid hesitates, then extends his hand. "Private First Class Johnson." He shakes my hand.

I consider trying to negotiate some of our food back, then decide against it. The most important thing is to get this group out of here. We can figure out the food situation later. At least they haven't found our real stash in the room across the hall.

"That's it," Johnny says. "They're full."

"Take the stuff and go," I say.

Johnson narrows his eyes. "I say when we go." He struts over to the plastic totes, riffling through the contents. "Nice," he says at length. "I can see you were being generous. Keep that up and we won't have a problem."

Johnson signals to the other soldiers and college kids, confirming to me that he's the ringleader. Even Ryan complies with his instructions. Everyone holsters their weapons. They grab the crates, retreating to the door with their stolen larder. The bottles of alcohol clink inside.

"Just so you know, the university is ours," Johnson says. "Anyone living here must pay a tithe. We'll be coming around once a week to have our crates filled. If you can't pay, we'll take our tithe another way." He throws a dirty leer at Lila. She shrinks back in on herself.

"Fine," I say, moving to block Johnson's view of Lila. "We'll have your tithe."

Carter shifts behind me. I sense his rising argument. I give him my most severe mom look. The one reserved for lies, missed curfews, and bad grades. And, apparently, for telling my son to back down when there are men holding us at gunpoint.

Carter snaps his mouth closed and keeps quiet.

"We'll be back in a week," Johnson drawls. "Make sure you have enough supplies to fill our crates." The last look he casts at Lila is a warning. "Come on, brothers. We're done here for the night."

Johnson and his lackeys file out. Roberts flashes me an apologetic grimace before he slips out last. He, at least, doesn't agree with what Johnson is doing.

As soon as the last soldier is out, I slam the door and lock it. I spin around, looking at my ashen-faced kids. Lila bursts into tears, crying quietly into her knees as she huddles against the wall. Jenna hurries to her side and slips an arm around her shoulders. Eric joins her, flanking Lila on the other side.

"How did they get through our front door?" I ask.

"They were lying in wait," Jenna says. "Carter and I went outside to get water, and they pounced on us. Held us at gunpoint and forced us back inside."

I close my eyes, struggling to tamp down my rage.

"What are we going to do?" Eric asks. "We can't just hand over a shitload of stuff every week."

Even though I agree with Eric, I don't reply. I don't know what to say that won't make the situation worse.

"Do you by any chance have a tip for dealing with bad guys in that *Thrive* book you're writing?" Carter asks.

Johnny shakes his head. "No. But I bet this is the group that College Creek gunman warned us about. I guess he didn't take care of them like he said he was going to."

He's probably dead, I think.

One thing is certain. This arrangement with Johnson can only go one direction. Down. He'll demand more and more of us over time. Eventually, he'll take everything. Possibly even kill us, or worse.

Being under Johnson's thumb is bad. Very bad.

41

Hazing

KATE

I don't have a solid plan in my head when I retrieve the gun from under the sofa. I slide it into the back waistband of my pants.

When I slip outside after Johnson and the others—leaving the kids to argue about how we're going to scavenge enough food to keep Johnson's crew off our backs—all I know is that I need to find him. I want to know where that motherfucker sleeps.

Once outside, it's easy to find Johnson and his lackeys. They make enough noise to draw the dead. Literally.

It's dusk. There are no streetlights anymore, making it easy to find concealment as I tail them. I hug the side of the road, taking cover behind the tall redwoods that grow along the street.

Talking loudly, Johnson and the boys pass one of our bottles of booze between them.

"Did you see the way those pussies ran around like mice?" says Ryan.

"You did good work in there." Johnson claps him on the shoulder. "They knew who was in charge."

"Incoming," calls one of the soldiers.

Three zombies stagger toward them, arms outspread

as they grope their way forward. The group moves back toward the center of the road where there are no obstacles.

"Let me waste these fuckers." Another college kid draws his gun.

"Don't be an idiot, Henry," Johnson snaps. "Gunfire just draws more of them. Use your knife."

"Cut his balls off," says a third college kid.

"Dude, Adam, *you* cut off his balls," snaps Henry.

Adam straightens. "Watch this." Raising his knife, he advances on the three zombies. "Ryan," he calls over his shoulder, "get the one on the right. I'll take care of these two."

Ryan shrugs, passing the booze bottle to one of his companions. He draws a knife. Casually, he strolls forward and dispatches his assigned zombie with a blade through the head.

"I want to see balls, Adam," Johnson says.

Adam cuts through the first zombie, letting the body fall to the ground with a thud. By the time his attention shifts to the remaining monster, the beast has zeroed in on him. Letting out a moan, it charges and knocks Adam to the ground.

Roberts takes a step forward, but Johnson flings out a hand to stop him. "Let Adam show us what he's made of."

Even in the dark, I see the strain in Roberts's body as he watches the scene unfold. It's clear he wants to help. I can't say the same for the rest of the boys. They watch the scene with sick glee, grinning at one another as they pass the bottle between them.

"Get that fucker," cheers one of the boys.

"Get his balls!" says another.

Adam thrashes underneath the zombie, grunting as the creature snaps his teeth and goes for his throat. The boy manages to wedge one fist against the zombie's chest and roll. The zombie crashes sideways. Adam's knife finds its way into the beast's temple.

The boys break into applause. Someone hands Adam the bottle.

"Not so fast," Johnson says, snatching back the bottle. "Show us his balls, Adam."

Adam hesitates before turning back to the corpse.

I look away. When the cheering of the boys starts again, I have no doubt that Adam has indeed produced zombie testicles.

"Now you're really one of us," Johnson tells Adam.

They continue down Granite Avenue, laughing and heckling one another. I wait until their voices become indistinct before following.

A light rain starts to fall, soaking my clothes within minutes. *Idiot.* I should have thought to grab a jacket.

I try to imagine Frederico here with me. *Suck it up, buttercup*, he'd say.

The soldiers disappear into one of the frat houses at the end of the street. From the front, no one would be able to tell people are living inside. There's no trash outside. The windows are blacked out.

Johnson has done a good job disguising their occupation. I'll give him credit for that, even as I shiver to think how close it is to Creekside. It's dumb luck they didn't find us before.

I crouch behind decomposing bodies as the group clomps around to the back of the house. As soon as they're out of sight, I hurry after them.

The back of the house looks pretty much like you'd expect the yard of a frat house to look. Lots of lawn chairs and sofas, many of them faded from years of use. Multiple barbecues. At the back is a stage with lights. Trash is everywhere. Some of it is in bags, but most is loose. Most of it is discarded cans and food packaging.

Kneeling in the darkness, I watch and listen. There isn't much to be heard, but there is the occasional creak of floorboards or the sound of a raised voice.

I steal closer, stepping onto the porch. A refrigerator sits next to the door, along with a collection of battered wooden chairs.

The house is old, a relic from the early nineteen hundreds. The redwood, even after all these years, is solid beneath my feet. A few of the steps creak, which makes me pause in alarm, but no one inside notices.

I press my ear against the back door. Inside comes the muffled sound of voices and music.

They're having a party. They extort us, terrorize us, and threaten us. Then throw a party.

I understand the sickos we're dealing with.

Now I just have to figure out my next move.

*

"Foot Soldier, this is Kate. Are you there? Over."

I sit alone in the living room, staring at the cluttered kitchen table. By now, everyone has gone to bed. A blanket drapes across my shoulders as I hunch over the ham radio.

"Foot Soldier? I know it's the middle of the night. I've never been a great sleeper. Over."

No response.

I think of Carter, see his frantic, worried eyes when I returned home a few hours ago.

"Mom, where have you been?" he demanded.

"Out," I replied, unsure how much I wanted to share.

"Out where?"

"Just . . . out. I needed to think."

"You can't go out alone," he said. "It's not safe. You see that, right?"

My son. I love him so much. I care about all these kids. I need to figure out a way to keep them safe.

Scenes from the day replay in my head. I see Johnson grinding himself against Lila. I see Johnson coercing Adam into a sick apocalyptic hazing ritual.

We'll be back in a week. Make sure you have enough supplies to fill our crates.

How long will we be able to keep those crates filled? How long before they demand more? How long before Johnson just takes the other things he wants?

"Kate, is that you? Over."

I close my eyes, raising the ham to my mouth. "Foot Soldier. Yeah. It's me."

"What are you doing up? Over."

"We had a run-in with some bad guys today."

"What kind of bad guys?" Alvarez drops the official radio talk.

"The kind you would expect in an apocalypse," I reply, swallowing. "They're bad people."

A long pause. "You can come here. You know you have an open invitation."

"I've looked at the maps. There's no way to get to Fort Ross without backtracking down highway one-oh-one for a hundred miles. One-oh-one is a death trap."

Another long pause. "Then you have to work something out."

"I know." My words come out a whisper. "It's just . . . I'm not coming up with anything that doesn't involve murder."

My words float around me in the darkness, made real and tangible now that I've let them out of my mouth.

"I've been where you are," Alvarez says. "I know, Kate. I know. My journey to Fort Ross was . . . hard."

I squeeze my eyes shut. Alvarez has made hard choices, too. Knowing this makes me feel not so alone.

"But it wasn't all bad," Alvarez continues. "I met some good people. Some of them seemed like bad people at first, but they were just scared. Maybe your situation isn't as bad as you think it is."

I can't bring myself to describe Johnson with Lila, or the hazing incident with Adam. They aren't pictures I want to paint.

But not all the kids are dark. Roberts wasn't like Johnson. Maybe there are others like Roberts.

"Here's something to consider," Alvarez says. "Human beings are few and far between. We can use friends more than we can use enemies. Maybe you can find a middle ground with these guys."

"I don't know. They held us at gunpoint."

"I held you at gunpoint when we first met."

That brings a smile to my face. I'd forgotten about that. "Actually, you tackled us to the ground. Then you held us at gunpoint."

"Whatever. My point is, look how it turned out for us. Don't write these guys off because of one encounter."

"What if you're wrong?" I ask. "I don't think these guys are like you. I think . . . I think they may have raped and killed."

A long stretch of silence follows this statement.

"Are you sure?" he asks at length.

"Mostly sure."

Alvarez lets out a long sigh. "If you're right, you only have one choice. Survival can be shitty. Feel things out. You can do this, Kate."

"I hope so," I whisper back. *God, I hope so.*

42
Assignments

KATE

"How's Lila?" I ask when Jenna and Carter emerge the next morning.

Jenna shakes her head. "She won't look at us. She has her head covered up with the blankets."

The poor girl was borderline agoraphobic before our run-in with Johnson. No doubt that will be worse after last night.

"I need you guys to scavenge today," I tell Carter and Jenna, showing them the pieces of paper before me. Each is labeled with the name of the four other dorms in the complex where we live: Juniper, Fern, Laurel, and Willow.

"These buildings need to be cleared and inventoried," I say. "Start with Fern today. Clear the rooms. Make a list of everything you find, but don't bring anything back here."

Carter takes the paper and pen from me. "This is for our tithe, isn't it?"

I nod, jaw clenched. "We don't want to be caught without enough food to fill their bins, but I don't want them to know how much we have. Do your workouts, then head to Fern. Oh, and one more thing. If you find a bottle of brandy, bring it back to me."

Johnny, Eric, and Reed wander out an hour later,

rubbing at their eyes.

"I have a job for you today," I announce, not giving them a chance to flop onto the sofa or go for the food.

"What sort of job?" Reed asks.

"Clearance." I hand them a sheet of paper with the name *Willow* written across the top. It's another neighboring dorm. The boys get the same instructions I gave Jenna and Carter.

"Clear out Willow. Make a list of everything you find that might be useful to us."

"But . . ." Johnny frowns at me. "Is that the best use of our time? Shouldn't we be packing up our stuff and leaving Creekside?"

"Where are we going to go?" I ask him. "Traveling is more dangerous than staying here. And Creekside is our home. You guys cleared this place and made it safe. It's fortified and well stocked. We're not letting anyone take it away from us."

"Okaaay." Johnny draws out the word, studying my face. "Whatever you say, Kate."

"Search for a bottle of brandy," I say. "If you find one, bring it back."

"What about Lila?" Eric asks. His gaze drifts to her closed bedroom door.

"I'll keep an eye on her," I say. "She'll be okay."

In the end, Eric leaves with the others. When I finally have everyone out of the apartment, I poke my head into Lila's room. She lays on her side in the bed, staring at the wall.

"Lila?" I sit down next to her, resting one hand on her shoulder. "How are you doing?"

She stares at the wall.

"Lila? Can I get you anything?"

She rolls over to look at me. Her almond eyes are puffy and unfocused. Her silky black hair is a messy halo around her face. "Do you know what it's like to be average in a family of geniuses?"

Her question catches me by surprise. "What?"

"Do you know what it's like to be average in a family of geniuses?"

"No, I don't. My family was pretty average." What is she trying to tell me?

"I'm the youngest of three sisters," Lila replies. "My oldest sister got a full academic ride to U.C. Berkley. My middle sister got a tennis scholarship to Stanford. Guess where I got a scholarship to."

"Humboldt?"

"Nowhere. I got a few dinky local scholarships, but nothing like my sisters. I was always the dull coin in the family. I was the one never mentioned to my aunties and uncles.

"But I have a plan. I studied articles on the cannabis industry in Colorado when that state legalized it. I know the money that was made by the people who got their foot in the door early. Cannabis is going to be legalized in all the states in the next decade. When I graduate from this place with my degree in botany, I'm going to start my own business with medicinal cannabis. I'm going to make more money than both my sisters. I'm going to give my mom something to brag about."

I search Lila's face. Her eyes are glassy, her skin pale. She hugs a pillow in her arms. She is dead serious.

"I know you'll make your mother proud," I reply, not knowing what else to say.

"I don't care if she's proud." Lila rolls away to once again face the wall. "I just want her to brag about me to my aunties and uncles. And I want to drive a Tesla to a family reunion."

I stare at Lila's back. She doesn't say anything else. When I finally lean over her to check, I see she's fallen asleep.

The poor girl is cracking. I've seen the world chipping away at her day by day, but last night's run-in with Johnson has traumatized her.

I don't know what to do. I'm no therapist.

Alvarez's words run through my head. *Survival can be shitty.*

*

It takes the kids two days to clear Fern and Willow. They manage to find not one, not two, but three bottles of brandy. They're all half empty, but that won't matter for my purposes.

"Now what?" Carter asks me. "Should we start gathering up the supplies and bringing them back here?"

"Not yet. There are two more dorms to clear and inventory." I hand out two more sheets of paper, one labeled *Juniper* and one labeled *Laurel.*

"Wouldn't it be better if we start transporting the food back here?" Jenna asks.

"Not yet," I say. "We need to focus on inventory and clearance."

"Do you need more brandy?" Reed asks.

"Nope. These three bottles are all I need."

No one asks what I plan to do with them. They all remember Johnson likes brandy.

"I guess you're right," Johnny says. "We have enough stuff for when those jerks come back. Though I'd feel better if the food were with us."

"Trust me on this," I reply.

"Come on, Carter." Jenna takes his hand, tugging him toward the door. "Let's go. The zombies won't clear themselves."

After they leave, I take the list of Fern supplies and tuck it into my pocket.

Next, I gather the three bottles of brandy. I carefully combine everything into a single bottle. When I'm finished, I have a single bottle of golden-brown liquid.

Just what Johnson likes.

On an errand, I scrawl on a scrap of paper, leaving it

on top of the ham radio where they're sure to see it. *Be back later. Don't come looking for me.*

I drop trail mix, a flashlight, and two bottles of water into a backpack. The last thing I put inside is the brandy, wrapping it in a towel to protect it. I take one of the guns from my hiding place under the sofa and stash it in my jacket pocket. Then I leave Creekside.

Carter won't be happy to find out I've gone out alone, but it can't be helped. I don't want to involve him or any of the others in my errand.

43
Errand

KATE

I return to the frat house, taking up position across the street behind some bushes. Zipping up my jacket and pulling the brim of a hat low to shade my eyes, I sit down and settle in to wait.

The house is quiet and dark. If I hadn't seen the group go in a few nights ago, I'd never guess this is where they lived.

The sun is high in the sky before I finally see signs of life. Two of the boys step onto the front porch to pee over the railing before returning inside. Neither of them are the one I'm looking for.

I munch on trail mix as the sun crawls toward the western horizon. The only sounds are those of the buzzing flies and the squawking vultures as they feast on the dead. If those two creatures ever go extinct, I will shed no tears.

I hear voices coming from the backyard of the frat house. They carry on for half an hour, then disappear.

Dusk comes. Still, I wait. They have to come out sooner or later. I don't care how long it takes.

Night falls. Under the cover of darkness, I creep into the backyard. The side yard next to the house is overgrown with weeds almost as tall as I am. I wade into them, stealing up to the side of the back porch. I flick on a flashlight.

As I had hoped, the siding along the bottom of the porch is rotting. I push against the boards with my foot. They crumble under the pressure like wet cardboard.

Doing my best not to think about spiders and rats, I drop to my stomach and crawl underneath. Once there, I spread out my tarp and pull the hood of my jacket over my head. The dull sound of voices comes from inside.

I think of poor Lila. The memory of her dull eyes makes me want to scream. If I can figure things out with Johnson, will she recover? Will she ever be able to adjust to the new state of things?

At some point, I drift into dreamless sleep.

I'm awakened by the sounds of boots on the floorboards overhead. My eyes snap open. I roll my freezing fingers into fists. I'm so cold I can hardly move.

I lay still as boots clomp on the boards directly above my head. A moment later, a long stream of urine hits the grass a foot away from my head. I recoil, drawing farther beneath the porch.

"Good haul from those tithers," says the boy above me. Not Roberts. It's Ryan, the college boy. "What do you think they'll have for us when we go back in a few days? Think they'll find Johnson a bottle of brandy?"

A grunt comes in response. Another stream of urine hits the grass on the opposite side of the porch.

I crawl through the dirt and weeds, trying to catch a glimpse of the second person. Spiders and cobwebs are everywhere. You'd think I'd be immune to creepy critters after dealing with zombies and dead bodies, but nope. Spiders are still icky.

A third stream of urine hits the ground somewhere in the middle of the porch. "There's more I want than brandy." This statement is followed by a lewd laugh.

Gooseflesh pricks my skin. Johnson's voice is unmistakable.

"I want the tall one," says Ryan.

"Patience, brother," Johnson says. "Good things come to those who wait."

"You guys are crossing the line," says the third boy. His voice is hard and angry.

Roberts. Finally.

He's the one on the far side of the porch. I army crawl the rest of the way toward him, wondering how best to get his attention.

"Calm down, brother," Johnson says, voice going from lewd to silky. "We didn't mean anything by it. Did we?"

"Nah," Ryan says. "I was just fucking around."

"Making them tithe food to us is one thing," Roberts says. "But that's as far as it-it—"

He falters as I shove a blade of grass up between the boards by his feet. We make eye contact through a knothole.

Don't give me away, I think as hard as I can, hoping Roberts will receive my silent message.

"Did you have something to say?" Johnson asks.

Roberts spins on his heel, zipping up his fly. "We should give them protection for the food. Give them something in return."

Johnson snorts. "We let them live, brother."

"That's not living," Roberts replies. "That's letting a nest of resentment grow. Offering them protection makes them beholden to us."

"We don't have to give them anything," Ryan scoffs.

"We have the guns," Johnson points out. That smarmy smugness is back in his voice.

"You're my brother," Roberts says after a long pause. "I follow where you lead. Just think on it, okay?"

Johnson's boots clomp on the boards as he heads back inside. "Sure thing. You coming in? Ash is going to make pancakes."

"Can you believe we got pancakes off those losers?"

Ryan says.

"I'm going to have a smoke," Roberts replies. "I'll join you in a few."

Johnson and Ryan go back inside, the door closing behind them without a squeak. I take note of this, wondering if the door was well greased before the apocalypse.

I crawl back to the hole I kicked in the bottom of the porch and emerge into the daylight. Roberts watches me, taking a long drag off a cigarette. I wipe a cobweb off my face, glancing around to make sure we're alone.

"No one else is here," Roberts murmurs. He grabs a chair and pulls it over to the railing closest to me. "You're lucky I didn't piss on you."

"Honestly, if I had to choose between piss and spiders, I'd probably pick piss."

"Really?"

"No."

He flashes a small grin at me before taking another drag off his cigarette. "How long were you under there?"

"All night."

"You must have something important to say to me."

I study his handsome face. Dark eyes, perfect skin, classic military haircut. He's not a guy to fuck with, but he doesn't give off the same predatory vibe as Johnson and Ryan.

"I want to make an offer to Johnson. Will you help me?"

"What kind of offer?"

"Creekside is our home. We want to live in peace."

Roberts snorts. "I don't think there's going to be peace for a long time, lady."

"Kate."

"What?"

"My name is Kate. And I heard what you said to Johnson about creating a nest of resentment." I meet his eyes. "You weren't wrong."

Roberts shakes his head, letting out a lungful of smoke. "You heard him. He's not interested in doing things differently."

"Give me a chance to convince him."

"What do you want me to do?"

"Take me inside. Give me a chance to talk to him."

Roberts waves an expansive hand at the frat house. "Door's open, Kate. Go on in and talk."

"I'd like to speak to him without having a gun in my face. That's not talking."

Roberts looks away, turning his gaze to the frat yard. "One of the first attacks was here," he says. "An infected girl turned and went ballistic at a party. Bit a bunch of other kids. Everything pretty much went to shit after that. Ironic that Johnson picked this place as our headquarters." He lets out a long, silent breath. "Johnson changed with the world. He wasn't always a bad guy."

"I'm not here to judge him," I reply. I couldn't give two shits about Johnson being a good guy before the apocalypse. "I want to find a way to live in peace with him. With all of you. In case you hadn't noticed, there aren't a lot of people left. We can work against each other, or we can work with each other."

"You sound like a politician."

"I'm a mom. I'm trying to protect my family. I heard what you said. You know what Johnson is doing is wrong."

Slowly, I lay out the negotiation I've constructed in my head. I show him the bottle of brandy and the paper with the list of supplies in Fern. Roberts listens, sucking away on his cigarette as I talk.

"Help me," I say when I finish. "Please."

Roberts looks me up and down. "You lay under the porch all night for a chance to talk to Johnson?"

"To talk to *you*," I correct. "You were the only one I was pretty sure wouldn't shoot me on principle."

"You're not wrong." Roberts stubs his cigarette out.

"I'll take you inside. I can't promise he'll agree to your offer, but I can keep him from blowing your head off."

"That's all I'm asking. Thank you, Roberts."

"Don't thank me yet." He rises. "Come up here. Let me pat you down."

I climb onto the porch, holding out my arms. "I have one gun. Right pocket."

Roberts pats me down, taking my gun and tucking it into his waistband. He lets me keep my knife, probably figuring I'm not much of a threat with it.

He isn't wrong. I might be able to take down a zombie, but it's unlikely I could take on any of the boys with it.

"You sure about this?" Roberts asks.

I nod. "Yeah."

"All right," he says. "Let's go get pancakes."

44
Pancakes

KATE

The bottle of brandy is heavy in my hands. As I follow Roberts into the house, I carry it in front of me like a shield. Like I can hide behind a glass bottle.

The back door opens into a large kitchen. Yellowed linoleum covers the floor. The cupboards are beat-up red oak that look like they were installed in the nineties. Christmas lights are tacked to the top of the cupboards, dormant with the lack of electricity.

Past the kitchen is an archway that leads into a sitting room. A large pool table fills half the opening. Surrounded by chairs, it looks like it does double duty as the dining room table.

Beyond the table is a mishmash of sofas. The boys are sprawled around a coffee table playing cards as they pass around a bottle of tequila.

Yuck. Tequila for breakfast? With pancakes? I'm sure that never made it onto any restaurant menu. Ever.

A girl in military fatigue pants stands at the kitchen table flipping pancakes on a propane camp stove. Like everyone else, she looks to be in her early twenties. Thick black hair is swept into a ponytail. Her wife beater tank top shows off well-muscled arms. She could be a poster child for CrossFit.

"I'm glad it's the apocalypse," she says without looking up as we enter. "Sooner or later you're going to run out of cigarettes. You won't—who the hell is that?" Her eyes narrow as she catches sight of me, her hand going to her gun.

"Woah, Ash." Roberts holds up his hands. "This is Kate. She's just here to talk. She's from the tithe group we established the other night."

From first glance, I wouldn't have thought the boys in the other room were paying attention to anything beyond their cards and their tequila. As soon as Roberts speaks, they explode into action.

Cards fly into the air as the boys leap to their feet. The soldiers draw their weapons. The college boys also pull out firearms, though not with the smooth efficiency of the soldiers.

Ash goes back to flipping the pancakes, letting the boys handle the situation. I try to get a read on her, but she's mastered inscrutable.

"What the fuck, Roberts?" Johnson demands.

"Kate is here to have breakfast with us," Roberts replies, unruffled by the agitated boys with guns. "She wants to talk."

"Unless she wants to suck me off, there's nothing to talk about," Johnson retorts.

My grip tightens on the brandy.

"Can you all just calm the fuck down?" Roberts asks. "She's just here to talk."

"How did you find us?" Johnson asks. "We don't advertise our location."

I bypass the question. "I brought a peace offering." I step around Roberts, displaying the bottle of brandy. I make eye contact with Johnson. I want to smash the bottle in his face, but I force my best mom smile. The one that promises cinnamon rolls and a cup of hot chocolate for good little boys. "Word has it that you like brandy. I had this bottle dug up especially for you."

A slow smile spreads across Johnson's face. I remember that smug, feral expression from the other night. "Why didn't you say so?" He holsters his gun. "Come on in."

I stay beside Roberts. I trust him to keep me in one piece, but he can't do that if I'm on the other side of the room.

Together, we cross to the pool table. I place the bottle of brandy on the worn green felt. My palms are sweaty from nerves. I press them flat against the table, meeting Johnson's gaze with a level stare of my own.

"Would you like a pancake, Kate?" Roberts asks.

"That sounds good," I reply. Seeing the bag of Krusteaz on the table makes my blood boil. That was *our* pancake mix.

I take a seat. Within fifteen minutes, everyone is gathered around the pool table eating pancakes. A bottle of Aunt Jemima syrup is passed around.

My stomach feels like lead. The last thing I want to do is eat, but I force down a bite. If it's one thing I learned from ultrarunning, it's how to push forward with a bad stomach.

No one speaks. The only sound is that of forks against plates. The boys stare at me with a mixture of curiosity, distrust, and arrogance. I count nine altogether. Four soldiers and five college boys, plus Ash, who is still in the kitchen making pancakes. What does she think of all this?

"So, Kate," Johnson drawls between bites. "What is it you wanted to talk about?"

I gauge the room as I take a bite of my pancake, determining the best way to move forward. Playing the scared sympathy card won't get me anywhere with this bunch. Neither will bravado or threats.

In the end, I decide to play the mom card. It's the one I know best, and it worked to some extent last night. A mom offering a reasonable compromise, not a mom trying to cram her opinion down a kid's throat.

"I want to talk about neighbors," I reply.

He snorts. "As in, we're neighbors?"

"Exactly." I set my fork down. "It used to be that everyone had neighbors. Sometimes you couldn't get away from them. I could tell you about periods of my life where I went out of my way to avoid certain neighbors."

A small murmur of agreement runs around the table as everyone continues to shovel pancakes into their mouths.

"These days, neighbors are scarce. If you want to play cards with a friend, you're shit out of luck because there are no neighbors. If you need someone to help you move furniture, you're shit out of luck because there are no neighbors." I tilt my head, letting my gaze linger on Johnson. "My point is, there are benefits to neighbors. We help each other out. We bring each other gifts." I gesture to the bottle of brandy.

"We don't need gifts," Ryan sneers. "We take what we need."

"Everyone needs gifts," I reply. "Everyone needs favors. Roberts." I turn to him. He sits to my left. "Would you mind reaching into my pocket and pulling out the paper there? I'd do it myself, but I don't want anyone to think I have a weapon."

Roberts complies. His hand dips into the pocket of my coat and emerges with the folded piece of paper. I take it from him and smooth it out on the table.

"This is a list of all the supplies in the Fern dorm," I say. "My kids cleared it. I'm giving it to you, Johnson. You and your people. A gift. A kindness. That's what neighbors do for each other. There's enough rations in there to feed you guys for a month."

His eyes narrow at me. "We don't need favors. We take what we need."

"Think of the big picture," I say. "You could have us working with you. We can clear buildings together. Your people and my people. We split everything fifty-fifty. You'll have more supplies that way. We can watch each other's backs. Everyone wins. It can be good to have neighbors."

"I don't see how we win in that scenario," Johnson says. "Sounds to me like you're trying to get us to do work for you."

I shake my head. "A community goes further when everyone works together. It doesn't have to be you and us. We can be on the same side. The real battle is out there." I pick up my fork, jabbing in the direction of the university. "The undead. We should be fighting them, not each other." I spear a piece of pancake and shove it in my mouth to keep from saying more. I'm skating too close to a mom lecture. That won't get me anywhere.

"Huh." Johnson grunts and returns to his pancakes. "Ash, bring me another hot one, will you?" When she delivers the requested pancake, he slaps her on the ass.

Ash whirls and slaps his hand with her spatula. Johnson bursts out laughing. The other boys all laugh, too. Ash, spine stiff, stalks back into the kitchen.

Johnson digs into his pancake. He watches me as he eats, chewing loudly. I return his stare, eating my pancake. I feel like throwing up. I've never been this nervous in my life.

This is for Carter, I remind myself. *For Carter and everyone else.* I have to keep them alive and safe.

"Do you want another one?" Johnson points his fork at my empty plate. "Neighbors cook for each other, don't they?"

"They do," I reply.

"Ash," Johnson barks. "Get our neighbor another pancake." He saunters around the table in my direction.

As Ash brings a pancake to me, the golden circle balanced on top of the spatula, Johnson smiles at me. Ash deposits the pancake on my plate, expression blank.

"Syrup?" Johnson holds out the bottle of Aunt

Jemima to me.

Unease slithers through me, but I force a smile. "Yes, thank you."

His eyes never leaving mine, Johnson pours the syrup over the top of my pancake.

His free hand whips out. It connects with the back of my head, slamming my face down into the plate. Hard.

Pain bursts behind my eyes and forehead. I reel back, syrup and mashed pancake on my face.

"Is this neighborly enough for you?" Johnson grabs a fistful of my hair, dragging me backward out of my chair. Then he shoves me, sending me sprawling across the dirty linoleum. The boys whoop, cheering him on.

"Kick her ass," one of them shouts.

"Show her who's boss," calls another.

Ash has abandoned her camp stove. She's cleared out of the kitchen, hovering just inside the sitting room. Her face is impassive, but her skin has paled. Her knuckles are white around the spatula.

Johnson leers down at me, advancing. I scrabble to my feet and back up, bumping up against the counter on the far wall.

Johnson laughs, a big booming sound that scissors across every nerve in my body.

He knows how to fight and kill. He's bigger and stronger and trained. I can't stand against him. The only way I'm going to make it out of this alive is if I surprise him. That means letting him get close enough to hit me again. I'll go for my knife when he strikes. It will be my one and only chance.

I swallow as he draws closer. His boots caress the linoleum, barely making a sound as he stalks near. I brace myself, mentally preparing myself for his next blow. My heart hammers with fear. It takes all my willpower not to turn and run.

Roberts steps between us. His arms hang at his side, hands loose. "I promised Kate she wouldn't be harmed," he says.

The boys around the pool table boo. "Why'd you do a dumb shit thing like that for?" one calls.

Johnson shoulders up to Roberts. The two young men are nose to nose. Roberts doesn't back down.

"Get the fuck out of my way," Johnson snarls.

"I gave her my word, Johnson," Roberts replies. "You know what that means."

"Fuck your word. Get out of my way."

"No."

"Motherfucker." Johnson is the first to back down. "God damn motherfucker."

Roberts glances over his shoulder at me. "Get out of here," he says.

I don't have to be told twice. I turn and run. I run hard and fast, not slowing or stopping until I get back to Creekside.

45
Eavesdropping

JENNA

"Where is she?" Carter brings both fists down on the back of the sofa.

He's asked this question at least a hundred times during the night. Seeing the anguish on his face makes my heart split in two.

I wish I could tell him where Kate was. I wish I could tell him why she left.

I wish there weren't two empty brandy bottles on the counter. I wish the third bottle wasn't missing.

"I don't understand where she could have gone or what's taking her so long." Carter paces up and down the dorm living room. "She's been gone the entire night!"

I don't point out that Kate survived outside for several days when she journeyed here on foot. She knows what she's doing out there. That won't make Carter feel better. It doesn't make me feel better. My anxiety ratchets up every minute that passes without her return.

Johnny, Eric, and Reed are with us, all of us having stayed up the entire night waiting for Kate to come back. We even left the downstairs door unlocked for her.

"Did you know your mom beat a guy with a metal chair?" Johnny asks.

"What?" Carter stops his pacing.

"Yeah," Johnny says. "When you guys were stuck in that rock shop. She went ape shit on one of those drug guys. He had a gun, but your mom charged straight at him and started beating him with the chair. He ran away like a little kid."

"Our mama did that for us?" Reed sighs happily. "I'm so glad I adopted her."

"Are you serious?" Carter asks. "You're not exaggerating?"

"No, man. Your mom turned into a total she-demon. I know you're worried about her. We all are. But your mom is insane. She'll be okay."

Carter returns to pacing. "My mom is tough. I know that. But she's been missing for almost twenty-four hours." He grips his head in both hands, pulling on his hair. "I have to look for her."

"Her note said not to come looking for her," Eric reminds him.

"I don't care what the note says," Carter growls. "My mom is out there somewhere. She could be hurt, or-or—"

The door opens.

Kate bursts inside. Her hair is matted and wet. Cobwebs cling to her clothing. Dirt smudges every exposed part of her body—her hands, her neck, and her face. A huge bruise swells on the front of her face. Dried blood crusts her upper lip. Bits of shiny brown residue are smeared across her face. Pale crumbs of something are stuck to the brown stuff. Her breathing is loud, her chest heaving like she's just run hard and fast.

She stands in the doorway, eyes wild.

I watch her wrestle with her emotions, watch her rein back whatever terror or fear drove her back to us.

Her breath slows. She swallows and closes her eyes.

When she opens them again, the Kate we all know and love looks out at us.

"What are you all doing here?" The slight hitch in her voice is the only indication of her true mental state.

Her voice is like a trigger. We all leap to our feet and rush her. Carter gets there first, wrapping her in a bear hug. Reed and I are right behind him, throwing our arms around them both. Eric and Johnny join in, the six of us standing in a group hug.

"Mom, where were you?" Carter demands. "We were worried."

"I didn't say it, but I thought the zombies got you for sure," Reed says. "I didn't say it out loud, but in my head, I was like, Kate is zombie food. My mama is dead."

"I thought you went back to Trading Post to get more shoes." Johnny leans back to look at her. "You didn't go back to Trading Post, did you?"

"She didn't go to get shoes," I snap. "Kate, let me get you a washcloth for your face." An ice pack is also in order, except there's no ice anymore.

"That would be nice, Jenna. Thank you." Kate extracts herself from the pack, crossing the kitchen to sink into a chair.

Carter gets her a bottle of water. "What happened to your face, Mom?"

Kate cracks open the water and downs half of it in a long gulp.

"Mom." It doesn't take a genius to see that Carter is about to lose it.

"My face had a close-up conference with a pancake and syrup. Thanks, Jenna." She takes a wet cloth from me and scrubs at what is apparently syrup and pancake on her face.

"A pancake? Mom, what the hell happened?"

Kate sighs. She sets down the cloth and squeezes Carter's hand.

"I'm sorry I worried you. I went to talk to Johnson."

Silence. We all stare at her. Is the woman completely insane?

Kate winces under the weight of our incredulity. She resumes scrubbing at her face.

"I tried to negotiate a peace treaty with him," she explains. "It didn't go well. Hence, my face meeting the pancake."

"He could have killed you," I say.

"That's why I went alone," Kate replies. "I knew it was a long shot, but I had to try. I didn't want to put anyone else at risk."

Carter yanks out a chair and flops into it. "God, Mom. You scared us to death."

"I'm sorry, baby." She gives us a short retelling of her overnight adventure, which included sleeping underneath a porch with spiders. "I had to try," she finishes. "For you, Carter." She looks up at the rest of us. "For all of you."

"Promise me you'll never do that again," Carter says.

The rest of us murmur in agreement. Kate looks away.

"Mom." Carter's voice takes on an edge.

"I promise, baby."

Am I the only one who sees the lie in her eyes?

"I'm serious, Mom. Promise me."

Her eyes sober. "I promise to keep you safe, Carter." She looks up at the rest of us. "I promise to keep all of you safe."

*

"Babe?" Carter stirs in the bed next to me as I sit up. "You okay?"

"I can't sleep." I keep my voice to a whisper so as not to disturb Lila. Not that Lila responds to much since Johnson's assault.

He exhales sharply, sitting up beside me. "Me, neither. I was just pretending because I thought you were sleeping." He scrubs a hand through his hair.

The moon outside the window is full. I love the way the light plays on the angles of his face.

"Do you think she was telling the truth?" I ask.

Carter doesn't ask who I'm talking about. "She was holding something back. I could tell. I just don't know what."

I nod, staring at the closed bedroom door and wondering if Kate is awake. It's no secret she was shaken by her encounter with Johnson, even though she tried to hide it from us. After she got back, she spent several hours napping on a sleeping bag in the living room.

Except I don't think she was really napping. Her eyes were closed, her back to us, but I never got the sense she was asleep. It felt like she was hiding from us.

It probably doesn't help we spent the day buzzing around her and fretting. The third time Reed offered to massage her shoulders, I think she was ready to throw something.

"I'm worried about her, too." A lump of emotion swells in my throat just thinking about what she risked for us. "I love that she wants to take care of us, but she doesn't need to fight this battle alone."

"She doesn't have to protect us. She needs to work *with* us."

"I know." I get out of bed and cross to the closed door. Carter pads after me. Hand in hand, we open the door and stare down the short hall that leads to the living room.

The room is dark, but not silent. A soft sound comes from the kitchen, but I can't tell what it is.

My eyes adjust after a minute. Then I see it: a lone shadow pacing back and forth.

Kate.

I nudge Carter. He nods, letting me know he's also seen her.

Is she okay? Should we go talk to her?

Kate leans against the kitchen table, hanging her head. Her shoulders shake.

She's crying.

I shift, ready to head out and comfort her. To find out what's really going on. Carter stills me with a hand on my arm.

Kate lifts something off the table. "Foot Soldier, are you there? It's Kate. Over."

The answer comes immediately. "I'm here, Kate. I've been waiting to hear from you."

Silence. Kate's breath hitches.

"Kate? You there? Over."

"I'm here."

"You okay?"

"Not really." Her voice wavers. A single, silent sob wracks her body. "You know how you said we need each other more than we need enemies?"

"Yeah. I remember."

"Well, turns out not everyone agrees with that statement. Those fuckers definitely don't agree with it."

"It's okay, Kate."

"It's not fucking okay!" Her voice is a whisper-shout. "I'm not fucking okay."

"I get it." Alvarez's voice is smooth and comforting. "I've been where you are. I know what you're going through. It's shitty. You could always run."

"No fucking way." Kate's voice is soft but vehement. "I spent half my life running away from problems. I don't run anymore."

"Doing the smart thing isn't the same thing as running away."

"Running isn't the smart thing. You've seen the roads. You know what waits out there. Traveling by car is risky. Traveling by foot is near impossible if you're not like me."

Alvarez doesn't argue this point. The ham is silent in Kate's hands.

"Oh, God." Her voice is ragged. "I can't let them hurt my kids."

"No. You can't."

Kate drops into a chair, slumping over the kitchen table with the ham pressed against her face. "I don't want to do this."

"You have to. You tried the peaceful way out. It's not your fault they spit in your face. Do you have a plan?"

"Yeah."

"Is it a good plan or a half-assed one?"

I watch the silhouette of Kate's back expand as she sucks in a ragged breath. "It's a good plan."

"Do you need to talk through the details?"

"No."

"Did I ever tell you that when I first saw you and Frederico running through the woods in Laytonville, I pegged you for two country hicks who smoked too much pot in the sixties?"

"I was born in the seventies," Kate replies drily.

"Whatever. You know what I mean. What I'm trying to say is that when you buried Frederico's daughter, I knew I'd misjudged you. I knew you were a tough mama bear and nothing was going to stand in your way. I knew you'd make it to Arcata. When you guys left the bar, I knew you'd make it."

"Is this your idea of a pep talk? Frederico died not long after we left the bar."

I glance up at Carter to see how he's taking this. His face is stony.

"But *you* didn't die. You're the mama bear. Mama bears are some of the most dangerous animals out there. No one fucks with mama bears, Kate."

"No one fucks with mama bears," she repeats.

She sits in silence for a long while. Slowly, her spine straightens. Her chin lifts. Resolve infuses every line of her body.

"Thanks, Alvarez. I'll talk to you tomorrow. Over and out."

"Over and out, Mama Bear. Take no prisoners."

46
Premeditated

KATE

I think back to the times in my life I've endured unpleasant things for my son. Cleaned dog poop off his shoes. Washed his vomit out of my hair after a particularly bad case of the stomach flu. Sometimes, as a mom, you just have to do shitty things for the sake of your kids. It's what you sign up for.

There are a lot of murder metaphors in the mom world. Plenty of moms, myself included, talk about wanting to strangle the bully on the play yard or wanting to kill the shitty ex of their child. We even sometimes talk about wanting to murder our own kids when they do something epically stupid, like steal the car keys or sneak out of the house.

Back before the world ended, plenty of people bantered around terms like "kill" and "murder."

There is no bantering in the new world. No metaphors.

Jenna might not be my biological child, but I still feel a maternal responsibility for her. I've grown to care for her and all of Carter's friends. I'm not going to sit around and wait for Johnson to give Ryan permission to rape her. Or for Johnson to rape Lila.

That's what waits for both girls. Maybe not

tomorrow. Maybe not a month from now. But soon.

Johnson has to die.

The words play repeatedly in my head like a skipping record player.

Johnson has to die. They all have to die.

I don't think too hard on what I have to do. If I analyze or dwell on it, I'll lose my nerve. Premeditated murder isn't exactly something I've had practice or training in.

I slip out of Creekside and into the night. When I reach the frat house, I kneel in the dark to watch and listen. There isn't much to be heard, but there is the occasional creak of floorboards or the sound of a raised voice.

I steal closer and slip around back, stepping onto the porch. I press my ear up against the back door. Inside comes the muffled sound of voices and music.

I study the voices, just to make sure. Yes, the telltale signs are there. The brandy is doing its work.

I consider my options as the sound of their laughter washes over me.

Pillowcases. That's what I need for the next part of my plan.

I enter the nearest dorm, one with shot-up windows and bodies spilled all along the walkways and planters. My shoes crunch on shell casings as I step around the dead. Dried blood is sticky underfoot. The smell gags me. I breathe through my mouth, doing my best to ignore the stench.

I draw my knife and flashlight. A moan sounds off to the left. My flashlight beam darts that way, illuminating a zombie girl under a bookcase. Her torso is pinned. Grooves have been carved into the linoleum floor from her scrabbling fingers. Her sightless white eyes roll, her nostrils flaring as she scents the air.

I step through the gore and shove my knife through her skull. I make it quick, both for myself and the girl.

As I straighten, something grabs my ankle. I yelp as I'm pulled off my feet. The flashlight and knife fly out of my hand, clattering as they hit the wall. I land hard on a dead body. Under normal circumstances—whatever those are these days—I would have noticed the awful squish of a rotting body. But all my attention is on the thing clinging to my ankle.

A single keen fills the room, sending another spike of alarm through me. I struggle into a sitting position, my free hand landing in the ruined cavity of the dead college kid beneath me.

The grip around my ankle is like a shackle. The crazy angle of the flashlight casts shadows on the zombie that drags me across the floor. I kick out with my free foot. When I connect, a viscous growl rakes the air, but my trapped ankle is not released.

I see it. A round shape in the dark, white eyes reflecting green like a cat's in the indirect glow of the light. Teeth gnash.

I kick a second time, driving the heel of my shoe toward the face. The crack of its nose is audible, the soft cartilage crumpling under my blow. But it wasn't strong enough to bash through the skull.

"Shit!" I hiss, floundering around for any sort of weapon. I plant my free foot right in the face of the undead fucker, pushing hard to block its mouth. The remaining gun from Rosario's man is in my pocket, but if I use it, I risk alerting Johnson to my presence. Johnson, and every zombie within hearing range.

Its second hand appears out of nowhere, clamping around my other ankle.

"Motherfucker!"

It keens again, struggling to draw me closer. The thing appears to be pinned, unable to do anything more than pull me. I lock my legs, desperate to keep my ankles away from its snapping teeth.

Something glints off to my right. A silver-white

rectangular object.

A laptop computer. I roll, reaching for it. The monster howls, yanking on me.

My hands close on the computer. I sit up, whipping it around. The brief shift breaks my leg lock. The creature's teeth snap and it jerks me forward.

The corner of the computer smashes into the zombie's skull. Black blood spills out in a languid gush. The monster goes still.

Breathing hard, I scramble back—only to run into the corpse I fell into earlier. Fuck and double fuck. I scramble to my feet and retrieve the flashlight with shaking hands.

That was a close call. Too close. The list of my mistakes tallies in my head.

Idiot. This is what I get for trying to rid the world of assholes by myself.

The flashlight beam catches the figure with the laptop buried in its skull. The sight makes me gag. It's not the ruined skull, but the bloody stump of a torso missing both its legs that hits me like a sucker punch. The poor kid's legs were blown off.

"Pillowcases," I mutter, searching about for my knife. I find the blade on a pile of dead bodies. "Pillowcases and string."

Outside comes a long, loud keen. Shit. The dead boy called his friends before he died. How many are out there?

"Mom?"

Carter's voice freezes me in my tracks. I flick the flashlight, illuminating Carter and Jenna inside the doorway.

"Are you bit?" Carter's voice spikes with panic.

"I'm fine. I . . . fell." Going into the details of my stupidity seems pointless. I take stock of myself, of the gore coating my back, hands, and arms. At least I can't smell myself, since everything around me stinks just as bad.

Carter and Jenna pick their way inside, both wearing the headlights we took from Trading Post.

"Mom, what are you doing out here?"

I shake my head. "Go back." I can't drag them into this.

"Not without you," Jenna says.

The vehemence in her words warms me, but I stand my ground. "Look, you guys don't want to be a part of this. Just go back."

"No way," Carter says. "We're not leaving you here alone."

I consider my close call. It *is* stupid to be out here alone. "How did you find me?"

Jenna opens her mouth, but Carter speaks first. "We were awake and heard you leave."

"Okay," I amend. "I could use your help."

"What are you planning?" Carter asks.

I shake my head, unwilling to put words to my plan. "Just help me find some pillowcases and string."

47
Zombie Catchers

JENNA

I don't ask any questions when Kate tells us to help find pillowcases and string. I have a sick feeling I know what her plan is. It's too horrifying to put into words.

"Now what?" I ask, staring at the pile of pillowcases we pilfered from a deserted bedroom.

"Now, we catch some zombies," Kate replies, tossing a spool of string onto the pile.

"There are some gathered outside." Carter hasn't said much during our search. I suspect he also knows what his mom has planned.

Kate nods. She looks like an extra from a zombie slasher movie. More precisely, she looks like she rolled in a dead person.

We peer outside. The moon is up. The stars are bright beads in the sky. Five zombies mill around, called by the keening of the one Kate killed inside.

"What's your plan for catching them?" Carter asks.

"Pillowcases and slipknots." Kate unrolls a length of string, snaps it with her knife, and ties a slipknot. In a few minutes, there are five nooses next to the pillowcases.

"I'll be the bait," Kate says. "Carter, you're in charge of the pillowcases. Throw them over the head of the zombies. Jenna, you put the noose on and cinch it tight."

Carter hesitates. I know he doesn't want his mother to be the bait. I also see by the steely set of Kate's jaw that she's dedicated to her course.

Johnson's face flashes in my mind. The memory of Lila's weeping sets my teeth on edge. I'm with Kate on this. I might not know her exact plan, but I know she's out here because of Johnson. Because of what he did. Because of what he wants to do. Living under his thumb is a bad place to live.

"Okay," I say, picking up the string. "Let's do this." I march toward the door, hoping to quell any objections from Carter.

Kate strides after me. Carter has no choice but to follow us.

Kate positions herself next to an abandoned car. "We use this for a barrier." She rests a hand on the hood. "We draw them to us. Bag them and move onto the next. Don't let them clump up. We move back around the car and keep them strung out." She looks to each of us, waiting for confirmation that we understand the plan.

I flex my hands around the nooses. Carter, adjusting the first pillowcase in his hand, nods.

Kate raps with her knuckles on the car. The zombies moan in response. They rotate, their aimless milling becoming a focused march.

The foremost of them runs straight into a pile of bodies and goes down. The second one passes him, nose lifting to scent the air. Kate keeps up her insistent knocking. She grips her knife in one hand, jaw set.

The first of the creatures reaches us. Kate grabs it by the front of the shirt and spins it up against the side of the car. It hisses, fingers clawing at the car.

Carter pounces, yanking the pillowcase over the zombie's head. I'm a heartbeat after him, dropping the noose and cinching it tight.

It all happens in less than thirty seconds. We don't have time to bask in our brilliantly executed zombie-catching plan. The second undead is hard on the heels of the first.

We fall back, trying to put space between us and the advancing monster.

I stumble on shell casings, almost losing my footing. Carter grabs me to keep me from going down.

And then the zombie is there, teeth bared as it lunges. Kate kicks, aiming at the knees. The creature falls with a howl. Kate slams her foot onto its back while Carter and I rush in and bag it.

I breathe hard as the third zombie approaches. The first two thrash angrily, biting and clawing at the pillowcases but unable to figure out how to get them off. They weave and twist like erratic pinballs as they struggle against the fabric that stands between them and their next meal.

Just as Kate lures the third zombie closer, one of the bagged creatures knocks into her. She tries to shove it away, but it grabs at her. They both go down right as the third zombie reaches them.

Carter yelps as the third beast lands on his mom. I lunge forward. Snatching my knife from my belt, I swing. The hilt cracks the zombie across the face, turning his teeth away from Kate.

Carter leaps into the fray, pinning the squirming creature as he wrestles the pillowcase over its head.

"String, Jenna!" he hisses.

I dart forward, cinching the noose tight around the zombie's neck. It thrashes and writhes, moaning.

Carter extricates himself and kicks the creature off Kate. As he does, another zombie staggers around the car.

Fuck this. I don't know what Kate has planned, but hopefully, she can do it with three zombies. I'm not leaving our lives to chance.

I intercept the undead and drive my knife through its forehead. When the fifth one comes around the car, I do the same thing to it.

"It seemed like a solid plan," Kate mutters as she extricates herself from the pile of squirming zombies.

"It was semi-solid," Carter tells her. To me, he says, "Babe, maybe this can be our new profession."

"What?" I ask, sucking in air.

"You know, since we can't have our mobile brewery. Maybe we can be a mobile zombie catcher service."

I stare at him, then smother a giggle. I love the fact that when Carter talks about the future, he talks about us being together. Even if he is being a goofball.

"Maybe we can find rogue scientists working on a cure for the zombie plague," I say. "We'll be their go-to team for bagging undead lab rats."

"Mom, hope you like being bait," Carter says.

"Fuck that," she says. "I'll drive Skip. The two of you can do the hard labor. I'm getting too old for this shit."

As soon as she says the words, the mood sobers. All of us are thinking about whatever it is that Kate won't talk about. About Johnson and his lackeys.

"Now what?" I ask, flicking blood off the end of my knife.

"Now?" Kate kicks a thrashing zombie as it rolls too close. "Now we round up our new pets and put them out to pasture."

48
Pasture

KATE

I can only conclude that Carter and Jenna have figured out the general details of my plan. Neither questioned me hard when I told them I wanted to catch zombies. Now, as we drag them along by the long cords wrapped around their necks, they're silent.

When we reach the frat house, I turn to them. "Go back to Creekside."

They shake their heads.

"This is our fight, too," Carter says.

I consider my next words. "Johnson and his crew are in that house. They stole from us. They threatened us. I intend to make sure they don't do any of that again." I pause, feeling my heart swell as I take in Carter and Jenna, standing side by side with their fingers laced. There isn't anything I wouldn't do to keep them safe.

"We're with you, Kate," Jenna says. "Tell us your plan."

I shake my head. Part of it is because I really don't want to involve Carter and Jenna anymore. But mostly, I can't bring myself to voice the plan I've put into motion over the last few days.

"You've done enough," I say. "I can take it from here.

"Good try, Mom," Carter says. "We're not leaving."

Jenna folds her arms across her chest, adding her resolve to Carter's.

"You guys sure about this?" I ask. "There's no going back."

"We're sure," Carter and Jenna say in unison.

So be it.

I force myself to form the words, to spell out exactly what I plan to do. I feel sick as the details of my plan fall from my tongue.

This is self-defense, I remind myself. Sooner or later, Johnson will hurt Lila. Ryan will hurt Jenna. One or more of us will be killed by those boys.

Jenna and Carter are pale by the time I'm finished. To my surprise, neither of them looks at me like I'm a monster. Neither of them tries to talk me out of my plan or proposes an alternate, less brutal one.

They disappear to secure the front door of the frat house while I lead the three moaning zombies by their leashes. The undead are so preoccupied trying to claw the pillowcase away from their mouths that they don't try to grab me. They stumble as I lead them around the back of the house, yanking at the fabric the whole time.

I take them up the porch. It's slow going because they trip on the steps. They make more racket as they hit the wooden planks with their knees, moaning all the while.

I'm not worried about being heard. Based on the sounds coming from inside the house, no one is in a state to notice something as mundane as tripping and moaning zombies.

I reach the back door and turn the handle. It's unlocked. Laughter comes from inside. I tug the zombies forward, positioning myself behind them.

Then I move fast. I yank the pillowcase off the first one, simultaneously planting my foot in his backside. I shove hard, sending him sprawling into the kitchen. He lands on his stomach, moaning.

I repeat the same procedure with the second zombie, kicking him harder than the first. They end up in a pile of rotting flesh on the chipped linoleum.

"Hey, guys, did someone let pigs in here?"

"Those aren't pigs, brother. They're turkeys. We should go turkey hunting!"

"Are you sure those are turkeys? They look like pigs. Smell like pigs, too."

"If I say they're turkeys, they're turkeys, motherfuck— ouch! Fucking thing just—ouch!" A bellow splits the air. "Guys, the turkeys are biting me!"

Someone laughs. "Johnson is afraid of turkeys! The big bad Johnson is—ouch! What the fuck—!" A second voice dissolves into screaming.

Heart pounding, I rip off the third pillowcase and kick the last zombie inside, then slam the door. I rush around the side of the refrigerator that stands next to the door. No doubt it's a beer fridge from the frat party days. I drive my shoulder into the side of it. It hits the porch with a *boom* that reverberates in my ears.

More shouts erupt from the frat house. Backing down the steps, I crouch in the shadows and wait, gun in hand. I need to make sure they're all dead. No loose ends. No stragglers to come seeking vengeance at Creekside.

A flash of movement catches my eye. Jenna and Carter scurry down the driveway to the backyard.

"Is it secure?" I whisper as they join me.

Carter nods. "We moved the sofa on the porch in front of the door. They won't be getting past that anytime soon."

I nod, embracing the sick sensation that sends gooseflesh over my body. I'm killing all those people inside the house. My action is cold blooded. Premeditated.

"Mom, I'm not sure this is going to work. Three zombies against—how many did you say were in there?"

"Ten." I signed the death warrant on ten people, Roberts included. The last part makes me ache the most. There wasn't a way to spare him without jeopardizing the entire plan.

"I think it's going to take more than three zombies," Jenna says.

"Not when they're all high on acid." I meet their eyes.

Carter's mouth falls open. Jenna blinks at me with wide eyes.

"Reed's acid," she whispers. "You laced the brandy with it."

I nod.

"You were never on a peace mission," Carter says. "You went there to plant the brandy."

"No." I shake my head. "The brandy was my backup plan. If Johnson had agreed to my proposal, there would be no zombies in there right now."

The shouting within the house escalates, followed by screaming. High-pitched keening punctuates the human voices. A second later, someone tackles the back door. The refrigerator shudders but stands fast.

"What the fuck!" a voice hollers. "What the fuck! Guys, the turkeys!"

The refrigerator vibrates again as the person on the other side tries to throw open the door. Gunshots rend the air, followed by more screaming and shouting.

I absorb the sight of Carter and Jenna, their entwined hands white-knuckled as they stare at the house. I know the decision was the right one. Whatever bad karma I bestow on myself for this act, it's worth it to keep them safe.

"This was my plan," I whisper to them. "My choice. This is on my conscious, not yours."

Several more gunshots go off, followed by the sound of shattering glass. A boot kicks out the remains of a second-story window. One of the soldiers crawls out.

I squint, trying to see who it is, hoping against hope

that it might be Roberts.

"Stay here," I hiss to Carter and Jenna, pushing them behind one of the faded frat sofas sitting outside in the yard. "Stay down. Don't come out until I tell you it's safe."

"Mom—"

"Damn it, Carter," I snap. "Shut up and listen to your mother."

I turn my back on his stunned expression, putting an end to the discussion. I hurry toward the house, relieved when Jenna and Carter don't try to follow.

My hand is sweaty around the gun. My resolve falters, mingling with fear and revulsion.

Ducking behind a barbecue, I stare up at the roofline. Even in the darkness, I recognize the profile of Johnson. The square jawline. The hard, Romanesque nose.

Fuck. Of all the ones in there, he's the most dangerous.

That should make him the easiest to kill. Maybe at some point, killing will feel easy for me.

Amid the shouting, moaning, and screaming from inside, Johnson shimmies on a downspout. He's naturally agile, making the trip to the ground look easy.

I sprint across the shabby lawn, gritting my teeth. Now isn't the time to second-guess my decision.

I raise the gun and take aim. Johnson, hearing my approach, spins around to meet my attack. I squeeze the trigger, but not before Johnson knocks it from my hand. He delivers a vicious punch to my jaw.

I'm thrown off my feet, pain exploding along the side of my face and neck. When I hit the ground, my breath leaves my body.

Before I can gather myself, Johnson is on me, pinning me flat. His knees land on either of my arms, grinding them into the damp earth. His hands lock around my throat, eyes bulging with rage as he looks down at me.

There are bite marks all up and down his arms. His

eyes are glazed and bloodshot.

The clouds open up without warning, dumping down on us in a chilly flood. My world narrows to the cold wetness, the crazed fury of Johnson, and the pair of hands squeezing the breath out of me.

"I can't tell if you're the bitch from Creekside or a pink leprechaun," Johnson snarls. "Whoever you are, this is your doing."

I don't try to deny it.

"I knew I was gonna have to get rid of you," he snarls. "I saw it this morning when you looked at me. I was planning to hunt you down. I was going to make it fun. Then you ruined it all, you sneaky bitch. You know, you have rainbows coming out of your head right now." He laughs, a wild, desperate sound. His grip on my neck never loosens.

Dark circles bloom in front of my eyes, vision narrowing to a small point. My mouth works as I suck for nonexistent air. The pressure of Johnson's fists is like a constrictor around my windpipe. I strain against his knees, trying to free my arms. I'm completely pinned, unable to move, watching the world fade and die around me.

Kyle. His name and blue eyes flash in my mind's eye. *Frederico.* I see the bob of my friend's gray ponytail as he runs down the trail in front of me. Two of the people I love most.

I'm on my way to join them. Just another few seconds and I'll see them both again.

The thought brings me peace. I stop struggling, accepting my fate.

Johnson's head explodes in a spray of red. I stare in dumbfounded confusion as he slumps sideways, hands sloughing away.

Oxygen rushes back into my airway. I suck it down in long, painful gasps. Rain sheets into my face, making the world watery and indistinct.

A figure appears above me. I blink, trying to find Carter or Jenna in the person.

But the figure above me is dressed in military fatigues. The dark skin of his high cheekbones shimmers with the rain.

Roberts. Recognition hits me as my wits return. I sit, coughing and sucking in air. My throat feels like it's been scraped raw with a file. Every breath is fire.

"I asked him to stop." Roberts' voice is thin and faint. "We were friends before all this started. He was a good guy. Helped me through boot camp. But something snapped. He hasn't been right since-since—" Roberts raises a shaking hand, pointing the gun at me. My gun. "You did this. You laced the brandy and set the zombies loose in our house."

I stare at him. After a moment, I nod, my eyes never leaving his. I could list out my reasons. Throw them at him like bullet points on a PowerPoint presentation. But it doesn't change the fact that I killed his friends. That I tried to kill him, even though I didn't want to.

"God damn it." Roberts lowers the gun, his free hand making a surreptitious trip across his eyes. "God damn it." This last part comes out half sob, half shout.

Carter and Jenna materialize out of the wet darkness. Jenna helps me to my feet while Carter plants himself between us and Roberts. He holds his knife, which looks ridiculous against the gun.

I didn't do the things I did tonight just to watch my son get killed. I shove him aside, shaking off Jenna.

"This was my plan," I tell Roberts. If he wants vengeance, I have to make sure he takes it out on me. "I'm responsible for what happened tonight."

"I know!" Roberts shouts. "And I know why you did it!" His chest heaves. Thunder booms overhead. The frat house stands quiet in the pelting storm. "You're a crazy bitch!"

I don't back down. I stand with my back straight,

refusing to turn away from the murder I committed. Roberts can do what he will. There is no apologizing for what I've done.

His eyes take in the lifeless body of Johnson. His shoulders slump. "Ryan and the other college kids were as bad as he was. They sold out their own friends to Johnson. If you knew the things—" He breaks off, making a choking sound. "I'd be dead with the rest of them, but I was pissed and went to bed without having any of the brandy."

He turns, looking back at the house. Then he looks at me. "We have to put them down."

"You can't go in there," Jenna says. "You can't—"

"I'll go." I cut her off, nodding to Roberts. This is my responsibility.

Carter steps up beside me, armed with his knife.

"Wait here," I tell him.

"No, Mom. We're in this together."

"You're not alone," Jenna adds. "We're family."

Emotion swells within me. *Family.* Carter and Jenna, both of them soaking wet, still stand by my side. Even after all I've done. I gather them both in a hug, a shudder of relief running through me.

Family.

49

Clean Up

KATE

The interior of the frat house is a gory tomb. I lead Roberts, Jenna, and Carter inside, my shoes squelching in the blood.

The first body I see belongs to one of the college boys. His face is scrunched in a rictus of pain. The body is on its side just inside the door, stomach and throat ripped open.

What have I done?

Recalling my interaction with the group this morning, my lips thin. I did what I had to do.

I pull out my knife, crouching beside the dead boy. He hasn't turned yet, but it's only a matter of time. My heart thuds as I place the tip of my knife against his temple. Forcing myself to watch, I shove.

Tears sting my eyes as the knife slides into the skull. He was just a kid. A stupid, lost kid.

A hand rests on my shoulder. Roberts. He gives me a tight nod of approval.

We fan out into the kitchen. There is blood and body pieces on the floor and counters. More gore is smeared on the cabinets and walls.

In the middle of the pool table is a body. Two zombies crouch on either side, gnawing on it. They're so busy enjoying their feast they don't notice us.

The dead boy on the table is Ryan.

Jenna falls in beside me, the two of us advancing down the left side of the pool table toward the zombie feasting on Ryan's forearm. Roberts and Carter move in on the right side, heading toward the other zombie.

My shoe scuffs against the floor, the blood on the bottom making a soft squeak. The zombies turn their white eyes in our direction, baring bloodied teeth as they snarl.

Jenna and I spring forward. Her screwdriver drives up through the beast's throat while my knife finds his skull. Carter and Roberts make short work of their zombie.

A wild howl slices the air. The last zombie leaps over a nearby sofa, charging straight at us.

I leap out to meet the creature head on. With a shout, I swing the knife. The front of its face buckles under the blow. Blood sprays everywhere. The zombie drops without another sound.

"You are officially the scariest woman I've ever met," Roberts murmurs.

I draw in a shaky breath. "I don't feel very scary."

"You are," Jenna and Carter assure me.

Roberts turns his attention back to the body of Ryan. "I got this one," he says. "Believe me when I say this motherfucker doesn't deserve mercy, but I don't want his sorry ass coming back to bite any of us."

He jams the knife through Ryan's eye socket. The body twitches under the force of the impact, then lies still.

I let out a shaky breath and turn my attention to the rest of the living room. The bottle of brandy lays on its side, the remnants of the brown liquid glistening on a scratched oak end table.

I count six other bodies in various states of ruin. None of them move. All bear a myriad of grisly wounds, most on the throat and abdomen. Zombies are efficient killers.

As I move into the sitting room, a muffled cry makes me jump. I spin around, knife raised. The rest of my companions do the same. The noise comes from behind a closed door at the back of the kitchen.

"The bathroom," Roberts says.

As a group, we creep toward the bathroom. Something is most definitely moving on the other side of the door.

"Did you hear that?" Jenna hisses. "I think someone is crying."

Dread makes my feet heavy. Is there a newly turned zombie behind the door? Even worse, could it be someone who's bitten but still alive?

"Get the door," I tell Roberts. "Jenna, Carter, get behind me."

Roberts hesitates. He's probably not used to taking orders from a middle-aged woman with bad hair.

"The door," I repeat, leaving no room for argument. It's my job to take care of whatever is on the other side.

Lips compressed, Roberts nods. I ready myself, tightening sweaty hands around my weapon. He wraps one large fist around the doorknob and yanks.

A figure inside screams, throwing her arms over her head. She cowers inside an old-fashioned claw-foot tub.

"Ash!" Roberts shoulders past me, pushing into the bathroom.

Ash. The girl who made pancakes. I might be sick. Am I going to have to put down the girl who made me pancakes?

"Don't touch me!" Ash screams, cowering on the bottom of the tub.

"Ash, it's me, Caleb."

"Caleb?" She raises a face streaked with tears. "You look like a talking reindeer."

"That's the acid talking."

"Acid?"

"The brandy was laced with acid. Are you hurt?"

Ash shakes her head.

"No bites?" Roberts demands.

Again, Ash shakes her head. My knees nearly give out in relief.

"I-I was on the toilet when the screaming started," she whispers. "Bugs started crawling out of the walls. Ryan kept yelling about flesh-eating turkeys." She shudders. "I was so scared. God, I wish you didn't look like a talking reindeer. With a green nose. Rudolf the green-nosed reindeer." The noise that comes out of her throat is half sob, half hiccup.

Roberts leans down, scooping Ash up into his arms. She leans her head against his chest.

"Are they gone?" she whispers.

Even though Ash is scared and high as a kite, it occurs to me she's not asking about the zombies. Those were not the scariest things in this house.

Roberts glances at me. "Yeah. They're gone."

"Ryan, too?"

"Yep."

Another shudder goes through her body. "Thank fucking God."

"It was the woman who came to have breakfast with us," Roberts tells her. "She took care of them. She's standing here with us."

"All of those dickwads? By herself?"

"Pretty much, though she had a little help."

Ash squints out at us, then shakes her head. "All I see are reindeer with tie-dyed fur. Oh, and walls with trees growing out of the side."

Roberts responds by tightening his arms around Ash.

"Come back with us," I say. "Our place is safe. We have supplies."

"Come back with you?" Roberts stares at me with narrowed eyes. Behind me, I sense Carter and Jenna shift with unease, but neither of them contradicts my offer.

"In case you haven't noticed," I reply, "there's a shortage of good people in the world. Well, a shortage of people in general, but definitely a shortage of good people." I glance at Jenna and Carter. "We can use good people."

"Caleb," Ash says, "I want to go with the lady who got rid of Johnson and Ryan. Tell her I'll make pancakes."

After a long moment of hesitation, Roberts extend one hand to me in greeting. "My name is Caleb Roberts. I'm from San Diego."

I grasp his hand and shake it. "My name is Kate. I'm from Sonoma County. This is my son, Carter, and his girlfriend, Jenna. It's nice to meet you, Caleb."

I look at Caleb's defeated shoulders, at the wrecked frat house looming large and bloody all around us. This could be the dumbest decision I've ever made. But maybe I can balance out tonight's dark deeds with a little compassion. Caleb did save my life, and Ash made me pancakes.

Caleb's gaze shifts to Carter. "That's one hell of a mom you got. She's got balls."

A grin spreads across Carter's face. "Tell me about it. She ran two hundred miles on foot to get here."

Caleb stares at me without blinking, absorbing this information with a long look that makes me want to squirm.

"I definitely want to go with you," Ash says, "even if you do look like a psychedelic reindeer."

A soft laugh rumbles in my chest, spreading warmth through my body. For the first time in a long time, I feel a twinge of optimism. Maybe, just maybe, everything will be okay.

"Come on," I say. "Let's go home."

Epilogue
Mama Bear

KATE

"Mama Bear, are you there? Over."

From my seat at the kitchen table, I pick up the ham. "Foot Soldier, this is Mama Bear. How are you? Over."

"I picked apples today. Can you believe it? There are seven different apple trees here. If you held a gun to my head, I couldn't name seven different kinds of apples. I always thought there was red, yellow, green, and those other ones that are sort of a blend of all three colors."

I laugh. "How do they taste?"

"Like heaven." Alvarez lets out a moan of pleasure. "I'm so sick of fish and seagull. It's a nice change of pace. How are things going with the track?"

"We managed to clear it of zombies. It took us almost five days, but we managed. The fence around the bleachers is intact, so once we got rid of the zombies it's remained clear. We've moved our daily workouts there."

"Your group isn't afraid to venture out anymore?"

"There's always a healthy amount of wariness, but it's not like before. Now that Johnson is gone, we go outside every day. Eric hooked up another two solar panels and managed to get the lights working in two of the apartments."

"Electricity, huh? You trying to make me jealous,

Mama Bear?"

"Is it working?"

"We have a grain mill. Beat that."

I chuckle. "Yeah, but you need horses to pull it."

"I'm working on that. We spotted some horses on a scavenging run. The problem is no one here knows how to ride. We'll figure it out, though. How are things going with the newcomers?"

"They're integrating. Things were a bit tense at first, but once I told them how Caleb saved my life, things loosened up. Oh, Carter, Jenna, and I moved out."

"Moved out?"

"Just into the dorm next door," I explain. "Things were pretty tight in the apartment. And I was tired of sleeping on the sofa. I have my own room now. So do Jenna and Carter. Caleb and Ash are rooming with us, too." I don't tell him my ceiling is covered with Grateful Dead posters, or that the closet smells like a gym locker. I haven't had a chance to make the place my own yet.

"What about the other girl?" Alvarez asks.

"Lila? She's better. She's twitchy around Caleb, but at least she leaves her bedroom. She won't leave the building yet. She's taken over daily meal prep for us."

"Aw man, you have a chef?"

"I wouldn't call her a chef," I reply, thinking of the cake Lila made on the barbecue, which had been more charcoal than cake. "But she's pretty good at heating up canned food."

"We started a compost pile. We integrated those techniques Jenna got out of the gardening book, but none of the seeds have come up yet. I feel like we spend a lot of time staring at dirt. And fishing. And plucking seagulls. Man, I still can't believe I eat seagulls. Those are dirty fucking birds."

I laugh. "Is there anything else you need us to get from the library?"

Alvarez's reply is cut off as the door to the dorm

swings open. Carter and Jenna file inside, followed by the rest of the crew. Even Lila is with them, dirt smudged on her cheeks from her work in the garden beds. She stands a little closer than necessary to Eric.

"Mom? I think you'd better come out here."

"I have to go," I say to Alvarez. "Good luck with that garden, Foot Soldier. Let me know if you need us to find more books from the library."

"Good luck with the track workouts, Mama Bear. Talk in three days?"

"Three days," I agree. "Over and out, Foot Soldier."

"Over and out, Mama Bear."

I switch off the ham. "What's up?" I ask my kids.

"There's someone here to see you," Carter says.

Wariness snakes through my gut. I try to read the expressions around me, but everyone looks as confused as I feel.

"Who's here to see me?" I ask.

Carter shakes his head. "You need to come downstairs."

I grab my gun belt, slinging it around my waist. My knife and screwdriver have a home in the belt alongside the firearm. Between the three pieces, I feel ready for just about anything, although the screwdriver is my preferred go-to weapon for dispatching zombies.

Thanks to Caleb and Ash—and the enormous stash of weapons Johnson had squirreled away in the frat house—we are now the proud owners of an impressive arsenal. Johnson had been smart enough to raid all the dead military bodies after the night of the massacre, which was why we hadn't seen any weapons among all the bodies.

Caleb and Ash are both eager to teach us all how to shoot, but I haven't figured out a safe way to do that. Guns might be necessary, but the sound draws zombies. Instead, the pair has started hand-to-hand combat practice with us. We tack the training on at the end of our runs. I'm getting decent at swinging a knife.

I push open the door to the downstairs lounge. The carpet has been pulled up and two raised garden beds erected in the center of the room. Lila and Eric have seeds started under the grow lights. A few tiny shoots poke their heads out of the soil. Reed laments that we're growing zucchini instead of marijuana, but he'll get over it.

The broad wooden door we built over the entrance is shut, the security bar in place. This does nothing to ease my nerves.

"Should I open it?" I ask them.

Seven heads nod. Not surprisingly, Lila didn't make the journey back downstairs with us. She only comes down with Eric to work on the garden, but whatever lies on the other side of our front door has her hiding upstairs again. Another not-so-good sign.

I pull off the bar. I almost set it on the floor, then think better of it. Instead, I brace one end against my hip and push open the door, ready to take a swing at whoever is on the other side.

A man in green military fatigues stands there. He looks to be in his late forties or early fifties. A dark crew cut is laced generously with gray. White stubble paints the lower half of his face. Sharp, dark eyes lance through me, drilling a quick, efficient assessment. I don't like the feeling of being under a microscope.

"This her?" His voice comes out raspy, like he hasn't used it in a long time.

"This is Kate," Caleb replies. The tall, dark-skinned boy wears a grim expression. "Kate, this is Ben Wheaton."

Wheaton and Caleb stare at each other over the sea of heads that separates them. The mutual hostility is palpable.

Wheaton looks away first. Somehow, he makes it seem more like a dismissal than a retreat. His gaze shifts to me, once again assessing me from my toes to my head.

"Like what you see?" I ask, narrowing my eyes at him. I know perfectly well how I look. I'm the skinniest I've ever been, my face and arms tan from the long track workouts under the sun. My gray roots have grown out another inch.

"You don't recognize me," Wheaton replies. "I was too far away for you to see the first time we met. But I know you, Kate."

My hackles rise. I know who this guy is. "You're the gunman from College Creek."

"I'm flattered you remember me."

"We thought you were dead," I reply. "We've been back to College Creek many times and never seen you."

Wheaton shrugs. "I moved weeks ago when I tracked Johnson and his crew back to their nest. I cleared out an apartment that overlooked the backyard of that motherfucker's den. I had a plan. I was going to go in while they all slept. The night I was going to attack, I saw you crawl under the porch. I decided to wait until you were clear so you didn't get shot in the crossfire." His eyes flick to Caleb. "I was going to kill every one of those motherfuckers for what they did."

"Caleb didn't kill any of those College Creek kids," Ash says.

"He didn't pull the trigger," Wheaton replies. "But when push came to shove, he went with Johnson and Ryan."

Caleb pales. There is shame in his eyes. He looks away under the scorn that radiates from Wheaton.

"Caleb saved my life." I plant myself between this cranky old man and my soldier. "Johnson would have killed me if not for Caleb. If you have a problem with him, you can turn the fuck around and march yourself back to wherever you came from."

Wheaton barks a laugh. "I knew I'd like you." He grins, but his dark eyes don't blink as they look into mine.

His intensity is unnerving.

I stare right back at him, refusing to back down. "Tell me what you want."

"Like I was saying, I postponed my attack until you were clear. I made plans to go in the next night. As I strapped on my gear, I looked out the window, and what did I see?" He points a finger at me. "I saw you shoving zombies through the back door of the frat house. After that, all I had to do was pull up a chair and watch the show. Their screaming was pure poetry. For that, I salute you."

And he does salute me. Right there in the doorway. His hand snaps up and out from his brow in a perfect military salute.

"But you only had three zombies," Wheaton continues. "That shouldn't have been enough to get rid of that viper's nest. I want to know how you did it. How did you get rid of those fuckers?"

I consider slamming the door in this whack job's face, except he's somehow maneuvered himself between the door and me.

"Acid," I say. "I laced a bottle of booze with acid."

Wheaton blinks. Stares. Then throws back his head and roars with laughter. He laughs so hard he doubles over. The sound is razor sharp, grating at my ears. He puts one hand out on the doorway to support himself. To my shock, a few tears of mirth slide down his cheeks.

He laughs, and laughs, and laughs. The sound takes on a maniacal edge. My hand inches toward my knife.

"And I thought he was scary when he was mad," Caleb mutters behind me. "This is way scarier." He's inched his way forward and planted himself directly to my left. His free hand rests on his gun in a stance that is pure protectiveness.

"Is he alone?" I whisper to Caleb.

"Yeah," Caleb replies. "Johnson killed all the other soldiers who opposed him. He would have killed

Wheaton, too, if he hadn't run."

I recall the soldiers we'd seen staked to doors and trees. More of Johnson's handiwork.

"Ma'am," Wheaton says, finally straightening. He huffs a few more times, trying to control his mirth. A few more maniacal laughs bubble up. "Ma'am," he says again, "I salute you. I. Salute. You." He rips off another three salutes in my direction.

"Are we done here?" I ask coldly. I'm ready for this fucker to take a hike.

"I hope not," Wheaton replies. "I was hoping you would be so kind as to let me join your band of merry men."

"No—" I begin, but he cuts me off.

"I don't come empty-handed." Wheaton steps to the side.

Next to the door is a giant tarp. I hadn't seen it before because of its angle to the door. Wheaton tugs on a string holding the tarp closed. The material crinkles as it falls away.

In the center of the tarp is a huge pile of food and guns. Wheaton grins at me as he takes in my shock.

"I've been busy," he replies. "I have three more bundles like this one. My contribution to the band, if you'll let me join."

I might be a newbie when it comes to guns, but I've seen enough of them with Caleb and Ash to have a newfound appreciation for firearms. I know a treasure trove when I see one.

To put off from answering, I ask, "Where did you get all that?"

Wheaton's grin broadens. "I may have raided a few military caches. I wanted to make a good first impression when I came calling. This is my way of showing you I'm ready to be a useful member of your tribe. I'll pull my weight. I'll cook. Keep watch. Clean up shit. Whatever. But I want to follow the woman who had the balls to take on those little prepubescent fuckers with three zombies and a bottle of acid."

I suppose I should be flattered. The guy is paying me a compliment, after all. His intensity is unnerving. He won't quit staring at me, which makes me wish I'd dyed my roots. Which is stupid. When did I start caring about my bad hair?

I'm about to turn him away when Caleb edges closer to me. He bumps me with his elbow.

"He's good people, Kate," he murmurs. "He stood up to Johnson. He tried to defend the College Creek kids before things went sideways."

Wheaton listens to every word, mouth twisting in distaste.

I look to Ash, who has shouldered up on my right side. "What's your opinion of him?" I ask, not bothering to whisper or be discreet. This Wheaton guy needs to know he's under assessment.

"He's a grouchy fucker," Ash says, "but Caleb is right. He works hard and his compass always points north. He might be an irritating old fuck, but he'll be a contributing member of our group." Based on the heat in Ash's words, I get the feeling she's wanted to say them for a long time.

"You'd be grouchy too if you'd spent the last thirty years of your life killing in the name of democracy," Wheaton replies. "This war is refreshing that way. It's the first time I've killed in the name of humanity. Brings it all home." He smacks a closed fist over his heart.

"Can we trust him?" I ask Ash and Caleb. When they both nod, I sigh inwardly.

I like the little family I've collected. We have good synchronicity. I don't want to change it by adding a new member.

But Ash and Caleb respect this guy. As much as they dislike him, both think he'll be a good addition to our group. I can't deny that we could use a trained military veteran in our midst.

"You can join us," I say, "but you fall in line with our routine. Endurance is an essential part of our survival plan. We work out every morning for two to four hours. We spend the rest of our time scavenging and fortifying our home. Sunday is our day of rest."

"When we're not undergoing sleep deprivation training," Reed adds.

"When we're not undergoing sleep deprivation training," I amend.

Wheaton's eyes take on an eerie brightness. If I didn't know better, I'd say he just perked up at the idea of sleep deprivation training. He's a little weird, I conclude.

"If you don't like the way that sounds, turn around now," I say, hoping he'll do just that.

No such luck.

"Whatever you say, ma'am," Wheaton replies. "You have my word that I will follow your orders."

"Welcome to Creekside, Ben Wheaton."

The kids shift behind me, forming a tunnel so Ben can enter Creekside. Ben laces up his tarp, slinging the rope over one shoulder to haul it inside.

"Reed!" a new voice rings out.

The tarp and its contents clatter to the ground. Every person, including Ben, draws a weapon as a dark-haired man scrambles out from behind a clump of bushes and dead bodies.

"Reed!" He runs forward and throws himself to his knees before us.

I realize in shock that this is one of the bastards who locked up Carter, Reed, and Jenna in the rock shop. The guy I beat over the head with a chair. There's a dent in his forehead, a ripple of skin and bone where I struck him. I can't believe he's still alive.

"Jesus!" Reed pushes his way forward. "I thought you were dead."

"Take me in!" Jesus wails. "Tell your Mamita that I'm

loyal. I'm handy in a fight and I never, ever turn my back on my people."

Mamita. I suppose that's me. I glare down at the drug dealer. "That's a bit hard to believe when you pointed a gun at Reed and locked him and his friends up in a closet," I say coldly.

"You've got it all wrong," Reed says. "Jesus is my friend."

"He tried to protect us when Rosario's men started shooting," Jenna adds.

"He held you guys at gunpoint," I argue. "I saw him."

Reed waves a hand, moving to stand beside Jesus. "He was just fucking with us. He didn't mean anything by it."

"You have an interesting definition of friend," Ben remarks.

"Jesus went outside to hunt Rosario's men while we stayed inside," Carter says. "He tried to protect us."

The man clasps both hands before him like he's praying. Could this day get any weirder?

"I've been on my own out here for weeks," Jesus says. "I can't do it anymore. I knew I needed Reed's Mamita. I came to the campus looking for you." He turns imploring eyes to Reed. "I need you, brother. Tell her we're brothers!"

"We're brothers," Reed says, turning an earnest expression to me. "Mama, Jesus is my friend."

"This she-wolf nearly beat me to death with a chair to rescue you," Jesus replies. "She inspires loyalty." He looks to me again. "I will follow you anywhere, do anything for you. I am your man, Mamita."

"You beat this fucker with a chair?" Ben asks.

"Yeah," Johnny says. "After she set a building on fire to rescue these guys." He jerks a thumb in Carter's direction.

"That's not exactly what—" I begin.

"You have a dent in your forehead," Reed interrupts,

peering at Jesus's head. "That wasn't there the last time I saw you."

"This is from Mamita." Jesus reverently touches his scalp.

"That's nothing," Jenna says. "You should see the guys she hit in the face with a cast iron skillet."

"Those guys didn't make it," Johnny adds.

Ben's eyebrows climb his forehead. He gives me another head-to-toe appraisal that makes me feel naked.

This is all more than I can take. I need to go for a run. A long one.

"Fuck it," I say. "Jesus, you can join us. But you play by my rules. You run your ass off every day. You scavenge. You clean. You be a functioning, committed member of our group. If you don't fall in line, your ass is out. Do you understand?" I feel like a mom grilling a teenager who wants to stay out past curfew for the first time.

"Just promise you'll beat someone with a chair for me," Jesus replies.

I let out a huff. "If some fucker drags your ass off the street at gunpoint, locks you in a closet, then proceeds to get in a shooting match over a turf war that doesn't matter anymore, then yes, I will beat someone with a chair for you."

"Thank you, Mamita." Jesus gets to his feet. I'm unnerved to see tears glittering on the edges of his lashes.

"You might throw up," Reed says. "I threw up, like, at least five times when I started running. She isn't joking about the running thing."

"I follow Mamita," Jesus says.

"I reserve the right to throw chairs at each of you," I say, pointing to Ben and Jesus in irritation.

"Yes, ma'am," Ben says, while Jesus says, "Yes, Mamita."

"We call her Mama Bear," Reed says. "You guys need to get used to that."

"This is going in the notebook," Johnny says. "I'm starting a new one. It's called *Dorm Life*."

"Whatever, dude," Eric says. "Not like anyone is going to read it."

"Dude," Johnny replies, "you never know. Two hundred years from now an archeology team could come through here to document the outbreak. My notebook could end up in a museum. It could be an international bestseller, like the *Diary of Anne Frank*."

"Now you're definitely giving yourself too much credit," Carter says.

I step to the side, gesturing to Jesus and Ben. "Welcome to Creekside," I say, hoping I'm not making a mistake. "I hope you're both ready to be immortalized."

Author's Note

Thanks so much for picking up a copy of this book! I hope you enjoyed reading it as much as I enjoyed writing it.

Please consider leaving an honest online review at your favorite book retailer. Reviews help independent authors spread the word about our stories. I sincerely appreciate every one.

Thanks for being part of the journey!

Visit Camille at
www.camillepicott.com
or follow on Facebook @ultrawriter

Acknowledgments

Many thanks to those who shared in the journey of *Dorm Life*!

Dani Crabtree
Victoria DeLuis
Chris Picott
Saundra Wright

Made in the USA
Columbia, SC
05 March 2021

33918632R00193